CW01269521

Hell's Super

(Circles in Hell, Book One)

by

Mark Cain

ISBN-13: 978-1517621438
ISBN-10: 1517621437

'Hell's Super' is published by Perdition Press, which can be contacted at:

hellssuper@hotmail.com

Additional cover art by Dan Wolfe (www.doodledojo.co.uk)

To all who walk this mortal plane, hoping that in the everyday we find more of Heaven than of Hell

Acknowledgments

Many people have read earlier versions of *Hell's Super* - too many to list here. I thank them all for their advice and suggestions.

Two readers, however, deserve special mention. Thank you, Linda, my wife, always my alpha reader, for your gentle, honest and clear-eyed criticism. I am also grateful to Maeve Sleibhin, whom I met through a writers' social network. A fine writer herself, Maeve has definite views on how a book should be crafted. We do not always agree, but she was so dogged in expressing her opinions about *Hell's Super* that she finally got even stubborn old me to rethink, and subsequently redo, parts of it. The result was a greatly improved book.

The rumble - a constant thrum thrum thrum of many feet pounding against flights of stairs - was not so distant now. The desperate and determined rhythm grew to an ear-splitting cacophony that threatened to overwhelm me.

I swallowed hard. Not long. Soon ten thousand Hellions would surge up the stairwell and trample me, if I couldn't stop them. And then all Hell would break loose.

I considered my assets: one tool belt, two rolls of duct tape, and a bullhorn. Not much, all told. At least I had a plan, though it seemed pretty lame to me now.

One against an entire horde. Not good. I had never felt so alone, though that would change soon enough.

I could hear the voices of those below, some angry, some jubilant, others merely feral, howls and grunts that sounded as if they came from stampeding animals instead of rampaging humans.

This was not in my job description.

My nerves got the better of me as the horde reached the landing immediately below. An index finger, slick with my own sweat, curled around the trigger of the bullhorn.

Maybe a bazooka would have been a better choice.

Chapter 1

The handle came off in my hand as I turned the knob. With a sigh, I reached to my tool belt, grabbed my hammer, and hurled it through the glass. Then I leaned into the hole I'd made and opened the door with the inside knob.

My office was in a single-wide trailer, the kind you'd find on a construction site for a small building. For big buildings, you'd usually find a double-wide. The trailer housed my desk and chair, a stool, some files, a collection of tools, and now a mess of broken glass.

I stepped over the shards and walked to the far wall where there was an old analog time clock. It showed two minutes to seven. Pulling my time card from its slot in the rusted holder mounted next to the clock, I punched in, then checked the stamp. It read 7:16.

"Minion!" a voice screeched over the PA system, which crackled and sputtered as if it would fail at any moment. "Late again!"

I thought to argue the point while stooping to retrieve my hammer, cutting myself on a piece of glass in the process. "Damn!" I said and sucked the blood from my finger, noting without surprise that the lurid red ooze was the same shade as the ink that had just been stamped on my time card.

"Damn straight! If you're late again, there'll ... well ..."

"There'll be Hell to pay?" I offered, trying to be helpful.

"Damn straight!" Then a piercing screech that all but broke my eardrums cut off Beezy's voice. The PA system had finally died.

I shrugged. *Gotta fix that one of these days. And the time clock too. Oh, and now the door.*

I went over to the ancient Mr. Coffee, grabbed yesterday's filter, which was by now dry, and dumped the old grounds into a nearby trashcan. I put the paper back in the brown plastic holder, filled it with fresh grounds and slid the holder back into position. Going to the sink, I rinsed yesterday's unfinished coffee from the carafe. Lime deposits on the side of the glass made the coffeepot more translucent than transparent; the stains from a never-ending cycle of burnt java had dyed the bottom permanently brown. These were details I noticed every day - not with interest, because they weren't particularly interesting - but I noticed them regardless. I was compelled to.

The water from the tap was that color of yellow caused by ancient, rusted pipes. The stuff looked like piss. Tasted that way too. I filled the carafe, then dumped the liquid into the top of the Mr. Coffee.

While the coffeemaker did its thing, I sat down at my desk. It was a small All-Steel job with a dent in the front that could have been put there by the wheel of a Harley doing ninety. The desk looked to have been assembled in the 1940s, yet it might as easily have been made just before I got here, especially for me.

I hated it. My old desk was rosewood with filigree carved along the edges. That fine piece of furniture was a work of art. My current workstation was more like a sardine can.

Glub, glub went the Mr. Coffee.

On the corner of my desk was a wire inbox overflowing with work orders. I rifled through the top few.

> ***HOTI Form ∞3971\PDYFF 666 - 327\?///WOE # ∞8911763987****: Priority:* **High***. Issue: Fix Plant and Non - Corporeal Facilities Departmental PA System.*

***HOTI Form ∞3971\PDYFF 666 - 327\?///WOE # ∞8911763986**: Priority: **High**. Issue: Fix Plant and Non - Corporeal Facilities Departmental Time Clock.*

***HOTI Form ∞3971\PDYFF 666 - 327\?///WOE # ∞8911763985**: Priority: **High**. Issue: Fix Plant and Non - Corporeal Facilities Office Front Door. Notes: Install a new door knob and replace glass broken by some asshole who threw a hammer through it.*

Glub, glub, splat. Ah. The coffee was done.

Grabbing my "I'm not With Stupid. I AM Stupid" mug from the desktop, I headed to the Mr. Coffee and poured myself some of the brown-yellow water that passed for joe in my department - well, hell, everywhere around here.

"It's going to be one of those days."

The door opened and one of the fattest people I'd ever known entered the office. Like me, he wore grimy coveralls - bright yellow ones, similar to those used in HAZMAT operations - but his uniform was so tight on his corpulent frame that every seam protested, threatening to break. A black oval of fabric was sewn above his pocket, which held a ballpoint pen and a small screwdriver - the type you'd use to fix a computer. Embroidered into the oval in blood-red lettering was 'Orson.' The fat man crushed glass beneath his work boot. "What the fuck?" he cursed in a mellifluous voice that contrasted sharply with his words, and his coveralls.

"Front door broke again," I mumbled over my coffee mug, taking my first sip of the day. Jeez, it tasted awful.

Orson was my assistant.

I glanced at the time clock as he punched in. The dial showed 7:16.

"You're late again. Show me your time card."

Orson took a look at the stamp and grinned wolfishly as he carried the card over to my desk, laying the paper before me as if he were a server in a fine restaurant delivering an appetizer. The stamp read 6:58.

"Figures," I mumbled, taking another sip and grimacing. The coffee seemed worse than usual this morning but that was impossible. It always tasted like hell. "How come I'm always early, you're always late, but your time card shows you to be the model of punctuality?"

"Oh, I haven't the foggiest, Steve," Orson responded in the superior tone he frequently used when addressing me, or anyone else, for that matter. He scooped up his time card and placed it in the metal slot beneath mine, next to a sticker bearing his name. He then ambled over to the rickety stool; it shouldn't have been able to support his enormous bulk but somehow managed. "Maybe it's because I don't give a damn about being late and you do," he commented, settling his extravagant butt with great care on the stool.

Orson was right, the supercilious snot. I'd always had a thing about punctuality. "I'm in Hell," I murmured.

"Really?" Orson's eyes widened at this revelation.

I grabbed ***HOTI Form ∞3971\PDYFF 666 - 327\?///WOE # ∞8911763985*** and tossed it at him. "Here, Mr. Director. Direct your fat ass over there and pick up that glass!"

Orson winced at the jab but nodded wearily. With the right words it was easy to take out what little fight he had left in him. His surrender was temporary - he'd be his old condescending self in no time - but for the moment I'd hit him where he lived.

Or used to. Orson Welles was accustomed to running the show and now he was reduced to being my assistant.

We all have our own versions of Hell, which is where we were, in case you hadn't picked up on that. Hell, Hel, Hades, the Inferno, Gehenna, Acheron, Cocytus, Phlegethon, Lethe, Tartarus, the Netherworld, etc. Got lots of names. Pick your favorite.

Poor Orson. I felt some remorse contributing to his eternal torment. He really wasn't a bad guy, once you got past the over-sized ego. Besides, I suffered from a bit of that too: the Sin of Pride. Hmmph. Probably was the reason half of us were in Hell to begin with.

Generally, Orson and I got along well. There was a lot about him that was pretty cool. He wrote, directed and starred in what many think is the greatest movie of all time, though between you and me I liked 'Casablanca' better. Orson was, in his prime - which was young, having reached his personal best with his first movie - a handsome as well as an astonishingly successful man. He'd even been married to Rita Hayworth, and not very many people can say that. (Well, five people can, but that's still not very many.) Hell's management, in its wisdom, though, had opted to freeze Orson for Eternity in the layers of fat that had imprisoned him during his final years. His mortal coil, there at the end, was less a spring than a big mound of Silly Putty.

Most people came to Hell the way they looked at the end of their lives, since we tended to get worse with age rather than better. Aside from sagging skin, age-spotted complexions and bulging bellies, there was also the chance of a deformity or two, a dowager's hump, hands gnarled by arthritis, that sort of thing. Sometimes people died while still looking good; maybe they'd had a brain aneurism or something. Got that with teenagers and young adults - those who hadn't been killed by drugs, booze, car accidents or some combination thereof - but when one of the young and beautiful died, the Lords of Hell would usually afflict that unfortunate with an eternal case of zits or perpetual bad hair day.

As regards my own appearance, I was luckier than many. Male pattern baldness was my main disfigurement, along with a nose that would have put Cyrano's to shame. Satan or Beelzebub, or whoever it was who decided these things, must have felt my bald pate and monstrous schnozzle couldn't be improved on, and so I appeared in death much as I had at the end of my life, when a crazed graduate student blasted me to oblivion with a .44 magnum revolver.

Things might have been worse. Management could have left my skull pulverized.

Before my ultimate incident, I had been a tenured professor of economics at Columbia. Even had an endowed chair, my professional zenith, for about a month anyway. Then said graduate student blew my brains to smithereens.

I saw him around here recently. We chatted. Not too bad a kid really. He was just thoroughly pissed off at me for rejecting his dissertation proposal, not to mention being high on angel dust at the time.

I refer here to PCP, not real angel dust, the latter being much more benign, but still kind of irritating. People high on the genuine article, i.e. the stuff that falls from those characters with the white wings, tend to act like Aunt Bee from the old 'Andy Griffith Show' of the 1960s, except they can't bake as well.

Hell has my former student parking cars over at the Styx Harrah's.

What? You think we don't gamble in Hell? Sure we do. We just always lose.

Anyway - Orson. I could hear him sniffling from here as he swept up the glass. "I was somebody," he mumbled. "I was big, really big."

You got that right, Dumbo.

Thinking that made me feel guilty all over again.

That's one of the purposes of Hell, you know: to make us feel really guilty, though mainly for the things we did in life, not in the afterlife. But what can I say? I have a conscience. And like I mentioned a second ago, Orson and I get along, which is more than I can say about my relations with many of Hell's denizens.

I walked over to where Orson was sitting on the floor, tears in his eyes, rocking back and forth as he sucked his thumb. My heart went out to him. This once-great man was blubbering and blubbery, like some monstrous infant who'd just hurt himself. Turns out he had; the fat man pulled his thumb out of his mouth and blood oozed from a cut he'd gotten from the glass.

Orson was mumbling something about the irony of his misfortune, from a life as director to an afterlife as gopher. 'Best Boy', I think he would have been called in the movie business. Or was it 'Key Grip'? I never could keep them straight.

Orson heard my steps and quieted. "Yes?" he sniffled.

"Look, Orson," I began, preparing to do something I'd regret but it was the only way to make the guilt go away. "About that crack back there, I'm ..."

He looked up, horrified. "No. Don't. You don't have to do that."

"Yes, I do," I replied, sighing. "I'm ... I'm s ... sorry."

A blast of Hellfire slammed into me, knocking me on my ass, singeing what little hair I had and giving my face second-degree burns. Pieces of broken glass poked through my coveralls. And then the *coup de grâce*: a coconut cream pie appeared before me and crashed into my face with enough force to make my back and head go thump on the floor.

It's always coconut. I'm allergic: gives me hives. Red lesions began to well up on my scorched face.

Orson pulled a rag out of his pocket and gave it to me. As I wiped my face, I saw him weighing his options. "No," I said, removing the final bits of cream from my puss, "don't make the same mistake."

He nodded, then helped me to my feet.

You never say 'thank you' or 'I'm sorry' in Hell, at least not with sincerity. Kindness and gratitude are generally frowned upon around here. Orson was about to thank me, almost certainly, and he would have gotten pretty much the same treatment I had, except with a lemon cream pie. He hated lemon. I could see the gratitude on his face, though, because he knew what that apology had cost me.

We smiled at each other, but I winced. "Shit, that hurts!"

"Always does, doesn't it?"

"Yeah." I could already feel the wounds healing, though. You can't be permanently damaged in Hell, even though it may feel like it sometimes. I handed him back his rag. "Can you pick the rest of the glass out of my ass?"

He sighed, "I guess so," and pulled out a couple of small pieces I couldn't reach.

He then swept the remaining shards on the floor into a pile and I held the dustpan for him as he brushed them into it. "Go get some glass and a new doorknob," I instructed, dumping the fragments into the trashcan.

"Can't for another thirty minutes. Parts doesn't open until eight."

"Right, right. Then pour yourself some coffee and help me go over some of these work orders."

While I had been helping him, an occasional *whoop* had sounded in the background. That was the noise of incoming work orders. The work order system used one of those old-fashioned pneumatic tube contraptions. The end, my end anyway, was right above my wire inbox.

Since yesterday, a hundred new work orders had arrived. This was far more than a staff of two could ever handle. Naturally, our bosses knew this; they simply didn't care. All of the work orders were marked 'High' priority, so we did our own little triage.

"Oh, crap. Not again."

Orson looked up from the pile he was sorting. "What?"

I waved the order at him. It simply said, "Replace burnt-out bulb on Sign at Entrance."

My assistant shook his head, sighing. (There's a lot of sighing in Hell.) "Dora should be in by now. Want me to pick one up for you when I go to Parts?"

"Nah," I replied, standing from my chair. "I'll go with you. Maybe the walk will ease the pain in my butt."

And so began another day in the work afterlife of Hell's Super.

Superintendent, that is. That's right. I fix things. Sort of. In all Hell, there's only the two of us to do the work. I'm not a very good handyman. Orson's worse, if that's possible, but he's not really allowed to do the fixing anyway. That would give him a sense of accomplishment, something he craves, so naturally it is never allowed. Orson can only assist me as I fumble my way to a solution.

No surprise why my eternal damnation had taken this particular form. In life, I had hated home improvement.

Everything always went wrong. I'd get upset, lose my temper and make things even worse, poking a hole in a wall, stripping a faucet connection, and so forth. When the job was thoroughly FUBARed - that means fucked up beyond all recognition ... you really should get out more or spend a little time on a military base - I'd end up hiring a carpenter or plumber or electrician to finish the job. I resented paying them, resented their skills, and, well, being an intellectual snob, didn't think much of them or their chosen profession.

So upon my death, naturally I was consigned to handyman Hell.

This is what some call divine retribution. Others call it ironic. The Devil just thinks it's funny. I've been Hell's Super for so long it's sometimes hard for me to even conceive that once I was an intellectual. I certainly don't think much like an economist anymore, or talk like one. Blue-collar through and through, that's me, except for my refined sense of sarcasm.

I left only two work orders on my desk: one for the door to our office and the new one, the important one. Meanwhile, Orson took the rest over to the corner of the trailer, where he placed the work orders atop a pillar of paperwork four feet high. The stack was only one of about fifty on our office floor.

When we ran out of room, or when we felt the weight of the ignored work orders threatened to tip over the trailer, we threw away the oldest pile.

We'd worked out this system a long time ago. There was just no way two people could fix everything that broke in Hell. Hell, things always broke in Hell. The best we could manage was to do the most critical things - and the things we felt like doing, like fixing our own door - and disregard the rest. If we missed something important, we'd hear about it quickly enough, either through a duplicate order or a scream over the PA system.

I thought it might be a good idea to ignore the PA request for a while.

If an "overlooked" work order was important, and we didn't get a duplicate, the original was likely to be in the most current pile. Might take us an hour or so to find it, but we would eventually.

I had a feeling most Physical Plant departments worked like this back on Earth.

Chapter 2

As we stepped out of our trailer, I looked to the sky. The morning was a typical one for Hell; the air had the uncomfortable damp warmth of a coastal city without the benefit of a breeze. A sulfurous cloud of smog was rising from the Mouth of Hell, which was a big opening in the center of all nine levels of Hades. The smoky fumes, generated in the fiery depths of the Underworld, reeked of brimstone. The haze would soon tint the air, giving everything a grayish-yellow hue, like an old jock strap that never quite came clean in the wash.

Parts was in a large warehouse, painted in the camouflage colors of an Army jeep, not far from the trailer. Well, usually it wasn't far, though every once in a while Beezy - that would be Beelzebub, my boss - or one of his buddies would move Parts to some other corner of Hell. When that happened, we could spend days looking for the warehouse. Work orders sometimes filled the trailer to the ceiling when Parts went missing, especially if, once we found it, we had to travel long distances to get our orders filled.

Someone had been in a good mood for a while now, though. The building sat a mere fifty yards from our trailer. The service window for Parts was a two-sectioned door. The top portion, the window part, was open, and Dora, looking bored, leaned out of it, smoking a cigarette. Dora was always smoking a cigarette

Dora had died of lung cancer, but since she couldn't be any more dead than she already was, she continued to smoke. I'd always heard that nicotine was the most addictive substance on the planet, and perhaps the known and unknown universe as well, and if Dora's afterlife addiction was any indication ...

She got no pleasure from smoking, though. She hated menthol cigarettes but that's all she could get in Hell. Other people could get the non-menthol variety, but she couldn't.

One time she confided in me, "I told George - he was my fourth husband, you know - anyway, I told George I'd be dead before I smoked a menthol cigarette."

Well, there you go.

Dora usually fed her addiction with a Kool 100, though sometimes she smoked Newports.

Like most former blondes who died of lung cancer in their seventies, Dora had wrinkled skin that made her look vaguely reptilian. Her bleached locks were up in a bun and she wore horn-rimmed glasses. They suited the leopard-print blouse she wore every day. I think Dora probably had on a skirt, but since no one had ever seen her bottom half, we couldn't be sure.

Basically, I liked Dora, though every once in a while she'd be in a mood.

"Hi, HOTTIES!" she chirped in false merriment.

Like today, apparently.

HOTI, short for Hell's Office of The Interior, the name of Beezy's division, was stamped in big maroon letters on the backs of our coveralls.

"That's HOTI," Orson replied for probably the millionth time. This scene had played out before. "Rhymes with goatee, sort of, like mine." Orson ran his fingers through his luxurious iron-gray beard. He may have been fat but he had a great beard ... and a full head of hair. More than I could say.

I put my hand on his arm. "Save it. She's just pulling our chains."

"Ha-ha!" Dora said. "I got one of those, too." She reached down and lifted a chain that I could only assume was fastened to her ankle. "Just like Jacob Marley."

Well, I mused, that would fit. In life, Dora had run a paycheck loan service, charging an exorbitant 390 percent APR, and an effective rate of 3,685 percent. She'd made quite a killing, until the government stepped in and changed the laws, limiting the amount of interest such a service could charge to twenty-four percent. If she couldn't gouge people, Dora really didn't see the point. She got out of the business, but by then she was already stinking rich, having made her fortune on the backs of poor people with too much month and not enough money.

The Sin of Greed: one of the Big Seven. You know: Wrath, Greed, Sloth, Pride, Lust, Envy, and Gluttony. As I said, in life both Orson's and mine had been Pride.

Not really much of a surprise that she ended up being head of the Parts Department. I firmly believed, that many times when we asked for something, she in fact did have the item, she just didn't want to let go of things, and so she hoarded her parts. Old habits die hard, I knew. Yet she suffered as well as her customers. Eventually, Dora had to part, so to speak, with her precious inventory. Each time she filled an order must have been agony for her.

Orson leaned on the counter built into the bottom half of the door and gave Dora his most winning smile. "I need a door knob to replace the one that fell off our office door. Oh, and a piece of frosted glass to replace the one that *somebody*," he looked accusingly at me, "broke this morning."

She shook her head. "Can't help you with the glass. It's on back order. At least a week. What model door knob do you need?"

Orson scratched his beard in thought. "I believe it's a Yale, as opposed to a Columbia, which doesn't make door knobs ..."

"Ha-ha," I mimicked Dora. "Very funny. Now, smart ass, can you tell her the model?"

He frowned. "Yale, uh, model ..."

"Cirrus, in gun-metal gray," I finished for him.

It's my job to know these things.

"Well, dearie, let me just check the computer." Dora kept her inventory on a machine that looked to be an original IBM PC, or at best an XT. It was slower than shit rolling uphill. After about five minutes, she turned away from the screen and looked at us. "Sorry. It's on back order, too. Shall I put a hold on both items for you?"

"What do you think?" Orson snapped. He had to deal with Dora more than I did, so his patience with her frequent antics was thin occasionally. But you were impolite to the Head of Parts at your peril, and he knew it, so he quickly recovered. "Sorry, Dora. I know it isn't your fault ..."

"I need something too, sweetie," I said in my most charming voice. Be nice to Dora, and maybe she'll be nice to you. Maybe.

"Well, let's have it."

I told her.

"Not again! That's the fifth one this week. Do they think five million watt red compact fluorescent bulbs grow on trees?"

I shrugged.

"I know I don't have that. You took my last one the other day. Back ordered. Three to five days," which usually meant weeks. Dora frowned. She looked really pissed now.

"Sorry, Dora. I don't break the things but you know how important the Sign is." I sighed. "Do you have anything we might use until the order comes in?"

She frowned, thumping her index finger on her chin in thought. Then she brightened. "Well, I have this." She pulled out a yellow, forty watt insect repellent bulb. "Think you could make it work?"

I rubbed my brow. A bad headache was beginning to form in there. For a moment, I closed my eyes, hoping that when I opened them, my surroundings would have magically changed. I cracked an eyelid just as a blast of Dora's cigarette smoke hit my face. Eyes watering, I stretched out my hand. "I guess we'll have to try."

"Okay, sign here, you little f … fucker. In triplicate."

I'm always caught off-guard when Dora swears. She just isn't the type. But everyone swears here; it's impossible not to. All those naughty words, they just seem to pop out constantly from every mouth in Hell, like bubbles from a boiling pot. My friend Oscar Wilde, who pays a great deal of attention to language, explained it to me one time over a shared bowl of treacle. (Yes, it's sweet, but a whole bowl is just as nasty tasting as the name sounds.) "My dear chap," he said, "in life, many of us swore anyway. Those who didn't, wanted to. We all come down here, and well, certain things in the Netherworld can only be properly communicated with a good curse. Some people who never swore in their lives might swear less than your average, but they still do the deed. Others, who never cursed, seem to take to it with relish, and you'll have grandmother types swearing like old tars."

I took the clipboard from Dora and rested it on the doorsill. "I know the drill, Dora."

"Just doin' my job."

"Me too," I said, signing and dropping the pen on the clipboard. I had to pry the bulb from Dora's fingers, and when it finally left her grasp, her whole body shuddered, looking like she'd just given me her first-born child.

Good grief, it was only a light bulb.

"Be careful with that," she rasped. "I only have a few of those left. The rest are …"

Orson and I looked at each other. "... on back order," we said in unison.

"That's right, HOTTIES," she confirmed, apparently fully recovered from her recent loss. "Oh, if you get a chance, pick me up a carton of Kools. I'm almost out."

"Sure thing, Dora." Orson smiled at her. He didn't look particularly sincere but he knew he had to stay on her good side. Better him than me, or as Orson would say, rather he than I.

At the moment I felt like slamming the forty-watter against Dora's skull. Instead, I just smiled and said I'd catch her later.

As I already mentioned, I like Dora. Compared to most of the creeps in Hell, she's a saint. Besides, she runs the Parts Department. I need her.

"I know we've got to replace the bulb," Orson said as we walked across the street to the trailer, "but we can't just leave the door open like that while we're gone."

Nodding, I reached for my duct tape.

While I'm really bad at fixing things, I've always been good with duct tape, the universal tool of last resort. Since my death, Satan's made me even better. I'm sure enhancing my skills was not a kindness on his part but a move of necessity. Even though my inept fumbling must provide for great hilarity among the devils and demons who run the place, at the end of the day even Hell has to keep the trains running, and if they gave me no tools at all, it wouldn't happen.

Not that Hell actually has days. Eternity is just ... well ... Eternity, but you get my drift.

Damn, I was fast with the stuff! If I had lived in the Old West and come upon Billy the Kid, I probably could have taped him to the side of the saloon before his gun had cleared its holster.

Billy's here in Hell. I see him every once in a while. He's a soda jerk at one of Hell's McDonalds. Still wears his guns, though. Maybe I should call him out sometime and settle this fast-draw thing once and for all.

I stood before the door of our trailer, both hands resting lightly on the two rolls of duct tape that hung from spools at my hips. *Draw!*

I grabbed at each roll, pulling the gray tape out with a dizzying rapidity. My right hand made a pass at the top of the window frame, tore the tape, and then my left hand made another pass, overlapping the strip above it. In seconds I'd covered the hole where the window had been. Then I ran a strip from the top of the door to its bottom, tearing the tape in a clean line and sticking the end to the door jam. Ten seconds flat.

"How do you do that?" Orson marveled.

I shrugged. "It's my job. Hell's handyman."

"Do you ... do you think you could teach me?"

"Sorry, Orson, I'd like to, but it's a gift. Besides, you know Beezy won't let you accomplish anything. You're only here to assist."

Orson scowled. "Screw you!" he snapped, putting his back to me.

Great. Now he was going to be impossible to work with for the rest of the day.

I reached down and pulled some of the tape away from the door. "Rats, I missed a spot. Orson, would you help me with this?"

Orson spun back to me, his face transformed. "Really? You need my help?"

Honestly, he could be just like a little kid sometimes. "Yeah, really. See?"

"Okay. Sure. What do you want me to do?"

"Would you hold the top flat while I smooth out this bottom section?"

Almost in reverence, Orson put his hand to the duct tape and held it in place, while I took my palm and smoothed down the tape. I made a point of wrinkling it a little so the job didn't look perfect. "Thanks," I said, rising. "Oh, Orson? Sorry, but I keep forgetting. Key Grip?"

His lips flattened immediately and he began making an impatient popping sound with his mouth. "No, 'Best Boy'. But please don't call me that."

"You prefer 'assistant'?"

"I guess."

"Why?"

" 'Best Boy' has too many associations for me."

"Okay, *assistant*. Oh, and Orson, I'd rather have you for my assistant than anyone in Hell."

"Thanks, Steve. I like you, too."

A few seconds later we were helping each other off the pavement, Orson cursing as he wiped the lemon cream from his face and eyes, me doing the same with the coconut cream missile that had hit me. I didn't have a rag, so I used duct tape.

"Let's just get the hell out of here before we get slammed again."

Orson grabbed a ladder from our storage shed and we began to hoof it the few blocks to Hell's Elevator.

I know the standard image of Hell: volcanoes, hot lava and Hellfire everywhere; people tied up to racks or placed on spits and spun slowly, like rump roasts, over staggeringly hot flames. There's plenty of that, I won't deny. Mostly, though, fire and brimstone is for the people who have bought into one particular notion of Hell. I mean, if that's what they think the Infernal

Realm is all about, who is Satan to disabuse them of the notion? There are also folks who have an extreme fear of pain and/or fire. Sure, we have here an image of the Netherworld that fits many people's preconceptions, and accordingly there's a bunch of infernal landscape devoted to it.

Me, I always thought Hell would be less about pain than about boredom, tedium and hopelessness. Seems I'm right, or at least that's how Hell appears to my senses. Who knows how other people see it? All a matter of perspective, I guess.

From my point of view, Hell looks like Scranton, or maybe Gary, Indiana. A little dirtier, perhaps. Some areas, especially the interstates, remind me of LA.

Across the street was an oil refinery, six blocks long, belching flames through numerous pipes scattered symmetrically across the tops of its buildings. If you squinted a little, the thing looked sort of like a really noxious birthday cake. In the center was an extra-large pipe for special occasions when the factory had to torch a boatload of extra gas. At those times, we seemed to have a small star burning on our street.

A few blocks away were the entry gates of an abandoned steel factory, acres and acres of dull, gray buildings that showed no signs of activity. On my side of the street, behind the little trailer Orson and I called our office, was a chemical plant as big as Manhattan. Pipes, like twisted pieces of cold spaghetti, connected building to building. These factories served no purpose at all other than to add to Hell's ambiance, giving it that 'Gary' quality I mentioned above.

After a short walk, we reached Hell's Elevator shaft, a towering obsidian monolith that stretched up into an indeterminate sky. It did end up there somewhere - had to - where the next Level of Hell began, but you couldn't see the terminus any more than you could spot the sun on a cloudy day back on Earth. For as far as the eye could see, things just looked like sky up there, gray, overcast and really polluted, but sky.

The queue for the Elevator on Hell's end was usually pretty short. Almost no one rode up on the Lift; very few were authorized to go beyond the Second Circle of Hell. Can't have damned souls taking the Elevator out of the Underworld anytime they wanted. You had to have a key to get to the top two floors. Orson and I, as Hell's maintenance staff, each had one.

We were in luck, if 'luck' were even a concept worth contemplating in Nether-Netherland. No one was standing in front of us. Still, we had to wait a long time for the Elevator to stop on our level.

Hell's Elevator was pretty big, designed to accommodate a lot of souls. Its door was a lot like what you'd have fronting a two-car garage. Unfortunately, on most Levels there was no automatic opener. I grabbed the handle on the elevator door, and with a little help from Orson, we shoved it up enough to slide inside, then let it slam down behind us. The arrow on the control panel was pointing up, and I punched the GL button. GL: that would be Gates Level, both of them.

Chapter 3

I swear. Hell's Elevator is possessed by some demon. The Elevator always takes forever to come to your level. The creature seems to sit between floors, smoking a cigarette, while waiting for the person pressing the call button to get thoroughly pissed off before deciding to show. But once you finally get inside, the Elevator takes off like a rocket.

We started to rise quickly and were hard-pressed to maintain our footing. Though the actual distances in the infernal firmament were more metaphysical than physical, you still got the feeling that traveling from, say, Circle Five, where my office was located, to the Gates Level was a very long way, yet we were there in seconds. The Elevator lurched to a stop, and Orson and I were suspended in free-fall for a moment before crashing back down to the floor.

Together we lifted the door and stepped out, Orson dragging the ladder behind him. The door snapped down like an alligator, pinning the ladder beneath a hundred pounds of metal.

"D ... damn this thing to Hell!" Orson stammered, as with my help he extricated the ladder from the mouth of the beast.

"Watch your language," I whispered. "Remember where we are."

We were standing on Cloud. In the distance, bathing the surroundings with opalescent light, were the Pearly Gates. Before them, St. Peter, Heaven's Concierge, sat at his high, podium-like desk. I nodded politely to him.

"Hmph. I still think I could do that better."

"Don't start again."

"No, I'm serious," Orson continued, handing me the ladder. He made a wide 'U' with his hands, the thumbs forming the bottom and the fingers the sides. He stared through the U, framing his shot of The Entrance to Heaven. "The Gates should be raised and at a distance. I've always said that, haven't I? And light should stream through, promising something special on the other side. Having the Gates glow, well, that's just garish."

"Orson ..." I warned.

"You know what I'd do?" he said enthusiastically. "Do you remember the scene in Citizen Kane where I'm standing by the fireplace? I'd do the same thing here. A deep focus shot with Peter in the foreground, big as, well, Afterlife, and the Pearly Gates behind him in the distance, both perfectly in focus. You know, your eyes can't really do that, but with the right lens you can do it on film."

"Yeah, I know. You've told me about a zillion times. Now, will you stifle? St. Peter can hear you." Peter gave Orson a hard-edged look, then turned back to the long line before him. Gates Level seemed pretty busy. "Besides, we've got work to do."

"Ah, right," he said reluctantly, taking the ladder back from me and shouldering it. "Sorry."

"Not a problem. Let's go."

Right now, with all the soon-to-be-sorted souls milling around, crowding the space before Peter's desk, and all but obliterating the view of the Gates themselves, The Entrance to Heaven didn't exactly inspire awe. Truth be told, Orson probably could jazz things up. He always did have a good eye, but Hell's administration never cared about something looking nice, and even if it did, Satan & Sons wouldn't give Orson the satisfaction that would come from doing the job. Not to mention that the Pearly Gates were under different management.

But that wasn't my problem, anyway. My immediate concern was the Entrance to Hell. A ways to the right of Peter's desk was

Hell's Escalator. Going down. Way down. The Escalator was the method by which most of the newly-damned entered the Underworld. Framing the Escalator were the Infernal Gates, which weren't really gates at all but three electric signs. The one to the left read: 'WELCOME TO HELL.' That on the right advertised: 'OVER 30 BILLION SERVED.' A large sign sitting atop and spanning the gap between the other two was dark. All three were wired independently, so one could go out while the other two remained lit, but each sign had to have all of its bulbs in working order or, like a Christmas tree, the whole thing would be dark. Like now.

The broken sign was an old one that needed replacing. I had been putting it in my budget request for years, but the item had been denied repeatedly. Yet the damn thing went on the fritz so often that Beezy had made one concession to practicality. He had put in a system that told me which bulb was burned out. Thank Go ... That was helpful.

(Oh, Hell's minions really aren't supposed to reference one of the Trini ... one of the Big Three ... by name, not even while cursing. The curious result is that swearing in Hell has been watered down a bit, with a greater reliance on 'potty mouth' to compensate for our inability to take the L___'s name in vain.)

In the old days, I had to block the Escalator for hours as I tested each bulb individually. Even so, the few minutes we were going to need swapping in the replacement would cause some backup in St. Peter's foyer. I took a strip of duct tape and blocked off a portion of space in front of the Escalator to give us some room to operate, then taped an 'out of order' sign on a small cumulus job floating nearby. "Step back, everyone!" Orson said theatrically. "We're working here."

We only had our five foot painter's ladder - the big one was broken - so this would be a stretch for me. With Orson steadying things, I climbed past the final step to the top platform. That really wasn't considered safe but there wasn't anything else to do. The sign had to be fixed. I just hoped no one would report me to the union.

That would be Satan's Employees Infernal Union. Membership is mandatory; we pay dues but never get improvements in wages or working conditions. Periodically, though, some of us are chosen to serve on the labor bargaining team, which means we sit across from a group of Management that might include Beelzebub, Baal, Ashtoreth, Hecate or one of those other jokers. They listen to our demands, we have a lot of arguing or dissimulation or the like that goes on for a few months, then Management will just laugh, thank us for all the entertainment we've given them, and tell us to go to Hell.

From the top platform of the ladder, I couldn't quite reach the burnt-out bulb. Orson might have been able to - he had an inch or two on me - but since he was not allowed to fix anything, that was out. *Damn*. Good thing we had a strong ladder.

I climbed back down to Cloud level. The crowd waiting to descend the Escalator had already thickened. "Orson," I said slowly. "I hate to ask you, but ..."

"Oh, come on, not again."

I shrugged. "Do we have a choice?"

"Guess not." Orson bit his lip. "You know, I feel like swearing but I'm having a hard time doing it. Have you noticed?"

"Yeah. I think it's the proximity to the PGs. Kind of puts a damper on bad language. Anyway, sorry about this."

I climbed up again, stopping on the last legal step. No point making this worse than necessary. Then Orson climbed up to the step just beneath me and, on the top platform, used his hands to brace himself. His shoulders were now more than two feet higher than the top of the ladder, which teetered dangerously, before a little balancing act on our part steadied it.

Don't try this at home. We're professionals.

Veeerrry carefully I placed one foot between Orson's hands, stepped up, put my free foot on one of his shoulders, and climbed up again. I could barely touch the bottom of the sign. Clutching its lip tightly with my fingers, I stepped off the platform and onto Orson's other shoulder. We wobbled some more, but now I had a firm grip on my target, so the wiggling stopped in pretty short order.

The bulb in question was just within reach. Before I could unscrew it, though, I had to release a latch. Funny. None of the other bulbs I'd ever changed on the sign had had a latch, but Hell's maintenance jobs often had little complications like this, just to mess with my head. The latch seemed completely superfluous to me, but whatever. From my tool belt I retrieved a screwdriver, but it was a flathead and I needed a Phillips. I dropped the thing to the cloud floor.

"Hey!" Orson snapped. "Watch it!"

"Sorry," I mumbled, reaching to the place where my Phillips normally hung. The belt loop was empty. "Shit!" I said, Pearly Gates or no. "Orson, could you pass me up your Phillips?"

"Oh, sure, no problem, it's not like we're going to lose our balance or anything." But he managed to extract the Phillips from his belt and hand it to me.

"Thanks." I unscrewed the single bolt holding down the latch, then slipped Orson's Phillips into the loop where mine normally resided. The latch was stuck, but after a bit of pulling on my part, it swung back, allowing me to access and unscrew the monstrous bulb that had burned out. "Orson, do you want me to hand this down to you or just drop it?"

"Are you kidding? Drop the sucker!" he gasped, straining under my weight. (Even damned souls are affected by gravity, but only when it's inconvenient.)

"Okay. Here goes. Close your eyes." I dropped the bulb, and there was a loud ***POP!*** as it hit the Celestial surface. St. Peter shot me a dirty look.

"Sorry, sorry. Lost my grip," I said vaguely in his direction while checking my pockets for the replacement bulb. Oh, right. I'd given it to Orson for safekeeping. "Orson, pass me the bulb."

"What am I, a hardware store?" he grumbled but reached into the chest pocket of his coveralls and retrieved the bulb. He almost dropped it. I almost did too when he passed it up to me, but I managed to keep my grip and inserted the bulb into the empty socket.

It didn't fit.

I really hadn't expected it to but it had been worth a shot. Now for Plan B. Pulling out the bulb, I reached into my own breast pocket and retrieved a piece of aluminum foil. I shoved it into the vacant bulb socket. There was the crackling sound of electricity trying to do something but not really sure what to make of a piece of foil. I did my best to screw in the insect bulb, then secured it with some duct tape.

The sign lit up, and both Orson and I yelled in triumph, which destabilized our precarious perch, sending us tumbling to the ground. The ladder fell on top of us.

After the stars cleared from our eyes, we looked up to find St. Peter hovering above us. "Nice job," he said, with all the sarcasm a saint can muster (which is more than you'd expect). "You know, if there were one more of you, you could be the Three Stooges. As you are, you're just a couple of morons. Now, have you finished making noise? I need to get back to work."

"Sorry, St. Peter," we both mumbled as we got to our feet, brushing cloud and broken glass from our coveralls. "Won't happen again."

Peter looked at us critically. "Forgive me if I don't bet the farm on that. Oh, and clean up that glass before you go." With that, he left us.

Orson glowered at him. "Why, that supercilious little pr ..."

I put my hand over his mouth. "Don't say it! Beezy doesn't like him any more than you do, but it would go bad for you if you said anything, especially up here."

The breath of a suppressed sigh dampened my fingers but he nodded, so I took away my hand. "Let's go." I said, pulling up the tape before the Escalator and removing the 'out of order' sign. "We're done here."

"What about the glass?"

"Leave it. It was made in Hell and will disintegrate up here, now that it's touching the clouds."

As we walked toward the Elevator, I started humming. For us, this had been a pretty smooth job. Abruptly I broke into song.

Comma, comma, comma, comma, comma, comma, comma
I'm your handyman.

"That's 'come-a,' " Orson corrected.

I stopped in the middle of a 'yaay.' "Really?"

"Sure. Why would you sing about a bit of punctuation?"

"I always thought James Taylor was saying 'comma.' "

"You mean Jimmy Jones, youngster. He did the song first. And you're wrong. It's 'come-a,' like 'come to me.' "

"Oh," I said, somewhat deflated.

Orson set the ladder down in the Clouds. "Oh, don't be a baby. Besides, you did fix the sign."

I looked up at my handy work:

> THROUGH ME YOU PASS INTO THE CITY OF WOE.
> THROUGH ME YOU PASS INTO ETERNAL PAIN.
> THROUGH ME GO THE PEOPLE LOST FOREVER.
> ABANDON ALL hope YE WHO ENTER HERE.

"Uh, not very impressive, is it?"

Orson squeezed my shoulder. It was the one I'd landed on, and it hurt like hell. "Best you could do under the circumstances. Besides, it's temporary. Next time, though, let's bring the big ladder ... once we fix it."

I rubbed my sore shoulder. "You said it."

We were waiting for the Elevator when a strong breeze, smelling of sulfur, dispersed a gaggle of clouds beside Hell's Escalator, and up through the Throat of Hell, straight up the funnel, flew a giant apparition. The monstrous thing was as big as a pteranodon. It screeched when it sensed me, banked right and dropped to the cloudy surface right beside the Elevator.

The newly-damned souls howled their terror. Even Peter looked disturbed.

The infamous Bat out of Hell, a.k.a. BOOH, was a giant vampire bat. Its fangs always oozed blood and its face was fixed in an expression of rabid ferocity. BOOH was clutching a scroll of paper with the claws of its left foot, which was about the size of a rake. The bat held out the scroll to me and, shuddering, I took it from the creature, being careful not to touch a claw or any of the noxious animal's skin or fur. With another screech, BOOH launched into the air and shot back into Hell's funnel.

I hated dealing with BOOH - he gave me the heebie-jeebies - but only one being used the Bat out of Hell for deliveries, the big S himself, so I told my heart to calm down and unrolled the paper.

"Ow! Ow!" I said, passing the paper like a hot potato back and forth between my two hands. It was a work order limned with flames. I let the paper drop and heard it sizzle as the fire melted away some of the cloud cover. Quickly I donned my leather gloves and picked up the work order.

Satan had filled this one out himself and marked it 'top priority,' which all of his always were. The Earl of Hell had three different handwriting styles and you usually could tell his mood by which one he used on a work order. Sometimes the script was fluidly elegant - that would be his Lucifer persona; he used that when he was pleased with himself or was showing off to somebody. Other times, his writing was thin and spidery; it just reeked of evil. That was the kind of script he used for a contract for somebody's soul. Most often, though, the handwriting on work orders looked like a doctor's: chaotic and almost completely illegible. That's what I had in front of me now, something I needed to decipher. "Hey, Orson, put down the ladder a sec and help me figure this out."

I heard a thud as Orson dropped the ladder once again to the cloud floor. He leaned over my shoulder. We must have made a pretty picture, the two of us frowning as we tried to puzzle out each word. "What's that?"

"I think it says 'Excalibur,' " Orson said.

I gave him a withering look. "Now, why would he be writing me about a mythical blade?"

Orson shrugged. "Beats me. Or maybe it says 'Eschallot.' "

"Well, that's even more stupid. Green onions?"

"That's scallion, not shallot, you peasant." Orson studied the work order some more. "No, I've got it now. 'Escalator.' "

I stared hard at the word. "Yeah, I think you're right, but I can't make sense of anything else, except maybe this at the end: 'Seemestat!' "

"Isn't that the succubus who does his nails?"

"You're thinking of Sir-ruššu, his pet dragon. I don't think that's what it says." My stomach got queasy as I figured it out. "No ... he's saying 'See me stat.' He wants to talk to me right away."

"Well, I guess you better hop on the Elevator as soon as it gets here."

"No time for that. 'STAT' means now, this instant." I had made the mistake once of keeping Satan waiting, and a year on the spit, being turned over flames while watching a 'Barney & Friends' marathon had driven the lesson home. Never, NEVER keep Satan waiting. I folded the now cooled work order and tucked it in my right pocket, then pulled off my gloves, unbuckled my tool belt and handed them to Orson. "Here. Take these back to the shop for me, okay?"

"Sure. What are you going to be doing?"

"Scaring myself shitless," I replied, taking off at a dead run toward Hell's funnel. Like Sonic the Hedgehog, I curled myself up into a ball and flung myself down the hole. "Geronimo!"

Chapter 4

"Aaaaaaaaaaaaaaaaaaaaaaaaaaaaaaaaaaaaaaaaaaaaaaaaaaaa aaaaaaaaaaaaa ..."

I screamed the entire time I fell through the infernal funnel. I had done this once before and knew it wouldn't permanently hurt me (after all, I am dead), but I'd always been a little nervous around great heights, or in this case depths, and a drop like this made a fall from the Empire State Building seem like hopping off a bike.

Besides, death doesn't diminish the survival instinct, even if being, well ... not alive ... makes that instinct sort of *ex post facto*. We humans are so hard-wired to avoid pain that even down here the prospect of going splat after a nine mile drop gets the old juices flowing.

While falling, curled up in my tight little ball so as not to touch the side of Hell's Throat, I watched some of the Circles of Hell go by. The golf course on Level One was being mown and a couple of foursomes were waiting to tee off. I saw some people in Lustland being denied sex, or getting sex they didn't really want, or dealing with partners having headaches. The big eaters in Glutton's Gap were discovering that platefuls of beef jerky weren't as delightful as they'd hoped. The hoarders would hoard then lose things, and the sullen were simply sullen. They'd been in Hell even in life.

Down I plunged, faster and faster, like a fallen angel cast from Heaven after the War, or a maintenance worker who had jumped into a very big hole with no real bottom. I reached terminal velocity, but already having been terminated, I sped up some more.

I was falling so rapidly now that nothing was visible except changes in light levels. There would be dark, and then there would be light.

The dark times were when I was 'beneath ground,' 'ground' not being exactly accurate but close enough to describe the metaphysical landscape on which a particular Level of Hell existed. While flying, or falling, through the hole in a level, I was completely blind, so my other senses took over. Smell mostly: the odor of sulfur was intense. There was another stench, though, like the overpowering 'gag me' of backed-up sewage. My ears couldn't pick up much more than my own screams, but when I paused to take a breath, I'd hear a whizzing sound, sort of a *zzzzzzzzzzzzz*. I guess that was what a body sounded like when it was falling really, really fast through a hole in the ground. As for taste, there was only the tang of my own blood. I'd bitten my tongue around Level Three. Finally, my sense of touch could pick up but one thing: heat, oppressive heat, like what might be found in a blast furnace, if a human were able to tolerate that and live. Being dead and in Hell, though, I'd already proven I could take the heat, so would not have been surprised if it really was as hot as a blast furnace.

Though now flying blind, I could sense the solid surface of the ring's exterior. If I wanted to reach out my hand, it would touch rock, superheated perhaps, but solid nonetheless. I tried it once, experimentally, but that was a really bad idea. The pads of my fingertips blistered in an instant and my hand felt as if it would be seared off, so I tightened back up into my little ball of ectoplasm and kept dropping.

Each time, the darkness seemed to go on forever, though it could not have been as long as a second, as fast as I was falling. Then I would see light, at first just a luminous patch beneath me, like the opening at the end of a long tunnel. The circle of light grew rapidly until I broke free into what passed for sky in the next level of Hell.

I don't know what was worse, the claustrophobic black of the infernal circles or the agoraphobia - inducing gray of the sky between them. Despite knowing intellectually that my descent was in a straight line - meaning that when I reached the surface of the next level, I'd just pass through it without harm - every human instinct in me screamed I'd soon go *splat*, like a parachutist whose silk hadn't deployed. The gray surrounded me and I was just as blind in it as in the black of a circle's core. I had no idea where the ground was. The heat was gone, and the thin air, at least at the heights, was cold. The *zzzzzzzzzzzz* sound had been transformed into a sort of *sssssshhhhhhh*.

I could sense the ground just before reaching it, and the inchoate fear of crash landing became oppressive. Then I passed into a hole in the surface and the cycle repeated itself.

I did this nine times.

"Aaaaaaaaaaaaaaaaaaaaaaaaaaaaaaaaaaaaaaaaaaaaa aaaaaaaaaa ... ***Ouch!***"

My aim had been pretty good. I went ***splat*** on the carpet before Satan's office, all of my non-corporeal bones shattering, but because they broke in Hell, they quickly mended themselves, and the excruciating pain of the impact was soon reduced to a mild headache.

I stood, did a couple of stretches to get the kinks out, and found myself face-to-face with Bruce the Bedeviled, Satan's effusively gay appointment secretary. In life, he had not been gay. He had in fact been a heterosexual in overdrive, not to mention a famous martial artist. But in Hell his only kickass moments occurred when he found you had missed your appointment by three minutes and must either wait in the iron maiden until Satan felt like seeing you or reschedule for three centuries from now.

Usually the Devil doesn't bother with the sexual orientation of his subjects, finding the focus of a soul's individual damnation in other aspects of its life on Earth. Satan is not prejudiced; he punishes everyone indiscriminately. In this regard, I respect him. However, every once in a while, he'll flip someone's druthers. Some gay guys are turned into macho pigs in Hell; some macho pigs are turned gay. Usually it's Satan's revenge on a life spent as a homophobe or a heterophobe. I think in this case, though, the Devil was just making a cheap joke out of the name 'Bruce.' Kind of juvenile, but I'm sure as hell not going to be the one to tell him so.

Bruce checked the wall clock above his desk, and was just getting ready to berate me for tardiness when the intercom buzzed. "Send him in," said a garbled voice.

Great. No Lucifer persona today, then.

I headed toward the door, hoping it wouldn't be the horned version. I stepped on his tail once and had to spend an hour in the Maiden.

Fortunately, Satan almost never appears in classic devil garb. He thinks it's gauche. He'll usually only wear it for the children. Satan will do anything for the little ones. He adores them, especially toasted and served with a good marmalade.

Maybe it will be the dapper, Ray Walston type, à la 'Damned Yankees.' I doubted it, though. Judging from the voice, it was probably ...

The door to Satan's Office swung inward. The smell of sulfur almost made me faint, but Bruce waved for me to go in.

One of the difficult things about dealing with Satan is that he's so unpredictable. That's because he represents Chaos - universal entropy. It's no accident that mathematically Entropy is represented by the letter 'S.' And that's what he was today: Chaos Incarnate.

Standing in the center of the office, before the large rosewood desk that stretched for what seemed miles in either direction, was a Protean figure, constantly changing from a ball of flame, to a cloud of dark smoke, to a winged demon, and then to television static, like we used to have before TV broadcast 24/7 and stations actually went off the air for the night.

You need to know something about me. I don't scare easily. The Wicked Witch of the West doesn't frighten me (not since I was a kid, anyway). Jason never did; neither did Freddy Krueger. Beelzebub, the great Lord of the Flies, he doesn't scare me, except when he's mad at me.

Shit, even my former mother-in-law didn't frighten me, and she was a nut case.

At this particular moment in my afterlife, only three things really scared me: BOOH, free-falling through the Nine Circles of Hell and Satan. Please note I'd just experienced all three in rapid succession.

Satan frightened me most of all. He wasn't Number Two in the Universe for nothing. It was for this reason that one of my mantras had always been: 'Don't screw with Satan.'

Let me say it again: 'Don't screw with Satan.' Just be unfailingly respectful and try to get away from him in one piece as quickly as you can.

"What took you so long?" the Adversary hissed.

At this point I soiled myself and fell to the ground in a dead faint.

A cloven hoof kicked me. "Oh, get up. I don't have time for this."

"Sorry, Lord Satan," I stammered, rising to my feet. "I came as soon as BOOH delivered the work order. May I leave now?"

"No. Oh, Hell and Damnation!" he said, and the constantly morphing figure resolved itself into a tall man in black suit and dark sunglasses. "There. Think you can handle this form?"

"Yes, yes sir. Thank you, sir."

"Sit," the Prince of Darkness ordered.

A chair materialized behind me. It was a small, folding metal chair, the kind I sat on when I played euphonium in my high school band. I tested the chair with my weight. It seemed solid enough, if uncomfortable. At least I didn't have the extra pounds of my old instrument in my lap. That would have made it worse.

Satan flashed me his biggest smile. "Would you like a euphonium to hold?"

I hate it when he does that. A man's thoughts should be his own, but you can't really hide much from Satan. If he wants, he'll just pluck thoughts right out of your brain. "No, thank you, sir."

"Then shut up, and listen to me. Something's happened."

"What, sir?"

The chair heated up abruptly and I could feel the hot metal, even through my coveralls. "Ouch!"

"Didn't I say shut up?"

I nodded rapidly, like a bobblehead doll.

"Hell's Escalator has broken down."

"But ..." It had been working fine a few minutes ago. Satan frowned at me and I remembered to hold my tongue.

"It happened while you were falling. And before you get yourself in trouble by opening your mouth again, yes, that's what the work order was about. I knew it was about to happen." He looked smug. "I'm Satan, after all, and this is my domain. Nothing goes on without me knowing it."

Behind the Prince of Hell, another chair materialized, though his was a bright red La-Z-Boy. He settled in it, kicking back to raise the footrest. Satan frowned as he rested his chin on steepled fingers. "I want you to get it fixed, of course. But more than that, I want you to find out who broke it."

"But don't you know?"

Satan briefly transformed into a giant King Cobra so he could hiss at me properly, then returned to his man-in-black form. "If I did, would I be asking you to find out? I know what happens in Hell but not always who is doing it, especially if there's more than one soul involved, as I suspect is the case here. This was a conspiracy, an act of sabotage, designed to create chaos in my domain."

"But I thought you liked chaos."

Satan smiled grimly and for a moment returned to constantly morphing from fire to smoke to demon to television static. My stomach began to roil but I was incapable of looking away.

Satan's like that. Love him or hate him - strike that, hate him or hate him even more - he's still mesmerizing.

Just before I lost my breakfast, he reverted to the man-in-black persona. "This is a public relations disaster in the making. Pete has already called to complain. He says the damned souls are stacking up."

"The Elevator ..."

"Can't handle the volume, as you well know. I don't much care if Peter is inconvenienced, but he can get me in trouble with our mutual Boss, and I don't need that." Satan got out of his chair, which promptly disappeared. "Now get going. Fix the damned thing or come up with an alternative."

"An alternative?"

"What, are you incurably stupid? Why did I make you Hell's Super?"

"To punish me, I thought."

"Well, yes, that's right. But you usually get the important stuff done." A small part of me felt a spark of pride. "If not very well," he added. The spark died.

"If you can't fix the Escalator quickly, you'll need to rebuild the Stairway."

Despite myself, I groaned. The Stairway to Heaven, a.k.a. the Stairway to Paradise, a.k.a. the Stairway to Hell, hadn't been used - or maintained - in decades. The only part in good working order led from the Gates Level to The First Circle, or Limbo, which was a gated golf community populated by virtuous pagans and unbaptized babies. These days, about the only person who used that flight of stairs was St. Peter himself, who liked to go down to visit his friend Socrates or play a quick nine holes.

In our spare time, of which we had little, Orson and I had been dismantling the Stairway, per Beezy's orders. We were down to the Fourth Circle. Rebuilding the Stairway would be a Herculean undertaking.

I cleared my throat. "Ah, couldn't people just walk down the Escalator until it gets fixed?"

Satan shook his head. "That's against code. The steps are too high."

"Oh, well, that makes sense, I guess." Fix the Escalator or rebuild the damn Stairway. Agghh. Orson and I couldn't do all that ourselves. No matter how frightening Satan was, I needed to screw up my courage and ask for more resources.

"If it comes to that, get whoever you want." Satan handed me a blank check, signed, "Lord Satan, Lucifer the Fallen, Earl of Hell." "Don't write anything in the amount blank," he warned, "or your hand will burn off for all Eternity. But just show it to others and you shouldn't have any trouble. You can approach anyone directly or go through Beelzebub."

"Thank you, Lord Satan." I stuffed the check in my inside pocket, then hesitated. "With the Escalator broken and the Elevator working to capacity, I'm going to need some way to get around fast."

The Lord of Hell slid his sunglasses down his nose and took a close look at me. His eyes were red and gouts of flame burst occasionally from the pupils. He grinned. "I thought of that, too. You can use BOOH."

"BOOH - Bat out of Hell BOOH?"

"Yep. Since you can't just will yourself to where you want to go, like I can, it's the fastest way to get you anywhere in Hell. Except my office. Freefall is still the best method for that."

Great. Just great. Being carried around by a vampire bat the size of a small Cessna. BOOH, who also just happened to scare me shitless. How could it get more perfect? "Uh, how do I contact him?"

"Oh, he's just like a big puppy dog. Whistle and call him by name."

Behind Satan there was a flickering, and a scene from an old black and white movie began to play. I recognized it: 'To Have and Have Not.' A sultry woman with big shoulders and light-brown hair was kissing Humphrey Bogart. She stepped away from him and started talking. The volume was turned down but I knew what she was about to say.

Oh good grief.

At the proper moment the sound kicked in, and Satan, in unison with Lauren Bacall, said, "You know how to whistle, don't you, Steve?"

Please.

"You just put your lips together and ... blow."

The movie vanished.

"Bwahahahahahaha! I kill myself!" Satan laughed for a good minute, bloody tears streaming from underneath his sunglasses.

Satan thinks he has a great sense of humor, and you never know when you'll fall victim to it. That's another part of his unpredictability.

I did my best to smile, though it probably came out as more of a grimace. "Good one, sir," I said without much conviction.

"Go ahead," he said finally, still chuckling. "Try it."

Whistling for Bacall was one thing, for BOOH quite another, but orders were orders. Lips together, mouth chalk dry and no wind to speak of, I finally managed a feeble tweet. "Whoo ... whoo ..."

"Louder, you weenie!"

After a few more attempts, I got out a decent one.

"Good. Now call him."

"BOOH! Here BOOH!"

There was a screech from the outer office and the giant bat burst through the doors. It settled on the carpet, walked over to Satan and rubbed against him, almost like a cat.

"Ah, BOOH, my pet. How's my BOOHsie today?" he asked, scratching the monstrous animal on its forehead.

And it purred. *Good grief.*

"You see? BOOHsie came when you called him, as I have willed it to be so. Now, BOOH, Mr. Minion here is working on an important project for me and is going to need to get around Hell pretty fast. Can you carry him around, for me, sweetums?"

BOOH nodded its head eagerly. If it had had a tail, it would have been wagging it.

Satan nodded. “Good boy. Minion, just tell him where you want to go. BOOHsie is very smart. Smarter than you, probably. Now, get out of my office and get the Hell to work.”

I had a thought. “Lord Satan … could I … could I have BOOH fetch people for me?”

The Lord of Hell considered my request. “Maybe, provided it scares the shit out of them.” Then he looked at me with suspicion. “Who do you have in mind?”

When I told him, he broke out laughing again. “Oh, those two! Sure! That would be great! I’ll have to make sure and *watch* for that. Now, begone!”

I swallowed hard. “Ah, BOOH, could you carry me to my office?”

BOOH stared at me with its beady little eyes. Bats were supposed to be nearly blind, but it looked to me like BOOH could see just fine; the creature just didn’t much like what it was looking at. Nevertheless, after hissing at me, BOOH jumped into the air, grabbed my shoulders in a bone-crushing grip with its claws, and bolted through the doors.

“Aaaaaaaaaaaaaaaaaaaaaaaaaaaaaaaaaaaaaaaaaaaaaaaaaaaaaaa aaaaaaaaaaaaaaaa …”

We had reached the Seventh Circle, on our way up to Five, and I could still hear Satan’s demonic laugh.

Chapter 5

"Aaaaaaaaaaaaaaaaaaaaaaaaaaaaaaaaaaaaaaaaaaaaaaaaaaaaaa aaaaaaa ... ***Ouch!***"

BOOH dropped me from ten feet above the pavement. On landing, I twisted my ankle. It hurt like hell and I hopped around on the other foot for a few seconds, cursing loudly, before walking off the pain.

Above me hovered the monstrous bat, drooling blood and screeching the whole time. It - he, it? I decided on 'he' - he creeped the hell out of me.

"Uh, thanks BOOHsie."

"SKREE!" the giant bat warned.

Oops. I guess only the Big Guy got to call him that. "Oh, sorry. I meant BOOH."

Did he nod? Never mind. "Uh, BOOH, could you fetch a couple of people for me?

The creature tilted his head to one side. I told him who. "They generally hang out together," I added, trying to be helpful, though BOOH probably didn't need the additional information.

The Bat out of Hell screeched again and banked quickly to his right. He flew off so fast he seemed to disappear.

"What's going on?" Orson was standing in the doorjamb of the trailer, my tool belt in his hand.

"Trouble," I said, fastening the belt around my waist and telling him about the Escalator.

"So that work order did say Escalator. I knew it!"

"Congratulations. You can read bad handwriting. Listen, Orson, this is big," I confided, patting my pocket to make sure the check was still there. "Satan has given me carte blanche to get the Escalator fixed, so I'm calling in a couple of experts."

The fat man leaned against the trailer's railing. It nearly buckled under the strain.

"Really? Who?"

"Aaaaaaaaaaaaaaaaaaaaaaaaaaaaaaaaaaaaaaaaaaaaaa aaaaaaaaaaaaaaa ..."

At that moment, BOOH returned, clutching Big Prick in his right claw and Little Prick in his left. As he did with me, BOOH dropped them from a height onto the pavement.

"Ouch!"

I grinned as Thomas Alva Edison, i.e. 'Big Prick,' and Henry Ford – 'Little Prick' - cursed and groaned.

"Thanks, BOOH," I said with genuine gratitude, then noticed with surprise the curious absence of Hellfire and pie. I was beginning to like the monster. "That's all for now. But you might want to stay close. If I need you, I'll whistle."

"SKREE!" And he was gone.

I was waving bye to him, like the little boy did to the gunslinger at the end of 'Shane.' A little embarrassed, I dropped my hand.

"Minion!" Edison snarled. "What's the meaning of this? Henry and I haven't finished our shift in the mines yet and Digger will skin us if we don't hit our quotas."

Digger is a first-order demon, responsible for running Hell's mines. He works for Adramelech, a.k.a. the 'King of Fire' - one of the Underworld's few arch demons.

"Relax, Big Prick," I said mildly. "Satan has us on another job that takes priority."

"Minion," he growled in warning.

"That's my name. Don't wear it out."

'Minion,' regrettably, really is my name. Don't be surprised. There are a lot of people named 'Minion.' Just take a look in the phone book. That didn't mean I liked my surname. In fact, in my early twenties, after a childhood spent on the receiving end of every 'minion' joke one could contrive, I'd sought relief from the courts and came out Steve Moulton. Hell's management, though, thought a minion named 'Minion' was just too perfect, so Satan changed my name back when I got here.

"Well, then, don't call me 'Big Prick.' "

"You heard him," said the smaller man behind him.

"Oh, shut up, Little Prick. I don't like you any better than I do him," I said.

I'd never gotten along with Edison and Ford. They'd always thought they should be running the Maintenance Department and were constantly telling me what I was doing wrong. But they would never have had a chance at my job. Both of them were too mechanically adept to be allowed to tinker with things. Instead, they were spending Eternity down on the Sixth Level digging sulfur out of Hell's soil. Sulfur was everywhere down here, but there was a constant demand for the stuff, so the Mine's output was a big deal, as were the daily quotas of BP and LP.

I didn't care. If they got in some trouble and were useful to me at the same time, all the better.

Lots of people called each other 'prick' down here, but for me these two were the originals.

Let me explain.

In my youth, I read lots of biographies of famous people, kid biographies that got the basic facts right but hid some of the less savory aspects of their subjects' lives. Edison and Ford were cases in point, and I'd only discovered as an adult what creeps they were in real life.

Not only did Edison take credit for, or outright steal, the inventions of others, he also ruined people financially. These actions were not consistent with my childhood image of the 'Wizard of Menlo Park.' Some of Ford's dirty laundry: he used intimidation tactics to keep unions out of his company; he also employed a form of secret police to monitor the morality of his employees. What most bugged me, though, was how virulently anti-Semitic Ford was.

I hate bigots of all shapes and sizes.

BP and LP had been friends in life, even owning adjacent properties down in Ft. Meyers, Florida. They really weren't that different in height. Edison was 5' 10" and Ford 5' 8½", but Edison had a much larger frame. They were both pricks in my opinion, so I differentiated between the two of them as BP and LP. Childish, I know, but in Hell, who cares? You've got to get your entertainment where you can.

"Look, guys, as much as I enjoy sparring with you two, I don't have time for this. Satan's given me an assignment and he says to call in whoever I want to help me." I looked at the two men critically. Both were wearing white coveralls covered with streaks of yellow sulfur. Digger required all of his workers to arrive for their daily shifts in pristine white uniforms, and like me, they probably had only been issued a single set of coveralls, so they must have spent hours every evening scrubbing out the stains.

Far different from their clothing in life: Edison liked bowties and vests; Ford long ties and suits. Even in death they'd managed to hang onto their ties. They were peeking out the tops of the men's coveralls.

"So why call us?" groused LP. "You hate our guts."

"True, but this project seems right up your alley."

"What is it?" Edison asked with suspicion.

"Hell's Escalator has broken. I want you to fix it."

"What?" Ford started pacing nervously. "The damn thing must be five miles long!"

"Eight." I smiled sweetly.

"How are we expected to fix that?"

"Don't know, don't care. Just do it."

"You can't make us," Edison spluttered. "It's not our job."

I waved the blank check in front of them. "Satan says it is. Would you like me to go back and tell him you refused?"

Both men blanched. "No," Ford said slowly. "But why'd you get us? Why didn't you bring in Seeburger or Reno, or one of those characters? They invented the things."

I shrugged. "I don't know them, and even though I dislike you two, you're both pretty handy. You can probably fix an escalator." And if not, I could get them in a lot of trouble. The thought made me smile.

Edison was frowning. "It's just ... it's just so fucking huge. Where would we start?"

Ford was pacing again. I could tell he was already mentally engaged in the project. "Escalators usually fail at one of the two ends. They're really simple devices, Tom, not all that different from the conveyor belts I used on my assembly lines. The problem is mechanical or electrical." Ford looked up at me. "I guess I can see why you called us."

"Yeah," I agreed and turned to Edison, "but, Tommy, this thing uses something called 'alternating current,' not direct current. Do you think you understand enough about AC to handle this?"

"Fuck you, Minion."

"While you're working on this, you can call me 'Boss.' "

"Fuck you, Minion," Ford echoed.

I waved the blank check at them again, and once again they paled. "Okay, okay, Boss," Ford intoned through gritted teeth. "If we need help, though, can we call in Seeburger?"

"Call in whoever you want. Just get the damn thing fixed. Oh, Orson, could you fetch a couple of spare tool belts from inside?"

Orson had been watching the exchange with amusement. "Sure," he said, chuckling as he stepped inside the trailer. In moments he returned with the belts. Edison and Ford put them on.

Ford nodded. "Come on, Tom, let's start on Level Eight. That's probably where the problem lies. If that doesn't pan out, we can head up to the Gates Level."

Edison frowned. "I still don't like it, but ..."

"But what are you gonna do, right?" This was great, *just great*.

"Um, right." He turned to the street and hailed a passing taxi.

Lazy bum. He couldn't even walk three blocks? Besides, did he really think I didn't see him shoot the finger at me? "What are you doing?"

"Uh, nothing," he said, putting the offending hand behind his back. "Just taking a cab to the Elevator."

I shook my head. "No time for that." I gave a loud whistle. "BOOH!!!!!!!!!!"

In two seconds, the bat was back, hovering in the air above us. "Please take these two to the bottom of the Escalator on Level Eight."

"SKREE!"

"Aaaaaaaaaaaaaaaaaaaaaaaaaaaaaaaaaaaaaaaaaaaaa aaaaaaaaaaaaaaa ..."

Clutched in BOOH's claws like two strips of bacon, they quickly disappeared into the sky. I walked to the trailer, humming.

Maybe things were looking up.

Orson grinned at me. "You really enjoyed that, didn't you?"

I grinned back, then quickly assumed a neutral expression. It didn't pay to look like you were enjoying yourself too much in Hell. "Just trying to get the job done."

Orson's face had also dropped the smile. He must have been thinking the same thing. "Now what?"

"Now we drink coffee and see if there's anything else we absolutely *have* to do."

As we were finishing the last of the brew from our Mr. Coffee, Orson turned to me nervously. "You're not going to make me travel by the BOOH Express, are you?"

"Not unless absolutely necessary. If you can catch a ride on the Elevator to wherever you need to go, by all means do it, but," I hesitated, "there may be a time when there won't be a choice."

Orson shuddered. "I understand. At least it's not as bad as what you did earlier today, cannonballing straight down the Mouth of Hell. That looked scary as ... well ... hell."

I sipped my coffee while idly flipping through the morning's work orders. There were about 100 of them. One in particular caught my eye and I pulled it out of the pile. "Yeah, it is. I wouldn't advise it. It's much worse than BOOH Air. Speaking of BOOH, we can't do anything on the Escalator problem for a while, so let's go do this job at the hospital."

Orson studied the work order for a minute. "Why? This looks like it could wait."

I shrugged. "Probably, but while we're there we might be able to pick up some treats for my new friend."

"Oh. Makes sense," he said, getting off his stool and grabbing a large burlap bag that lay crumpled in one corner of the trailer. "Best to stay on his good side. Besides, it will give you an opportunity to see Flo."

"Don't know what you're talking about," I mumbled, dumping the dregs from my cup into the sink.

"Yeah, sure."

The hospital was also on Level Five, as were most operations that served all Circles of Hell. You had to be centrally located to cover the entire Netherworld, but a consequence was that most of the damned, except those of us who worked on Five, had been crowded out of the level by Hell's administrative bureaucracy. The hospital was a short walk from our office.

In minutes we stood before a metal monstrosity that looked a bit like two United Nations buildings glued together. Or maybe it resembled a gigantic version of an old-fashioned toaster, the kind that could really toast, before Cuisinart, Williams-Sonoma, and their like got a hold of things, making sleek, sexy devices that couldn't brown your buns worth a crap. The hospital was tall, forbidding, a hulking, steel thing that towered over the other infernal offices surrounding it. It was big, really, really big.

It has to be. The hospital is essential to the workings of Hell. Not that anyone gets sick down here but there are billions of lost souls absolutely terrified of hospitals. Most of us spend our final hours in one, hearts in our throats, knowing that soon the Grim Reaper will come and collect us. (And when he does, you're toast, which is another reason I liken the hospital to a toaster.) Almost all of us, at some level or another, are frightened by the Giant Toaster, but some more so than others. These include people who are afraid of doctors, needles, pills, germs and health insurance premiums.

To Hell, the hospital is as essential as lava flows, racks, spits, and devils with pointy pitchforks. For many, eternal damnation can be summed up in a few words: 'lengthy hospital stay.'

A lot of the fear a hospital elicits is caused by anticipation, often anticipation of the worst possible scenario. Most of the time patients, whether in the ER or a hospital bed, or even just at their primary care physician's office, sit around waiting - in the front office waiting rooms, in examination cubicles or behind drawn curtains in wards while wearing humiliating gowns that open at the back, exposing butt cracks to cold plastic chairs - flipping through two-year-old issues of 'People' or pamphlets that describe in clinical detail things like skin cancer, gingivitis, heart disease and emphysema. You wait for the nurse, for the doctor, for a needle that seems way, way too big to plunge beneath the surface of your skin; you wait for a diagnosis that is the first ring of your own personal death knell; but mainly, you wait to receive some surety, good or bad.

In the end it's always bad. To quote my friend and fellow economist, John Maynard Keynes, "In the long run we are all dead." No wonder they call economics 'the dismal science.'

This waiting, while you are mired in uncertainty, may be the worst of it.

The hospital isn't just for patients who feared them in life. Doctors have a special place in Hell also. Not all of them. The vast majority, I suspect, sail right through the Pearly Gates as reward for all the good they did in their lives. But for those doctors who have won the booby prize, an all-expense paid trip to the Netherworld, the hospital is here for them as well.

There is a small subset of damned MDs who don't come to the Toaster. They are the truly evil ones, such as those who worked for Hitler, doing abominable experiments on Jews and Gypsies, small children - you know the kind. They would never have been allowed near the hospital, for fear they might have enjoyed themselves too much.

But these exceptions were few in number. Over 90 percent of the damned members of the medical profession were toasting in the Toaster. A number of them, those who had let the 'power over life and death' thing swell their egos to the size of dirigibles, were made interns or medical school students for all Eternity. These arrogant, authoritarian god-wannabees had to suffer as medical gophers for demon doctors: going on rounds, only to be humiliated for invariably offering up the wrong diagnosis; doing rectal exams without the benefit of rubber gloves; emptying ever-full bedpans; that sort of thing. Others spent their afterlives in insurance hell, filling out endless forms and struggling with fax machines that never worked properly, on the telephone with Aetna, Humana and so forth, trying to get approval for a procedure or a prescription that was off the formulary. The remaining damned docs had their own ward in the hospital where they suffered the same indignities their patients in life had endured: the endless waiting, the embarrassing examination robes, the cold-as-steel plastic chairs on their butts, hands up their asses and down their throats (usually the same hand), probes up their noses, frequently all at once. It didn't make for a pretty picture.

Needless to say, with the vast numbers of damned souls consigned to Hell's Hospital, the place had a very large waiting room, which Orson and I had to traverse as we headed to the stairs. Thousands of lost souls were there, a sea of the decrepit, maimed and contagious, sitting cheek-to-jowl with people who looked completely healthy, except for the fact that they were scared witless.

We exchanged a glance, shook our heads, and hurried to the nearest stairwell. As the door slammed behind us, we heard the receptionist say, "Just fill out these forms while I make a copy of your insurance card. The wait to see the doctor shouldn't be too long."

Right.

The work order was for the blood bank which was located down two flights. As we emerged from the stairs, we encountered another queue of patients. Junkies, people with blood-borne diseases, skin-pocked teenagers, germaphobes, hemophobes and trypanophobes - people with irrational fears of germs, blood and injections by hypodermic needle, respectively - stood in a line that wrapped around the far corner of the hallway. We stepped ahead of them all and entered the office.

The purpose of Hell's blood bank was not to provide whole blood or plasma to the sick, but merely to torture the donors. The needle they used was roughly the size of an awl. Okay, it *was* an awl that was pounded into the donors' arms with a carpenter's hammer.

Orson and I stepped inside the back room just in time to see a demon dressed in a female nurse's uniform, complete with paper hat, extract the awl from an arm of a whimpering donor who was strapped to a semi-reclined donor chair. Blood spurted from the hole like water from a geyser as the creature shoved a plastic tube entirely too far into the opening. Interestingly enough, despite the size of the wound and the large gauge of the tubing, the blood flowed slowly, and no doubt, painfully from the donor and into the plastic collection bag that was suspended like a hanged man from a scaffold attached to the chair.

"There, now," said the demon, patting its agonized victim on the shoulder, "that wasn't so bad, was it?"

"Mmmmph."

I recognized the demon. His name was Uphir. I say 'he,' though like angels and devils, demons aren't of a single sex, even if their tails seem pretty phallic. This particular demon looked like a 'he,' so I always thought of him as one, even though at the moment he was in drag. "Hey, Uphir."

Hell's demonic physician dropped his fake smile when he saw me. "It's about fucking time. You here with the replacement needle?"

I shrugged. "The work order you submitted wasn't very specific. What's the problem?"

Uphir threw the awl at me and I ducked. It sank so deep into the far wall that Orson had to help pull it out. I examined it for a sec. "Hmmm. The tip's broken. And why would that be a problem? Seems like, from your perspective, this would only, uh, enhance the experience."

Uphir put his hands on his hips, pulling his skirt slightly above the knees in the process. I noticed with some amusement that he was bow-legged. "Yeah, well that's all you know, smart ass. The needle makes too big a hole in the vein. The blood flows faster than I want."

I examined the awl once more. "How did you ever manage to break off the tip?"

Uphir smiled nastily. "I hit a tough vein. 'Course, I missed six times before I finally sunk it. Now, you and fat boy here quit wasting my time. I've got a lot of donations to take. Do you have my replacement needle or not?"

I thought for a second, reached to my tool belt, and pulled out my awl. "Will this do?" I asked, tossing it to him.

Uphir caught the tool in one claw and examined it closely. "What do you use it for?"

"Not much, really. I can't remember the last time I needed it."

Orson chimed in. "You cleaned your ears with it last month."

Uphir smiled, delighted. "Ear wax? Perfect. I'll take it."

"Sign here, please." I indicated the spot on the work order where the customer showed the work complete. Uphir scrawled a really creepy sigil on the paper.

The bag of blood dropped on its scaffolding. Uphir wrenched the tubing from the arm of his donor and slapped a BAND-AID over the hole. The demon then pulled on a lever beside the chair, which released the restraining bands and catapulted the unfortunate soul over the wall of the cubicle. "Next!" Uphir screamed as a messy splat sounded from the next room.

"Say, what do you do with the blood you collect?"

Uphir glanced momentarily at the bag in his claw and tossed it over his shoulder to a pile of similar bags in the corner. They looked like giant cherry sours. "Nothing, really. The dumpster sometimes. Or we burn them."

"Mind if I have a few?"

The demon eyed me suspiciously. "What are you going to do with them? Will it be disgusting?"

"A bit," I replied after some thought.

"Then take as many as you want and get out of here."

Orson and I put a dozen full collection bags into our burlap sack and left by the back door.

The donor had been shot over the clinic's wall and into a pile of medical waste stacked in the next room. The poor guy had old hypodermic needles hanging from arms, legs and even his cheeks, and he was crying hysterically as a glowing vision of mercy helped him to his feet.

The person assisting him was a rare sight in Hell - a beautiful woman. She looked to be in her early twenties. She had the face of an angel and a body that - even though I was sure she didn't realize it - was built for sin. In her left hand she held a lamp, like the one Aladdin's genie lived in, except this one had a wick coming from its tip. The soft light of the lamp illuminated her face, making her beauty even more ethereal ... and out of place.

"Hey, Flo." A familiar warmth built in my cheeks. This often happened when I encountered the 'Lady with the Lamp.'

Florence Nightingale shushed me with a gesture. She whispered a few words to the man as, with great tenderness, she removed the syringes from his body. Even after the last needle pulled clear of his skin, he continued trembling, so Flo held him in her arms. He hugged her back with a gratitude that was palpable. Then he swallowed hard, composed himself and headed for the end of the donation line.

A few tears fell from her eyes as Flo looked up at me and Orson. "I do what I can, but it isn't very much."

"It's plenty," I said quietly, going up to the one truly good person in Hell. "Nice to see you."

Nightingale smiled, though her expression was tinged with sadness. "You too, Steve ... Hello, Orson," she added.

Florence Nightingale had never been consigned to Hell. When she died in 1910 at the well-seasoned age of ninety, St. Peter had personally escorted her to the Pearly Gates, but she refused to enter Heaven. Nightingale had always been strong-willed. Against the wishes of her family, she had become a nurse - no, *the nurse* - and changed the course of medicine forever. In life she had dedicated herself to helping the sick, so she figured in death she'd be of more use in Hell than Heaven. With a polite, "Thanks, but no thanks," she took the stairs to the Netherworld. (Back then, Hell was reached primarily by the Stairway. The Escalator wasn't installed until the 1920s.)

Even Satan couldn't dissuade her from trying to ease the suffering of the damned, so he decided to use the situation to his advantage. He had her appear as she had in her youth:

beautiful, chaste, virginal - emphasis on the virgin. According to some accounts, Florence Nightingale had lived and died without ever having sex. Like Galahad, she was an unconquered knight, strong because she was pure.

Oh, let's not mince words here: Florence Nightingale was a knockout. And Satan knew it, even if she didn't. In Hell, Flo embodied all the girls we guys could never have - the head cheerleader, the prom queen, the woman you loved from afar but could never touch. Love unrequited. Satan adored the whole concept: a subtle, exquisite torture delivered by one of the kindest souls who had ever lived. Flo never even realized she was being used.

Satan also took advantage of Flo in one other way that was, well, devilishly clever. Nightingale had always been very good at math and she especially loved pie charts. She was, in fact, an early proponent and user of them. Satan often asked Flo to make presentations to the damned on such topics as the conditions in Hell or the distribution of sins across the Nine Circles. ("While you would think that the Second Circle, per Dante, is mostly populated by the Lustful, this pie chart clearly demonstrates that only 23.7 percent of all sinners there are, in fact, fornicators. Forty-two percent are Gluttons, seventeen percent are Sullen, and the remaining 17.3 percent are of various categories, as indicated by the wedge here marked 'Other.' ") She couldn't resist using pie charts to illustrate her points.

Poor Flo. She had no idea how mind-numbingly boring her presentations were. None of us had the heart to tell her, either, but everyone I knew dreaded receiving an invitation to an event where the featured speaker was Florence Nightingale.

In life, I was an economist. Statistics were my bread and butter, yet even I had seen enough pie charts in my lifetime to last me until the end of Eternity. If it was painful for me to watch one of her presentations, it must have been torture for other folks, like fry-cooks or janitors or dentists.

Flo had no official role at the hospital. She just haunted its halls, providing succor wherever it was needed - which was everywhere.

She stared for a moment at the pile of medical refuse and shook her head. She blew out her lamp, sticking it in her purse. "Gentlemen, let me walk you out. I promised I'd help in the waiting room for a while."

"That would be great, Flo," I said, offering her my arm, and a little thrill went through me as she slipped her delicate hand into the crook. Orson grinned but kept quiet as he took a place on her other side.

We walked in silence for a few minutes, climbing the stairs together. "Flo," I asked at last, "why do you do this? You don't have to torture yourself. You don't even have to be here."

She smiled her sad little smile. "It's what I do." That seemed to say it all for her.

"I understand, I guess, but you could at least get out of the hospital occasionally. Look, Thelonius Monk is playing at the Red Note tonight. Why don't you come with me and listen to a couple of sets? It would do you good."

Flo gave my arm a squeeze. "Why, Mr. Minion, are you asking me out on a date?"

Orson sniggered but I ignored him. "I don't know. Maybe, but mainly you just look a bit down. How can you keep up other people's spirits if you don't take care of your own?"

She looked thoughtful. "That's a good point, Steve. May I think about it, gentle sir?" she said as we reached the front doors of the hospital.

"Sure! Excellent!" I said, with perhaps too much enthusiasm. "I'll check back with you later."

She smiled a happier smile this time. Oh, she was exquisite! "That would be fine. Goodbye for now, Steve. Enjoy your day, Orson." Then she gave my arm a final squeeze and headed back to the waiting room.

Chapter 6

Orson was chuckling as we walked across the street. Finally he couldn't restrain himself.

> *Steve and Florence sitting in a tree*
> *K I S S I N ...*

"Knock it off."

My fat friend shifted the bag on his shoulder to a more comfortable position and laughed. "You're sweet on her!"

I started to protest but didn't see the point. "Yeah. Me and every other guy in Hell."

Orson slapped me on the back, still laughing. "Well, not *every* guy. Bruce, for instance, but I get your point. Still," he added a bit more seriously, "there's a difference here."

"What's that?"

"I think she may be sweet on you, too."

"What?" Florence had always seemed glad to see me, but then she was kind to everyone. I shook my head. "No, that's impossible. And even if it were true, Satan would never allow it."

We climbed the stairs to our trailer, me pulling the duct tape away so we could open the door. Orson set the sack full of blood bags in an empty orange crate. We dumped some ice from our fridge on top so they wouldn't spoil.

You might be wondering about the crate but anyone down here will tell you that Hell's minions eat a lot of oranges. I don't know if we need them exactly, being dead and all, but the afterlife in Hell is not that different from sailing on a long voyage. Can you imagine what Magellan's crew must have felt like, two years into their circumnavigation of the globe, in the middle of the uncharted Pacific, with no end in sight? That's a lot like Hell. Hell doesn't end, and the last thing we need is scurvy, so we eat oranges.

Orson glanced at the crateful of blood bags and shook his head. "You're right about Satan never allowing you to get anything on with Flo. In fact, I was a bit surprised you didn't get hit by Hellfire when you asked her out."

"Yeah." That had puzzled me, too. "What's up with that?"

"The Powers that Be probably knew she'd turn you down." Orson stroked his goatee, thinking. "Although she didn't exactly do that, did she?"

"No," I said, brightening. "She didn't. Think I have a shot?"

Orson put on another pot of coffee.

Along with oranges, we consume a lot of caffeine. Hell's interminable, and since you don't really need to worry about how well you sleep, since you never sleep well, you might as well drink as much coffee as you'd like.

He didn't answer until he'd poured us each a full mug. "Nah. Shit, Steve, this is Hell. No one has a shot, sort of by definition. Still," he hesitated for a moment, "if this were the real world, I'd say yeah."

"Hope springs eternal." I felt gloomy but not entirely defeated. A little fire yet burned in my eyes.

He patted my shoulder. "Yes, I suppose it does, but so does disappointment, and that's what Hell specializes in."

I considered all the time I'd spent in Hell. Time couldn't really be measured here. Shit, this was infinity we were talking about. Even what year the mortal world was involved in right now was a bit murky to me, though I'd get clues from the more recent residents of the Underworld. For instance, Global Warming, which was just being talked about when that graduate student blew my brains out in the 1990s, was a reality now. Both the Great Icecap of Greenland and ice of Antarctica were almost gone, and soon good beachfront property could be had in Pittsburgh, but I really didn't know the year. My best guess was somewhere in the Twenty-First Century, maybe 2050.

My point here is that, regardless of the year on the outside, I'd been in Hell for quite a while, where personal observation and experience had shown things never went right in the long run. There was no chance of having something with Flo. Satan or one of his underlings would see to that - and yet letting go of hope was difficult.

Oh no! I realized in horror. I was probably in love with her. I was totally screwed.

Orson spoke, shaking me out of my thoughts. "Shouldn't we have heard something from the two pricks by now?"

With an effort, I shoved the sublime Florence Nightingale from my brain and rose to my feet. "You're right. Maybe I should get BOOH to fetch them."

"Maybe. You probably want to call him anyway," he said, looking meaningfully over at the orange crate.

"Right." I grabbed a few pints of blood from the burlap bag and headed outside, Orson following.

"Tweet!" I whistled, holding the donor bags behind me. "BOOH! Here, boy!" I added a bit hesitantly.

"SKREE!"

How did he do that? He was so fast!

"Skree?" the monstrous bat shrieked, as if he were asking me what I wanted.

"Oh, I don't really need anything." I had decided to give Ford and Edison a little more time to get back without having BOOH fetch them. "I ... well ... I have something for you."

BOOH just hovered. A vampire bat the size of a helicopter, suspended above you in midair, was more than a bit unnerving, but I soldiered on.

"Uh, BOOH," I began with some hesitation, not certain now that this was a good idea. "I really appreciate all you've been doing to help me."

BOOH's head tilted to one side quizzically.

"Anyway, I brought you a treat." I suppressed a shudder and drew a donor bag from behind me. "You probably like to get your own, fresh and all, but this was drawn just this morning, so it's *practically* fresh. Would you ... would you like it?"

And then BOOH did the most astonishing thing I'd ever seen him do. He settled on the ground, reared up on his feet, and begged, just like a cocker spaniel.

I was stunned. Orson looked equally surprised, then, trying to act cool in an 'Oh, that's just what giant vampire bats do' sort of way, he shrugged.

"Here, catch!" I tossed the bag to BOOH, who snagged it deftly with one claw. He bit into the plastic, creating two precise punctures, and laid the bag on the ground.

Vampire bats, contrary to popular superstition, do not suck the blood from their victims. They make a bite, infuse the wound with an anticoagulant which, believe it or not, is called draculin, and then lick at the oozing blood.

Like a gargantuan puppy, BOOH cradled the donor bag in his claws, and with a foot-long tongue, licked away the slow trickle of red. Periodically he'd give the bag a little squeeze to get some extra ooze going.

Hmm. He was really kind of cute - in his grotesque, monstrous, scary way.

In no time BOOH finished his treat. He sat up and begged for more and I threw him another bag.

At that moment Ford and Edison walked up.

"About time. I was getting ready to send BOOH for you." The two men trembled. "What did you find?"

"This," LP said solemnly and handed me an object he'd been holding behind his back.

I look at the thing in disbelief. "You've got to be kidding. A monkey wrench? Someone literally threw a monkey wrench into the gears?"

"Yes," Edison chimed in, "and we had a devil of a time getting the thing out."

Orson cleared his throat. "Ah, you might want to choose your metaphors more carefully," he said, pointing down meaningfully.

Edison flinched. "Right. It was," he stammered, "it was very hard to get out of the gears."

"So the Escalator is working again?"

"No," said Ford.

"What?"

Ford looked uncomfortably at his companion. "Well, we're not exactly sure the monkey wrench caused the failure."

Edison brightened. "But now we're pretty sure the problem is electrical, not mechanical."

"Yeah," Ford agreed. "We're heading up to the Gates Level. If the problem isn't at the bottom, it's probably at the top."

"Electrical, huh?" I said, looking at Edison. "Think you can handle it?"

Edison straightened his bowtie with as much dignity as being a minion in Hell would allow. "Who better?"

I scratched my chin. There was someone better, and putting him on the job too would drive Edison nuts, so it was worth doing, regardless. I smiled innocently. "Why don't you two head up there, then?"

The two men stared in horror at BOOH who had just finished his second bag of blood. He looked expectantly at Ford and Edison.

"No, you guys take the Elevator. Orson, they don't have keys, so would you go with them? I may send someone else up to help as well."

"Sure, boss," Orson replied. He always enjoyed watching me go a round or two with Ford and Edison. "Where are you off to?"

"To report to Satan." Imagining the long ride down made me cringe. "I'll be up directly to check on your progress." I tossed BOOH a third bag of blood. "BOOH, be right back, okay?"

"Skree! Slurp, slurp, slurp."

With Orson leading the way, the three men headed toward the Elevator. I stepped into the trailer and went to my phone. There was a lot of static on the line, as usual, but the call went through.

"Halloo?" a thickly-accented voice answered.

"Nicky, it's me, Steve - I need a favor." I explained what I wanted as Nicky started cursing in Serbian. "No, listen, it will be great! This will drive him crazy and I really could use your help." Nicky argued some more. "No, don't worry about your boss. Tell him Satan gave me a blank check to bring in anyone I needed. So, will you do it?"

There was a few second's pause before Nicky responded. "Da."

"Great!" I grabbed a spare elevator key from my desk drawer and popped it into the pneumatic tube. "I've just sent you a key through the tubes. You'll need it to get Topside ... It's there already? Super! See you in a bit." I hung up the phone.

This was getting complicated. Now I had four people reporting to me, five if you counted BOOH. I wasn't used to directing the efforts of so many. A former faculty member didn't get many opportunities to supervise others. Professors usually only got administrative experience if made a Department Chair, a task most of us avoided like last night's dishes. Almost all senior faculty members had to take a turn as chair, but fortunately I was murdered before my number came up. That is, my number came up before my number came up.

I knew someone, though, who was very gifted at complicated projects. The idea was worth discussing with Beezy later. For now, I needed to get down and see the Earl of the Underworld.

On my desk the work orders were piling up as fast as ever. I rifled through them quickly.

Uh-oh. There was one that needed attention. I had standing instructions that anything involving this poor soul was always to be resolved immediately. I shoved the work order into my pocket and put the rest atop the newest stack on the trailer's floor.

On leaving my office, I smoothed the duct tape back down to hold the door in place. BOOH, treats all finished, was cleaning his fur like a cat that had just swallowed the cream. *Ugh!*

I headed over to Parts. Dora was leaning out her window, looking bored, as usual. "Hi, Steve," she said as she lit a cigarette with the still-burning stub of her previous one. 'Steve,' not 'Hottie.' That was a good sign. Her mood had improved since this morning. "What can I do you for?"

"I need a 4Real 4D/VR console."

"Oh, dear," she dithered. How she could talk with a cigarette in her mouth, the smoke rising up and enveloping her head, was beyond me. "I'm not sure I have one in stock."

With a sigh I showed her the name of the customer. Her eyes widened. "Oh, *him*. I always have one set aside for *him*. Satan's orders. Just a second and I'll get it." Dora disappeared from her window. A few minutes later she returned with the console. I signed for it and whistled for BOOH.

I only had a chance to blink once before the bat was hovering over me. *"Skree!"* Was it my imagination or was his screech a little less strident than usual?

"Could you whisk me up to the Third Level? I have to take care of this work order before reporting to Satan."

Two levels of Hell were nothing for BOOH, and in seconds I was standing before a modest bungalow in the Underworld's version of a suburb. Other similar houses fronted the street on both sides. The neighborhood looked to have been built in the 1950s and the trees were getting a little long in the tooth. Many of them had dropped half their leaves, though it was not autumn.

Autumn doesn't exist in Hell. Like spring, the fall is too pretty. All we ever get are summers that make those in Death Valley seem balmy and winters that put Siberia to shame.

Other trees looked rotten to the core; across their trunks someone had painted bright red Xs. A work crew would eventually come to cut down the trees that had been marked for destruction. Yards in this particular neighborhood were overgrown, riddled with weeds, patched with dead spots, or completely dead. In the driveways, lots of cars were propped up on cinderblocks.

As I stood before the house of my client, a truck drove through the neighborhood, spraying insect repellent, probably DDT, into the air. Back on Earth, this was a common practice in many mosquito-prone neighborhoods in the 1950s, before people figured out the stuff could kill more than insects. There didn't seem to be any mosquitoes around, so the spraying was probably just one of those special but gratuitous services for which Hell was famous.

This was a seedy version of a Beaver Cleaver neighborhood, complete with sidewalks. These, however, were cracked and broken, and some mean-looking teenagers with skateboards were being regularly tossed on their asses as they tried to ride over the fractured pavement.

Most adolescents you see in Hell really did die in their teens, usually killing themselves by doing something unbelievably stupid, like driving drunk or overdosing on drugs. Sometimes the deadly deed was as mundane as trying to ride a bike with no hands or popping a wheelie, or doing a really rad move on a skateboard, unaware that a Mack truck was going to take the kid out in midflight, or that the young bozo would just break a neck or pulverize a skull in a spectacular fall.

Most of the teenagers who died in a bike or skateboard-related accident were boys, the girls generally having too much sense or insufficient levels of testosterone to make them attempt death-defying stunts. I felt sorry for the boys and occasional girls who died this way. They seemed more stupid than evil, and in their final act of dying, they actually did the world good service by taking themselves out of the gene pool.

In Hell, teenagers usually spend Eternity reenacting the mistakes that got them dead in the first place, this time with the knowledge that what they're doing won't work and that "it's gonna hurt ... real bad."

I stepped past a mass of broken bones on the sidewalk - a kid who had, for probably the ten thousandth time, attempted a back flip while barreling downhill on his skateboard - and headed toward the front door of the bungalow. After a polite knock, I let myself in, noting that the boy was already back on his feet, preparing to execute the maneuver all over again. *Kids*.

They healed so quickly. Why, in his place I'd still be on the concrete watching my tibia mend itself.

The little house was furnished with American traditional furniture. Knickknacks, photos of devils dressed like human family members, doilies, and an odd assortment of pillows were scattered everywhere. All of the furnishings looked like what you'd find in grandma's place, except for the TV. It was a hundred incher that pretty much filled one wall of the room.

Four feet in front of the TV was a couch, the kind I remembered from my youth in the middle of the Twentieth Century. It was covered in dirty beige fabric; a dust ruffle of the same cloth extended from the bottom of the couch to the floor. The couch had three legs; the fourth leg had broken off and been replaced with a couple of bricks not quite the right height. As a result, the couch did not sit in stable fashion on the floor but wobbled slightly as weight shifted. Like right now, when the dweebish, nervous-looking fellow in glasses and vintage short-sleeved shirt turned to face me. He was drinking a lemonade, a very sour one judging from the expression on his face.

"H ... hi, Steve. I've been ... expecting you."

"Hey, Bob. Got here as soon as I could, but I've got the unit," I said, holding the 4Real console over my head.

Bob, or 'Virtual Bob' as the tabloids called him in life, as much for his reclusive lifestyle as his company's product line, took off his glasses, cleaned them on his shirt, and hooked them back on his ears. As usual, he was working very hard to avoid eye contact with me. "Great." He didn't sound very enthusiastic.

Bob's situation was unique in Hell, because all of his eternal punishment was delivered virtually. The 4Real 4D/VR was the first fully-immersive game console. Coupled with some human interface technologies, it provided an experience indistinguishable from reality. As soon as it came out on Earth,

Satan switched out Bob's eternal torment of cocktail parties and crowd scenes with a computer-simulated equivalent. He couldn't tell the difference, and Management was amused by the irony of using technology to torture the man who pioneered virtual reality.

Oh, more irony: In life, Bob owned 4Real Enterprises. At the time of his death, he was one of the richest and most powerful men on the planet.

There's more to the decision to use virtual reality than just Satan getting his jollies. Bob's virtual torment is an experiment. There are only so many devils to go around. I mean, it's not like they fall in love, get married and have little devil babies. All devils that exist have been around since the dawn of time, since the War to Begin All Wars, a.k.a. the 'War in Heaven,' during which, and I quote: 'That ancient serpent, who is called the Devil and Satan, the deceiver of the whole world - he was thrown down to the earth, and his angels were thrown down with him.' (Revelation, 12:7 - 9).

Hell can create the occasional demon, but not a devil, which is just another name for a fallen angel, so Satan's workforce is somewhat limited, and at the rate the ranks of the damned are swelling, he's going to need something like virtual punishment if he's going to keep up. But a device is simply not as dependable as a devil. Devils never break down; they are tireless. What's more, they love their work. Game consoles dispense punishment efficiently, if dispassionately, yet they sometimes break. Since, as far as I know, Bob is the only one receiving virtual eternal punishment, Satan has any malfunctions of the game console treated as a top priority. That's why, even with all the other stuff going on, the Lord of Hell would have wanted me to handle this immediately. And so I did.

"Okay, Bob," I said, tightening down a final cable. "You're all set."

Bob began trembling, but he set his lemonade on an end table and put on his virtual reality suit, which looked a lot like a scuba diver outfit, except it was riddled with wires, diodes and the like. Especially long wires ran from it to the game console.

"Thanks ... I guess," he said, signing off on the work order. Then he sat back on the couch, took a deep breath, slipped on his facemask, gloves and goggles, and entered full immersion. His body started jerking, as if he were having an epileptic fit. He was probably screaming, too, but the mask muffled all sound.

Everybody had his own version of Hell. This was another mantra of mine. Shuddering, I turned away.

Bob didn't seem like such a bad guy. In life, I guess he'd been a pretty ruthless businessman, but he'd also created a charitable foundation fueled by a large chunk of his own massive personal fortune. That happened shortly before I took a bullet to my brain, but from what I had been told by people who died after me, Bob did a great deal of good with that foundation.

I wondered, for not the first time, why some people ended up in Heaven and others in Hell. The judgments seemed so random, though maybe they were the workings of a divine, if inscrutable, plan. Just thinking about it gave me a headache, though. The whole issue was way above my pay grade.

Now where was I? Oh, yeah. I needed to report to Satan.

"BOOH?"

BOOH appeared from nowhere, as usual. Once again he clutched me by the shoulders, but his grip was gentle, and when he took off, he did it more smoothly, as if he were trying to make the ride a little bit easier on me. BOOH banked slightly as he reached the center of the Third Level, then began a slow spiral down to the Ninth.

I hardly screamed at all on the way down.

BOOH deposited me with barely a thump on the carpet before Bruce the Bedeviled's desk, then flew over to a telephone pole that had been mounted sideways into the wall before Satan's office, by the door of the Elevator. BOOH landed on the massive perch and commenced grooming himself while he waited for me to complete my business.

Bruce looked up in surprise. "Minion? You already had one appointment today. I'm sure you're not in the Book for another one." He began flipping through a large black tome that spanned the surface of his desk.

Satan's doors flew open, and a fist of flame knocked Bruce on his ass. "Send him in," said a harmonious voice that charmed me to my soul.

Ah, Lucifer mode. Good.

I helped Bruce off the floor. "Why does he even need a secretary," Bruce said tearfully, "if he's going to manage his own appointments anyway?"

"Status, dear boy, status." Lucifer stood at the entrance to his office, one arm resting artfully on the door jamb. He was naked. Golden skin covered the muscled perfection of his body. Curly, blond hair hung freely, falling a little below his shoulders. Behind and above him stretched two magnificent white wings. God, he was a beautiful bastard.

Lucifer looked at me and raised an eyebrow. "I appreciate the compliment, but don't bring Him into it."

Bruce looked like he would swoon at the sight of the Light-Bearer.

"Sorry, my lord. I wanted to give you my report personally."

"Come in, my fine fellow," Lucifer said. As I stepped behind him into the office, the doors closed. "Have a seat."

Two leather wingback chairs stood before a gentle fire. Between them sat a small table with a decanter full of a tawny liquid. Lucifer settled in one of the chairs, his wings just brushing the outsides of the leather back. A little hesitantly, I sat in the other seat.

To my surprise, the chair was very comfortable. Lucifer was in a good mood.

"Sherry?" he asked, pouring some for both of us. It wasn't so much a pleasantry as a command with a question mark at the end.

"Sure. Thanks." I took a sip and found to my surprise that the sherry actually tasted the way I remembered. "Say, this is good!"

"Naturally, Minion. A fine amontillado. Nothing but the best for me, and since I'm in the mood for sherry, you're the beneficiary. Besides, who wants to drink alone? Cheers!" Lucifer said, holding his glass forward. I gingerly clinked my crystal against his. "Cheers, my lord," I said and finished the pour.

Lucifer put his empty wine glass down on the table, which disappeared, leaving me with no place to put my own. I held it awkwardly in my hands. "Now," he said, all cordiality at an end, "what do you have to report?"

I told him what Edison and Ford had discovered.

"A monkey wrench? How trite. Still," he said, stroking his chin in thought, "the purveyors of this mischief must have little imagination."

Couldn't argue with him there. "We're not sure that it even caused the Escalator to fail. Ford and Edison removed the wrench, of course, but the Escalator still doesn't work. The problem appears to be electrical. They've headed Topside to check out things there. They tell me escalators usually fail on one of the two ends."

"Yes, yes, that would make sense. Do you think they can fix it?"

I shrugged. "I don't know, my lord, but I've sent for someone else to help them."

"Oh, really?" he asked with mild curiosity. "Who?"

When I told him, the 'Satanic laughter sound' burst from his angelic lips. "Oh, very good, Minion! You know, this is not the first time you have demonstrated a knack for cruelty. You have a real flair for subtle, yet exquisite, torture."

Great. Nothing boosts one's self esteem like being complimented for cruelty. "I ... I guess I don't like them very much. Especially Edison, that Big Pri ..."

Lucifer had stopped listening to me. "I'm serious about your talent. That delicate touch, it's a gift even some experienced devils haven't been able to master. Maybe I should move you. How would you like to be a lesser demon?"

I blinked. Man, I hadn't seen that coming! It would be a huge promotion. People, well the damned anyway, would treat me with more respect ... or fear ... which down here was pretty much the same thing. I'd get one of those nifty forks, uh, tridents. Probably score with the babes, too. And ...

And I'd have to be a demon. Images of Uphir ran through my head. Ugh.

Think of something. Quickly!

"Ah, thank you, my lord, but I can probably serve Hell better in my current position. Besides, it's sort of my eternal damnation, you know?"

"Too true," said Lucifer, sighing. "I was forgetting myself." He rose from his seat, his wings stretching up and out seemingly to infinity. "Head up to the Gates Level and see how they're doing.

If they can't get the Escalator working right away, go to Beelzebub and get a construction crew to rebuild the Stairway."

I groaned inwardly. What a ton of work, and meanwhile other work orders were piling up in my office faster than snowflakes in a blizzard. "Yes, my lord."

"In the interim, I'm taking some temporary measures. The D&D Squad will soon head up Topside. Peter is having a fit. The damned are stacking up like your work orders," he said, giving me a meaningful glance.

Right, right. The old 'mind reading' thing. Gotta keep remembering he can do that.

D&D: short for Devils and Demons. "What are they going to do?"

"Why," replied Lucifer with an angelic smile, "they're going to consign souls to Hell the old-fashioned way."

I shuddered.

The Lord of the Underworld waved a hand dismissively. "It's not good for public relations, but what else can I do? Besides, the boys need some exercise."

So that was why he was in such a good mood. He had an excuse to employ 'temporary measures.'

"Not an excuse, Minion. Merely a necessity. You can explain that to Peter for me, after you check on the Escalator. Speaking of which," he added, taking the glass from me, as if he expected me to try stealing his fine crystal, "it's time for you to get back on the job. From now on, work through Beelzebub. I don't want to see you again until you've accomplished all three of your tasks."

"All *three*?"

Lucifer shook his head. "You humans can't keep a thing in your heads, can you? One, fix the Escalator; two, if you can't do that right away, get a crew working to rebuild the Stairway."

“I had those two. What’s the third?”

He shot me a withering glance. It seemed worse, somehow, coming from such a beautiful face. “Find and stop the saboteurs.”

“Right, right! I knew that one, too!” I said desperately.

“And you’d better get on that quickly. My, my,” Lucifer said in mock concern, “so much to do. You may need some more help, even have to do some delegating.”

“I’m on it, sir!” I said, and found myself saluting.

“We’re finished,” is all he said, pointing a finger vaguely in my direction. A blast of hot wind lifted me from my feet, pushing me through the door and depositing me in front of Bruce’s desk - the desk that looked to have been recently split in two by a single blow from the hand of a very frustrated martial artist. Behind it sat Satan’s secretary, head in his hands. He didn’t look up at me, but kept mumbling: “He’s just so damn beautiful, so damn beautiful ...”

That must be why he was called the ‘Bedeviled.’

I got up from the carpet. You were thrown around a lot in Hell, but you got used to it. “BOOH? Could you take me to Gates Level now?”

The bat was still in mid-cleaning but stopped when he heard his name. BOOH stretched his wings, tilted his head back and forth. I could hear loud popping sounds as he loosened his neck muscles. Then he bounded from his perch, grabbed me, and took off.

Chapter 7

We were rising at a much slower pace than last time, and the wind was only a loud whooshing in my ears. "BOOH!" I shouted to make myself heard above the rush of air. "Thanks for taking it easy on me but I'm getting used to it."

"Skree?"

"Yeah. And ... and I trust you. You can go faster if you want to."

BOOH screeched again and took off like a bat out of hell. Which he was.

I tried to suppress the scream that threatened to explode from me at any moment. Then we were moving so fast that screaming would have been pretty difficult. My lips and cheeks flapped in the wind, distorting my face, as happens to kids when they're on a really fast roller coaster.

Maybe I should have just kept quiet. A slow ascent seemed pretty good about now.

Gulping back my fear, I pretended to be a flying super hero - BatRider. (Batman had already been taken and BatPassenger, while technically more accurate, didn't have much panache.) The name beat the hell out of Duct Tape Man.

With just this slight shift in perspective, I found myself exhilarating in the experience as we hurtled up the Throat of Hell. I could get used to this. I really could.

We caused quite a stir when we exploded from the Mouth. BOOH had a flair for the dramatic and he gave a wonderful screech, which scared the bejeezus out of the crowd that was queued up before the Elevator. They made lots of space for us as BOOH, in a power dive, swooped for the cloud floor. I landed on both feet, hands behind me, like a ski jumper. My work boots skidded slightly as BOOH released me and took to the sky, but I kept my balance. I bet it looked really cool.

BatRider to the rescue.

With a bit of a swagger, I walked over to Hell's Escalator, noting at the same time that the new bulb was still working. Orson, Edison and Ford were standing behind a yellow, easel-style 'out of order' sign. They were making like construction workers on a highway project; that is, they were standing around doing nothing, watching the one person who was actually doing something.

Correction: Edison was doing something. He was glowering, in red-faced anger, at his in-life competitor.

Nikola Tesla was a lean, old man (he had died at the age of 86) with a nearly full head of hair, swept back to reveal a thin widow's peak, a triangular face and a set of ears far too big for his head. He was dressed in peasant's garb - he spent his time in Hell working on a farm. As eternal damnations went, it wasn't bad fare, but in life Tesla hadn't been all that bad a person. Not particularly good with money, and with a serious case of Obsessive-Compulsive Disorder, but not bad as a human being. Still, he must have done something wrong to earn the eternal 'thumbs down.' Probably the Sin of Pride. That's what got most of the smart guys to Hell.

Currently, Nicky was crawling at the base of the Escalator's handrail. He had removed the landing platform. "See?" he said in his thick Serbian accent. He was talking to Orson, pointedly ignoring Edison and Ford, who probably knew this anyway. "Most of the work of any Escalator is done by the motor here at the top. This is where the main drive gear is. It moves the stairs. The bottom holds the step return idler sprockets. Hello, Steve."

"Hi, Nicky," I said nonchalantly. "How are you four getting along?"

Edison spat at me. "I didn't need this foreign charlatan in my way."

I looked at him as if something was puzzling me. "You're standing. He's crawling around on his hands and knees trying to figure out what's wrong. How is he in your way? Oh, Nicky, have you found anything?"

"Da. Yes," he amended. He was holding a multimeter in one hand.

A multimeter, also known as a Volt/Ohm Meter or VOM, can be used to test voltage and current. I know this in theory, but since fooling around with electricity scares the crap out of me, I have never used one. That's what assistants are for.

"See this here?" He indicated a wire in the compartment that would normally be covered by the landing platform. "It is the power source for the motor that drives the gears. Yet it is dead. No current at all."

"So you've found the problem?"

"Da."

"*We've* found the problem," Edison and Ford chimed in together.

I stared at them skeptically. "I don't see you two down there."

"We're a team," Ford said between clenched teeth, Edison being incapable at the moment of saying anything. "Besides, we're on our break."

"There are no breaks in Hell," I murmured, turning back to Tesla. "So, can you fix it?"

"Nema. No." He shrugged, putting the panel back in place. "I've tried tracing the wire, but it disappears into the ether. I cannot tell where it comes out."

"Can you rig an alternate power source?"

Tesla got to his feet, dusting cloud particles from his knees. "If I can find a source, yes, but everything is sealed closed." He pointed at the signs to Hell. "They are probably powered by the same circuit, but I cannot see how to get open them and run a wire to the Escalator."

"So, you're sure the problem is electrical, not mechanical, meaning," I pointed at Ford, "that he can't help us anymore."

The Little Prick turned pale.

Tesla smiled slightly. "I don't see how."

"What about Edison?"

Tesla shrugged. "Moguće. Possibly he could assist me, no?"

"Maybe. Edison, help Tesla in any way you can."

By now, Edison's face was purple. "Work for *him*?" Edison glared at Tesla. "Work for you? Why, you used to work for me!"

Nicky nodded slightly. "Da, and you never paid me the $50,000 you promised for fixing your inefficient designs."

Edison looked like he had been slapped. Then his eyelids narrowed. He smiled at Ford conspiratorially. "He never could take a joke."

"Adjusted for inflation, that amount should be in the millions by now." As a former economist, I often felt the need to point out the power of inflation to the uninitiated. Those who owed money to others found it a particularly irritating trait of mine.

So sue me.

"Yeah, back on Earth. Fortunately," Edison added, an evil look in his eye, "we're in Hell."

"You said it, not me. Just take orders from Tesla. He found the problem. He's likely to be the one to solve it."

"But," the Big Prick stuttered, "but I'd have figured it out sooner or later."

"Later, probably," I said, turning my back on him. "BOOH?"

Out of nowhere, the giant bat appeared, hovering in the air above us. *"Skree?"*

"Please take Mr. Ford back to the mines, as quickly as you can. We don't need him anymore, and he has a bunch of work to do to make up his quota."

"Aaaaaaaaaaaaaaaaaaaaaaaaaaaaaaaaaaaaaaaaaaaaaa aaaaaaaaaaaaaaa ..."

How fun this was, putting Ford and Edison in their places, but then I shuddered. Jerking them around was a little too much fun. In my mind I heard Satan chuckle. Long-distance telepathy. Scary stuff.

I shook my head, trying to clear it of the infernal laughter. "Nicky, now that you've found the problem, keep trying to find a solution. Oh," I added, "if this Big Prick gives you any trouble, just let me know, and I'll have BOOH take him back to the mines also."

"I will do my best, Steve. Come along, Mr. Prick, we have work to do." Edison, totally defeated, followed Tesla back to the Escalator.

Orson and I stood silently watching them go. "Having fun, are we?" he asked.

I grinned wryly. "Well, that at least was fun. What I have to do now won't be, though."

"Oh? What's that?"

"I have to talk with St. Peter."

Orson smoothed back his hair. "Good luck with that. He's in a state right now."

"No doubt. Listen, Orson, after I finish up here, I'm going down to talk with Beezy about a construction crew to rebuild the Stairs. Head on down to the remains of the Stairway on Level Four. I'll meet you there shortly."

"Right, boss. Kind of a busy day, don't you think?"

"A bit," I deadpanned, then started shouldering my way through the crowds, trying to get to St. Peter, who looked pretty flustered over the chaos engendered by the broken Escalator.

I was just about to say hello when he turned on me. Peter looked mad enough to spit bricks. "You! When are you going to get the Escalator fixed?"

"Sorry, Saint Peter ... lord ... uh ... sir. We're doing our best but we're having difficulty tracing the circuit."

"Look around you, man!" he said, waving his hands at the huddled masses. "This is completely unacceptable."

I winced. "I know, sir. We'll get the Escalator fixed as soon as possible. Meanwhile, we're going to put a couple of workarounds in place."

"What workarounds?"

"Well, we're going to rebuild the Stairway."

St. Peter snorted. Theoretically I knew he could snort but never thought I'd actually hear it. Yet having witnessed the phenomenon, I now had first-hand knowledge that snorting was among the many powers of a saint. "That will take forever."

"Uh, no, sir. Satan has given me a blank check to put together as big a work crew as we need. All trained carpenters and construction types, sir. I'll be heading down to see Beelzebub, right after we finish talking, to get started."

Peter eyed me suspiciously. "You said a couple of workarounds. What's the other one?"

DING went the sound of Hell's Elevator as it reached the Gates Level. "That," I said hesitantly, "that would be them now, sir."

The doors to the Elevator opened and a gang of fifty devils and demons, each carrying a pitchfork, rushed out.

"You can't be serious. We haven't done that in three hundred years!"

"Can't be helped, sir. We have to clear the crowds somehow."

The D&D Gang began herding the damned toward the Mouth of Hell. The sounds of wailing and gnashing of teeth filled the air as the crew used their pitchforks to drive the condemned souls into the hole. They fell, scrabbling futilely at the cloud-rimmed edge before falling in like so many marbles.

The Guardian of the Gates of Heaven almost spat in disgust. "This is barbaric!"

"It doesn't actually hurt them, you know. I mean, they're dead already. A few burns here and there is all, and they'll heal right up. Besides, it's only a temporary measure," I finished, noting to myself that Satan had called this atrocity the exact same thing. He chuckled again in the back of my brain.

"Well, it's bad for morale," Peter said. He tapped nervously on his desk with a pencil.

I looked over at the D&D Gang and grimaced. "Not everyone's, sir."

The minions of Hell were singing, "Heigh-ho, heigh-ho," as they prodded soul after soul into the Mouth. I hadn't seen the boys in such a good mood for a long time.

The pencil snapped in two in Peter's hand. "Just get me another solution," he said through clenched teeth, "as soon as possible."

Feeling vaguely threatened, I backed up. "Yes ... uh ... your Saintship." Then I hurried away.

"BOOH!" I yelled, and he was there. Impressive that he had taken Ford all the way down to Level Six and was back already. "To Beelzebub's office, please."

BatRider took to the skies.

Chapter 8

The Eighth Circle of Hell is one of the oldest. This, I know, is non-intuitive, since you would expect Satan to have started on top and (metaphorically) dug down. However, just the opposite is true.

After the War in Heaven, he and the rest of the Fallen had dropped just as far as possible. There was nowhere to go but up, so, as the devils and their thralls ran out of room, they tunneled upward and outward, making each higher level bigger than the one beneath it.

Hell has had nine levels for over a millennium, though we're beginning to get a bit crowded and, since we're shoved right up below Gates Level, if Satan ever needs more room, I guess he'll have to dig lower and relocate his own space to a tenth or eleventh circle. Maybe he could widen existing levels or go sideways, making circles perpendicular and tangential to the main event. I don't know. It's sort of beyond me.

But, like I said, the Eighth Circle was one of the oldest in the Netherworld. That was where Beelzebub, Lord of the Flies and, not insignificantly, my boss, had his office. Beezy's compound sat in the middle of a sweltering hot desert, with white dunes of sand as far as the eye could see. The settlement looked a lot like an ancient Middle Eastern city, such as Babylon, or the ghetto portions of that fabled place, anyway. No shining minarets here. Instead, ramshackle buildings surrounded a large square on which a merchants' bazaar operated. The plaza was always crowded with sellers, buyers, beggars, cripples. If you wanted to get a cheap set of devil horns or a hookah, a blanket, a scarf or a camel whip, this was the place to go.

BOOH dropped me before a low-slung building at the north end of the bazaar. Atop the roof, in stark contrast to the ancient structures around and beneath it, was a neon sign that perpetually flashed Beezy's Arabic name, "بعل ذباب الذبـ."

For those who can't read Arabic script, this says "Ba'al Azabab."

I don't know why he clung to this affectation; perhaps because in another life he was a Semitic god. Still, an ancient language displayed on a sign that would have been more appropriate in Vegas than Gehenna seemed quirky to me. Oh, well. Beelzebub was very old, and as one of the Seven Lords of Hell (second only, though still junior, to Satan himself), I guess he was entitled.

There were a couple of things about Beezy's headquarters that didn't square with the rest of the settlement. For one, Beelzebub Central was more of a screened-in porch than a building. The second oddity was that the entrance was a revolving door. It wasn't designed, though, to keep out the heat of the arid landscape. The door was all about the flies.

Beelzebub: Lord of the Flies. That's literally what his name means. And, Hell's Bells, the flies - and the mosquitoes - really love him. He isn't very fond of them, though. They are always trying to be near him, and the revolving door, which Orson and I installed some years ago, is intended to keep the flies, mosquitoes, no-see-ums and other buggables from getting at him.

I spun through the door and found myself in Beezy's office. Beelzebub wasn't much on ceremony. He didn't have a secretary - he considered them a waste of time - so he didn't have a waiting room. Beezy's stronghold was a large rectangle of a room. A fan suspended from the center of the ceiling circled lazily. The devil's desk sprawled across most of the screened-in porch, and in a broad chair behind it sat Beelzebub. He was wearing his readers and studying a scroll in his left hand, while muttering under his breath. In his right, he held a flyswatter. Despite his best efforts, the bugs still got to him, and they flew around his head, forming a buzzing cloud. Occasionally one would land on his desk and Beezy would swat it, almost without noticing, but always with deadly accuracy. Then he would snort as he shoved the dead critter off the desktop with his flyswatter.

Beelzebub was quite fat, even fatter than Orson, which was unusual for one of his kind; devils tended to be thin to the point of being cadaverous. Beezy, though, was fond of what was, to him, a relatively recent invention - junk food. All the burgers, pork rinds and moon pies he'd eaten over the past century were catching up with him. He was dressed in an immaculate white suit, and atop his head, canted back slightly to clear the horns that grew from his temples, was an ancient black fez.

"Minion," he growled, looking up at me. "Report."

Beelzebub wasn't one of those devils that liked to jerk you around, inflicting modest torture just for fun. He was all business. If Beezy wanted to indulge in some torment, he'd grab and spit you, place you over hot coals and turn your carcass on a rotisserie. *Nothing done by half-measures*, he always said.

I stood at attention as I brought my boss up to date on the status of the Escalator. "Satan says I should get started on rebuilding the Stairway."

He cursed in a language so old I couldn't translate it, and I know all the best swear words in hundreds of tongues.

"I know. I've put together a list of workers."

He took off his readers, laying them on the desk next to a dead fly, which he idly brushed to the floor with a finger, and handed me the scroll. "They all know their stuff and have already been told to report at the base of the old Stairway on the Fourth Circle."

I looked over the list and whistled. "There must be over a thousand names here!"

"More like 1,323. And you'll need them all to get that dinosaur rebuilt in any decent kind of time."

I swallowed hard. "Beezy, er, Lord Beelzebub, I've never supervised this many people before, and I'm also trying to get the Escalator fixed. Not to mention my spook work, which I haven't even started on."

Beezy slapped at his face where a mosquito had just bitten him. "Nasty little buggers," he mumbled. "You mean the saboteurs?"

"Yes, sir."

He looked at me critically. "I heard you asked out Nightingale."

News certainly had a way of traveling fast in the Underworld. I swallowed hard. Dates were frowned on in Hell. Even asking someone out could put you on the rack for a year.

Beezy swatted another fly. "Oh, relax. I think it's a good idea."

"You do?"

"Yeah. I don't know much about this group of conspirators, but they call themselves the Free Hellions. From what I've heard, they like to gather at local jazz clubs. Going with someone else will make you less conspicuous, and the Red Note is as good a place to start as any. That's where you're taking her, right?"

I cleared my throat. "Well, uh, she hasn't exactly said yes, yet."

Beezy cracked a smile for the first time in I couldn't remember when. "Can't even get a date, huh? What's the matter, Minion? Your pecker too short?"

"Yes ... no," I floundered. "I mean, Flo has never been much on dating, not even in life."

The Lord of the Flies killed another of his insectoid worshippers and flicked its carcass at me. "Just tell her she'll be helping you spy."

I looked at my boss as if he were daft. "And why would that convince her to go out on a date with me?"

He chuckled, a sound much like a chainsaw running out of gas. "To ease suffering, of course. That's what she's all about."

"*Ease suffering?* Whose?"

"Why, those poor schmucks on Gates Level who are being pitch-forked into the Mouth of Hell. The sooner we wrap this all up, the sooner that will stop."

I scratched the stubble on my jaw. It had been a while since I'd had time to shave. "Do you think she'd go for it?"

He smiled again, a big grin that gave me my first look at his very long, pointy canines. One of them was black. I found that unnerving for some reason. "I guarantee it," he said.

Get a date by promising her she'd get to go spying. That was one hell of a pick-up line.

"Oh," Beezy continued, "and call on Pinkerton up seaside on Level Seven. He's already working on ferreting out the little conspiracy twerps. The three of you should be able to deal with whoever you find."

I turned to go, then slapped my forehead. It wasn't a fly, though there were a damn lot of them swarming around. All this talk of Flo and the saboteurs had almost made me forget one of my main reasons for reporting in person to my boss.

"Lord Beelzebub," I began, as I turned back to face him. He was frowning at me but that wasn't unusual. "This Stairway job - it's big, really big, bigger than anything I've ever done."

The Lord of the Flies snorted again. "Don't think you can handle it?"

I stared him straight in his beady red eyes. "Honestly, no. I need someone who can direct all these people. I need ..." I hesitated for a moment. "I need Orson to manage the job."

"No."

"But, look, Beezy," I said, forgetting myself, "Orson is perfect. He's made movies, directing hundreds, perhaps thousands of people at the same time."

"I said no."

"Why not?"

Beelzebub pushed out of his chair and stood up. He leaned over his desk and I was caught up in the vortex of insects surrounding him. "It's his punishment," his voice buzzed in my ear, in synchronization with his flying minions. "You know that."

I swallowed hard and reached to my pocket. I withdrew the blank check and handed it to him.

Flames erupted around me. Beelzebub grew in size before me, until his head crushed the ceiling fan above him. "ACCURSED HUMAN!" he screamed. "YOU DARE DEFY ME?"

"B ... blank check," I stammered. "From ... Satan ..."

The flames rose higher, then abruptly died. Beelzebub shrunk back to his normal size. He frowned again as he handed the check back to me. "Very well. Just this once."

"Thank you, my lord," I murmured. "I'll try to keep him from enjoying himself."

"See that you do!" he said, as I headed for the exit. "And tell him to stay within budget for a change."

* * *

Level Four, near the site of the old Stairway, is a vast plain, much like the Great Plains that stretch across the middle of the United States. High, dry and desolate, the landscape looks deserted; there is hardly any activity to be found beyond the occasional tumbleweed that wanders aimlessly along the prairie. Compared to Level Four, even Beezy's desert-like circle seems crowded, but perhaps that's just the bazaar area, where my boss has his office. I've never really been anywhere else on Eight. Things tend not to break in Beezy's domain. He has no patience for downtime.

This was big sky country, the perfect place to torture an agoraphobic. I might have only seen a tumbleweed or two down there, but somewhere across the vast wasteland below, sprinkled so thinly that they were unlikely to encounter one another, was a number of damned souls whose notion of Hell was exposure, visibility to Satan's all-seeing eye, with no place to hide, not a sod-roofed hut anywhere, nor rocky crevice nor spindly tree. The ground looked too hard to dig a hole in which to hide yourself.

Even BOOH had a little difficulty finding the work crew in the vast anonymity of the Plains, but finally, which for him was all of three seconds, he spotted the ruins of the Stairway. Around the dilapidated structure milled a vast throng. BOOH circled above the multitude until I spotted Orson, looking a little daunted, standing by a pile of metal risers. I pointed, and the bat set me down by my assistant.

Orson didn't seem intimidated by BOOH anymore, even when BOOH settled on the ground next to him. The big man had far bigger things to worry about. "Hey, Steve. I guess you got your work crew."

"I guess I did. Beezy certainly knows how to get the old collective ass in gear, doesn't he?"

"I'll say." A cement mixer pulled up nearby. How Beezy had managed to get heavy equipment to this isolated place so quickly was beyond me. With a shrug, I looked at my assistant. "If you were in my shoes, what would you do first?"

Orson scratched his goatee as he thought. "Probably sort the workers by skill set, while someone drew a design for the stairwell. That wouldn't have to be very complicated. We have the pattern of the lower stairs to go by." Orson retrieved the pen and some paper from his pocket and rapidly sketched a pretty accurate drawing of a portion of the Stairway, as it would look running between two circles of Hell. "Then I'd stage the work. The Stairwell is open from this level down. See?" he said, indicating the intact, if wobbly, stairs at his feet. "I'd have some of the men do repairs on the lower levels and send a crew of workers, supplies and equipment up to Three. We might be able to have two teams building toward each other, or maybe build two shafts at the same time, one on Four, another on Three. We have enough workers for that." He was quiet for a moment, then shook his head. "Not sure. I'd have to think about that some. Regardless, we need a substantial amount of concrete poured first to support the shaft. The distances between each circle is pretty staggering. We'll have to run hundreds of flights of stairs between them. Yes," he concluded, "first pour the foundation for the stairwell housing, then build the housing, then lay in the risers, and finish with the steps. Do that three times, and we're done."

"Wow!" I said, genuinely impressed. "You just thought all of that up?"

He shrugged. "Just seems logical. That's the way I'd do it."

I patted him on the back. "Then have at it, my friend."

A puzzled Orson looked at his boss. "What do you mean?"

"I mean, go to it. You're the general contractor here."

"*What?* Oh, quit kidding, Steve. You know I'm not allowed to do anything but assist."

I reached over and scratched BOOH's ear. He seemed a little surprised but didn't pull away from me. Without looking at Orson, I said, "This time you get to do a bit more than that. I got Beezy's permission for an exception. You're to direct the whole operation."

My friend gasped. "Did you say *direct?*"

"Yep. Think of yourself as the director of this show." I turned to Orson. "Look, you know I never supervised this many people in my life, let alone my death. But you, you're perfect for this job. You know how to organize people, put together really complicated projects and get them done." Well, if you ignored the fact that in life Orson Welles left some of his movies unfinished. I tried not to dwell on that inconvenient biographical detail.

My assistant's eyes were glowing with a manic light.

"So, Mr. Director, shall we get this show on the road?"

Orson was giddy with excitement. "You bet, Steve. I won't let you down." He started to turn toward the people who were still milling around ineffectually, as construction workers generally do if not supervised very closely, but paused. "I don't know how you pulled this off, but, well ... thanks."

Ten seconds later, after he wiped the pie from his face, I helped him to his feet. "Forget it, Orson. Besides, we both know you can do this better than me."

"Better than I, Steven," he said, winking at me. "Better than I."

"Okay!" he shouted, turning to the workers. "How many of you can work concrete? Right, stand over there. Who of you are experts in stairwell construction? Good, good. Over there, please. Truck drivers? Who has worked as a foreman? So few? I guess most foremen go to Heaven," he said, to much laughter. "Oh, and is there anyone who is an architect or draftsman? I have a crude sketch here that I want someone to turn into blueprints."

Orson continued to organize the workers and he did it with complete confidence.

I smiled.

Chapter 9

The Seventh Level of Hell, at least that portion of it where Allan Pinkerton was to be found, was a port, like what you'd find in a Northern European city. As a working harbor, there was a constant bustle of activity as workers loaded and unloaded ships. The cargo was inconsequential; the work involved was all that mattered. This provided many an opportunity for a net to break, tumbling the not-so-precious cargo on the pier or in the water, or for a foot to slip and pitch a dock worker or two into the drink. Every once in a while, an entire ship would sink, as the crew tried desperately to control an uncontrollable vessel that, suddenly possessed of its own infernal will, had determined to slam its wooden hull against the quay. On special occasions, ships would burn as they were tied at port. Sometimes the docks themselves would burn as well.

Few oceans existed in Hell, so seeing one was always impressive. There were no calm, brilliant blue waters, with sandy beaches. No Caribbean scenes here, not even a reggae hint of one. Hardly. This was an ocean that a Moby Dick would travel, that kraken would inhabit, waiting in submariner fashion for the unsuspecting vessel that would have the misfortune to float above the creature. And then the leviathan or the monster squid or, frequently, both, would haul the ship and its crew to the sea bottom, where the panic-stricken sailors experienced the terrors of feeling their lungs fill with water, of drowning without dying. Some poor bastards - the ones with extreme cases of hydrophobia - got to drown multiple times a day, always in spectacular fashion. Great stuff.

And the shoreline was beyond rocky. Sharp, jutting cliffs were always waiting to embrace the storm-driven vessels as they crashed against the jagged rocks, hulls to shatter, crews to drown, ships to, well, sink.

With all the sinking and burning of sea vessels, this portion of Hell stayed pretty busy. The major industry here was, unsurprisingly, ship building, along with various related trades, such as net-knitting (well, I doubt it's called net-knitting, but that seems as good a description as any, and nicely alliterative too), fishing (usually for trash fish), fishmongery (gotta love any business with a name like that).

Oh, and barrel making. They use a lot of barrels aboard ships, because ships have cargo holds, and barrels stow neatly in holds. They look good down there.

I took in the panorama of ocean and port as we hovered over the city, while the giant bat got his bearings. In a second, he did his screech thing and shot down to the pavement.

Pinkerton's workshop was a dilapidated wooden structure wedged between two skyscrapers that were incongruous in a place that otherwise seemed like an Eighteenth or Nineteenth Century seaport. After putting me on the ground, BOOH settled on the shop's small roof. I heard the trusses groan under his enormous weight, but the structure held, and the giant bat folded his wings to get comfortable. As he sat there, he hung slightly over the edge to look down at me. He reminded me of a gargoyle, except he was way too big. Hell, even for a Gothic cathedral, he would have been out of proportion. I waved at him and stepped inside the workshop.

The dim interior was crowded with planks of rough wood and metal hoops, and some of the shoddiest barrels I'd ever seen. Between the wooden staves that formed the sides of the casks were gaps as big as my thumb. The hoops holding the slats together on each end, turning what would otherwise be piles of wood into cylinders, were crooked. Hanging from the back wall were adzes of all shapes and sizes, key tools of the cooper's trade, for that's what Pinkerton was: a cooper, or cask maker, and, apparently, a very bad one.

In the center of the workshop, a man in a leather apron was leaning inside one of the rickety barrels. As he worked, he swore loudly in a Scottish brogue so thick he was almost unintelligible. With his head stuck in the barrel, his curses echoed against the wooden sides, making him sound like he was in a tunnel.

Curious to see what he was doing, I walked over to the barrel and peered over the man's shoulder. Pinkerton, for surely this was he, was using a Swiss army knife to smooth the wood of the cask's interior. "Why are you using a Swiss army knife?"

"Ouch!" Pinkerton dropped his knife to the bottom of the barrel and stood up, his left hand bleeding from where he'd just stuck himself. "Damn yer eyes, ye daft eejit! Look what ye made me doo!"

"Uh, sorry, Mr. ... Pinkerton?"

Pinkerton had a strong brow, penetrating eyes, a receding hairline, and a beard that made him look like third runner-up in a Ulysses S. Grant Lookalike Contest. He nodded once while sucking on the cut. "Dinae matter. I jalousie be guid as new in a wee bit. Though," he frowned, "I almost went ma dinger on ye."

I scratched my head. "Excuse me if I seem stupid ..."

"Numpty," he mumbled, still sucking on his hand.

"Fine, *numpty*, then, but what the hell are you talking about?"

"Ach, mon, sorry. Scots English. Ah dinae get out much these days, since Ah died, ken whit Ah mean?" The man showed me his hand, which was now completely healed, but he seemed to sag a little. "Ah'm fair jiggered, er, *exhausted*. Them barrels," he said waving vaguely at his miserable handiwork with a good measure of embarrassment, "Ah'll *never* get them proper. Feel like Sisyphus, Ah doo, tryin' to roll his rock up the damn hill. Ah'm fair sick of them."

I nodded. "This is your hill, right?"

"Aye, laddie. My personal version of eternal punishment."

"But why barrels?"

He shrugged. "Ah was born in Glasgow. Being a cooper was my first job. Ah hated it, partly because Ah was ne'er very guid, never very good, at it. One of the reasons Ah left for the States was to get away from barrel building."

So, of course, Hell made him a cooper again. "We have something in common, then. I'm Hell's Handyman-in-Chief, but I'm all thumbs."

Pinkerton turned his intense eyes on me again. "Ah. Ya must be Steve Minion. Beezy told me to expect ya."

I choked. "You call him 'Beezy', too? I thought that was my personal pet name for him."

"Nah." Pinkerton said, chortling. "Been callin' em that for near as long as Ah've known em. Lots of people doo. Beelzebub's a mouthful, aye?"

Pinkerton took off his apron and dropped it to the workshop floor. "Ah need a bevvy, sorry, a *drink*." He went over to a nearby table and poured himself a short glass of amber liquid from a half-empty bottle. "Want some?" he offered, picking up a second tumbler. "Can't get steamin', ah, *drunk* on it, a course, but old habits die hard, ken whit Ah mean?"

Yeah, I kenned what he meant; still I reached out my hand to accept the glass he'd just filled with Scotch for me. I tasted it experimentally. The liquor was like motor oil - really, really terrible - especially so when contrasted with that sherry of Lucifer's. Funny how Satan could use an ephemeral pleasure to drive home the eternal misery of damnation.

"Sorry 'bout the broo," Pinkerton said. "But it's the thocht that counts, aye?"

"Right," I agreed and clinked glasses with him. "Cheers." I swallowed the nasty stuff in a single gulp and felt my stomach lurch in shock.

Pinkerton politely waited until I'd finished coughing before he spoke again."Noo to business."

"Yes," I agreed provisionally, "if 'noo' means 'now' instead of 'new' or something else."

Pinkerton settled himself in a rickety chair next to a crooked table. He'd probably built them himself. He indicated the chair's companion, and I sat down also. "Ah've been hangin' around the mines today," he began. "Miners alwae blather on. A guid place to get the talk o' the steamy."

"What?"

"Pick up gossip. Oh, Ah was there when BOOH returned Ford. Good work that. The Little Fuck had pissed all o'er himself. Scared shitless."

I grinned. Seems we had something else in common. "You don't like him much either, huh?"

"Nae. After Ah died, he hired the Pinkertons to bash the heads of workers who were trying to unionize. That's nae what we Pinkertons were aboot, leastwise, not when Ah was boss."

Pinkerton had already learned a bit about the Free Hellions. Turns out they had been around for a while; most of the famous rabble rousers in history were rumored to be members. "Anarchists, by the looks o' them. Ah'm pretty sure Marx is part of the group."

"Groucho?"

"No, Karl." He shrugged. "Groucho may be, too, fer all I ken. I don't know him well, but he seems loony enough. Ah think Lenin and Trotsky are members also."

"What about Stalin?"

"Nae. He wanted ta be, but, from what Ah heard, Trotsky dinae let him join. Ah think Trotsky is still a bit put out about that whole assassination thing."

I nodded. "Yeah, I guess that would piss me off, too. But you said they were anarchists. These guys don't seem to fit the bill."

"Marx and Ah lived around the same time, so Ah know a wee bit about him. He was involved wi' an early anarchist movement, though he moved things in the direction of his own ideas. Still, he preached revolution, so he'd want to be in on this. And Ah bet Lenin and Trotsky, if they really ur members, just went along for the ride. They worship Marx."

"So Marx is the leader?"

Pinkerton poured himself another drink, offering me the bottle, which I politely declined. My stomach already felt like an oil spill from the first glass. "Well, Ah'm still not sure he's even a member, but Ah'll get that confirmed soon. He's not the leader, tho'. No one can tell me how many are atop the hill. What little Ah know, Ah got on the sly. Some say there are three leaders, some four, others say as many as seven. But there's one high heid yin, er, brains of the Hellions, 'tis for certain, and the others are his lieutenants. Twixt them, they're supposedly the greatest anarchists of all time."

"Who would they be, then?" I didn't know much about the Anarchy movement.

"Well, William Godwin was the first gadgie, Ah mean, man who called himself an anarchist, but that seems a might obvious. And he was more a scholar's anarchist. Never really did much wi it. Whoever the leaders ur though, their identities ur kept secret."

"How is it that I've never even heard of this group?"

"That, laddie, is 'cause you been slingin' a deifie."

"English, please."

Pinkerton pulled on his right ear. "Deaf ear." I didn't know if he was talking about me or himself. "Ya haven't been paying attention. Ah doo. Ya must aye be paying attention when yer snoopin', and habits of my lifetime carried over into my afterlife, if ya ken whit Ah mean. Free Hellions propaganda is all over the place, if ya just look for it."

"Where?"

Pinkerton shrugged. "Graffiti on walls, flyers tacked to bulletin boards, whispers in back rooms, that sort of thing. Check out the building to the left of my workshop before ye leave. Ya'll see whit Ah mean."

"Is there anything else you can tell me about them?"

"No, except that they're planning something big. Really big. Ah should know more when Ah see you later."

"We'll see each other later?"

"Aye. Beezy said you and Nightingale - nice lass, by the by, and another contemporary of mine - were going clubbing tonight. Meet me at Red Square at nine o'clock."

"We were going to go to the Red Note."

"Make it Red Square instead. It's on Level Five, too."

"I know where it is." When you're Hell's Super, you pretty much have to know the location of every building in the Netherworld.

Pinkerton nodded. "Ah have a tip that some of the Free Hellions will be gathering there. Besides, Miles Davis is playing at Red Square, and Ah ken Flo likes Cool."

"Good to know," I said, standing. "Now I just have to get her to go with me. Guess it's time to head to the hospital and see if she can be talked into going clubbing."

"Good luck." Pinkerton gave me his hand. Odd, shaking someone's hand in Hell, as if there were honor and good will even here. I found I liked Pinkerton quite a lot. Besides, anyone who hated Ford was okay in my book. "See you this evening. Just keep your eyes open and see what else you can find out."

"Dunna worry about that. As we used to say in my old firm, 'We never sleep.' "

"Yeah, well," I opined, "there's a lot of that going around in Hell."

Pinkerton grinned. "Figger of speech, laddie."

Right." I turned to go, then thought of something. "Oh, you never answered my question."

"Which one?"

"Why were you using a Swiss army knife to clean up that barrel, when you have all this great equipment here?"

"Och. That." Pinkerton looked at the rack of blades behind him. "Hand me that adze there, will ya?"

I went over to the wall and removed the sharp and shiny tool he had indicated. When I handed it to him, he walked over to the barrel he'd been working on. As he reached toward the cask with the adze, it jumped out of his hand, flew across the room and settled back in its original place on the wall.

"Ah," I said understanding. "You're only allowed to use the Swiss army knife, right?"

"Aye. And this." He held up a rubber mallet so small it couldn't even have been used to hammer down the lid on a can of paint. "Ah was always a right terrible cooper, but not having proper tools ..."

"Can really be Hell." I patted his shoulder sympathetically. "I can relate."

Opening the door to the shop, I looked back at Pinkerton. He threw his hammer at the barrel in frustration. It promptly flew apart. Hurriedly, I left the world's greatest detective and spy. To see a grown man cry was never a pretty sight.

BOOH shifted on the rooftop, preparing to launch down and grab me, but I waved him off for a second and walked over to the building Pinkerton had told me about. I noticed that it was the corporate headquarters for a plastic container company. The entire skyscraper, in fact, looked to be made of plastic, in sharp contrast to Pinkerton's all-wooden workshop. The building was probably there just to irritate Pinkerton. Hell was like that: no expense spared when it came to making its denizens miserable.

Just around the corner, I encountered a small bit of graffiti, no doubt applied to the wall with a can of black spray paint. The writing looked like a little kid's block letters. It said:

WHOOP THE DEVILS!
WHOOP, WHOOP, WHOOP, WHOOP!
FREE HELLYONS, FOREVER!

What the hell? Maybe they meant 'whip' - or 'whomp.' Whoever heard of 'whoop'? Well, maybe as a loud yell, but that was just stupid.

Childish scrawls on buildings. Monkey wrenches. And they can't even spell 'Hellions.' What kind of idiots were these people? Yet Satan found them to be a threat?

I was a simple economist turned handyman, and this was all too much for me. My brain was beginning to hurt from having too many things on my mind: a broken escalator, a stairwell that needed to be rebuilt and a clandestine group of conspirators that apparently had a collective IQ of about twelve. And I was supposed to sort all this out?

First, though, I needed to score a date with, of all people in Hell, Florence Nightingale. To be fair, she was about the only person in Hell I would be interested in dating, but she was also about the least accessible. I still didn't understand why Beezy was so keen on having her involved in all this cloak and dagger business.

But whenever feeling overwhelmed, I remembered what my dad used to say: 'One step at a time.' Pretty obvious, but my father was better at platitudes than any real wisdom. Who wanted to go around taking two steps at a time? That was too much like hopping, tiring, and with a greater risk of falling over. So one step it would be, or rather a flight. I waved to BOOH, and he carried me to the hospital.

Chapter 10

I stood before the Giant Toaster, gathering my courage. The metallic gray of the hospital put me in mind of my high school locker, freshman year. Funny. Even in death I could remember the combination: right 36, left 22, right zero.

My locker had been on the bottom. All freshmen lockers seemed to be there, or maybe it was just those for the guys, because the person with the locker above me was also a freshman - a girl.

To me, a bepimpled adolescent, she was a goddess. She had shapely legs, which I got to see at least twice a day, all freshman year, because back then high schools had dress codes, and girls had to wear dresses or skirts. April, for that was her name, had frequently pushed the limits of the code, and while the hems of her outfits always fell below the knees, per the rules, they landed just below, always exposing a generous amount of calf. And she wore heels, not too high, because they weren't strictly allowed, but an inch worth anyway, and they gave a wonderful curve to her legs. When she wore a skirt instead of a dress, it would tend to be a bit tight. God, her ass was divine! She was the same age as me, but she'd already developed breasts (fortunately, I hadn't), and she showed them off by wearing clingy blouses, a classic sweater girl look. To top it off, she was a beautiful young thing, with porcelain skin and long, black hair that went halfway down her back. She had a habit of tossing her sable mane regularly in a coquettish fashion that was most appealing.

Why was it that girls blossomed so early and guys looked like geeks into their twenties? There were some compensations. Men tended to look better later in life than women of the same age, though in my own case I hadn't lived long enough to become a dashing older man.

Once again I stared in apprehension at the Toaster.

Who was I kidding? With my receding hairline, I would have never looked dashing or distinguished, just bald. Maybe I would have bought a wig or gotten hair plugs. Hair Club for Men? Or perhaps that fake spray-on hair substitute.

No, I decided firmly, I wouldn't have done any of that. I probably would have shaved my head and grown a goatee. That might have worked for me, as a college professor. The look was just coming into fashion around the time my life ended.

Back to April. I had the hots for her through most of high school, even screwed up my courage once to ask her out. She laughed at me. She actually laughed, then said she was dating the school's quarterback, who was a senior, and so why would she want to go out with a little twerp like me?

Her nasty rejection of me should have been a clue that I wouldn't have liked dating her, the vapid little tramp, yet instead I carried a torch for her the rest of high school.

We ran into each other at our twentieth high school reunion. Ugh. April had gone fat, bleached her hair platinum. Her once divine breasts were huge, repulsive and pendulous things that hung on her chest like two giant butternut squashes. April had married Tully, that very same football star who had been her high school sweetheart. They'd tied the knot right after her graduation. Tully was there with her that night, another fatso in a too-tight blazer that he'd buttoned over his enormous beer gut. Tully sold insurance and, according to his wife, was soon to be made office manager. April, who had apparently completely forgotten how cruel she had been to me in high school, spent a great deal of time that evening - between mouthfuls of food she onboarded from the snack table - telling me about their life together, including their six kids, about how wonderful her marriage was.

A year later, Tully ran away. He didn't run off with another woman, as the middle-aged stereotype would suggest. He just couldn't take April anymore. Two years after that, April died of adult-onset diabetes.

In the immortal words of Kurt Vonnegut, 'So it goes.'

April was probably around Hell somewhere; most people were. Fortunately, I hadn't run into her. She had been pretty grotesque at the reunion and would be only shoddier now. Hell tended to make everyone a little worse-for-wear. Thinking about the way April had ended up, helped steady me a little as I stood beneath the Giant Toaster, which for a brief moment had been transformed by my imagination into a colossal version of her locker from high school.

Yet middle-aged April was a minor consolation of memory. Mostly I remembered a beautiful young woman, along with the sting of rejection I felt when she wouldn't go out with me.

April was the unattainable beauty from my adolescence, but she had nothing on the unattainable beauty I was about to ask out now. At least Flo wouldn't treat me like April did. Flo was nothing if not kind, and if she said no, she would let me down gently.

With a sigh, I spun through the revolving door and into the hospital.

The waiting room was rowdier than usual. In addition to the huddled masses, insurance cards and information sheets in hand, a conga line had formed. In front was Uphir, shaking his pointy-tailed booty for all he was worth. He led perhaps a hundred patients, all in hospital gowns, and every time they went *shuffle, shuffle, shuffle,* ***KICK***, their gowns parted in back, exposing their butts for everyone to see. Most people in the waiting room averted their eyes, but some were mesmerized. The participants in the conga line - with the exception of Uphir, who looked exalted, having become one with the dance - looked completely mortified.

I stopped a burly man in a nurse's dress, who was walking through the waiting room, smoking a cigarette. He moved awkwardly, having a little problem with the high heels he was wearing. I'd seen him around the hospital before, though we'd never talked. My guess was he had been something like a truck driver in life.

"Uh, Jim," I asked, spotting his nametag, "what's with the conga line?"

Jim casually stubbed his cigarette out against the hospital wall and put the butt behind his ear. I guessed he'd finish it later. "Oh," he said, pointing to the demon leading the procession, "it's Uphir. He's celebrating."

"Celebrating what?"

"He just performed a brain transplant using only a can opener and an ice cream scoop." Jim looked at my tool belt. "Oh, yeah, and some duct tape."

"Jeez! No anesthetic?"

Jim rolled his eyes. "Certainly there was! Uphir was doped up the entire time."

"No, I meant for the patient." It was a stupid question, but I had to ask.

"What do you think this is, the Mayo Clinic? Nothing for the patient. The Chairman was awake for the entire procedure."

"Chairman?" My thoughts ran to Frank Sinatra, John D. Rockefeller.

Jim cracked his knuckles, gave his neck a quick back and forth tilt. It cracked, too, and at that moment he reminded me of BOOH. "Mao."

"Mao? Mao Tse-tung? What's he doing in Hell? He's Chinese!"

"Clerical error."

I chuckled. It was small and mean of me, I know, but I was an American who grew up during the Cold War. Mao was no favorite of mine. For some reason, it made me very happy that he had ended up in the Western world's Hell instead of Diyu, the Chinese version, though how a clerical error could result in something like this was a little mind-boggling. "So," I asked, trying to dismiss this metaphysical anomaly, "what body did Uphir put the brain in? A giant panda?"

Jim snorted with laughter, which triggered a nicotine cough. "Good one," he wheezed, "but you've got nothing on Uphir. No, he switched Mao's brain with that of a chicken."

"A chicken?" There were all sorts of possible candidates for a brain swap with the Chairman - Chiang Kai-shek, Nixon, Madame Mao all came to mind - but I would never have come up with this. "Why a chicken?"

"Because," said a jubilant voice behind me, "a chicken is the ultimate proletariat!"

I turned to face Uphir as Jim slipped away in the direction of the butt hut, probably to finish his cigarette. "And why is a chicken the ultimate proletariat?"

The conga dance was continuing, with the encouragement of several demons with whips and pitchforks. "Did you know," said Uphir in a professorial tone, "that there are nearly six billion chickens in China? That's four times as many as there are Chinese people. I wanted the Chairman to bond with his true comrades."

I don't know why I kept this conversation going but couldn't seem to help myself. "So how is the patient doing?"

"Thank you for asking," Uphir said in his most sincere insincere voice. "Both patients are adapting well to their new bodies. It's quite gratifying to see the Chairman's body move around with such energy, though it seems to have a little difficulty pecking the birdseed off the floor of his room. Chicken Mao mainly hasn't done much but sit around and smile. Honestly, though, isn't that about all Mao did in the last ten years of his life?"

"Sorry I asked."

"My pleasure." Uphir turned to rejoin the dance.

"Oh, Uphir, do you know where Flo is?"

The demon doctor put a finger to his nose. "Let me think. Ah, yes, I can sense her now. She's in the nurses' lounge, crying her eyes out. I guess something I did upset her." He grabbed the butt of the last man in the conga line and was gone.

I hurried up the stairs to the second floor, where the lounge was located. Opening the door quietly, I peeked in.

Flo was sitting in a leatherette seat, sobbing inconsolably. Quietly I walked up to her, pulling my handkerchief from my pocket. It was gray and dingy, but cleaner than most things you'd find in Hell. I kneeled next to her. Flo took the offered cloth as she looked down at me.

Even in Hell, I thought it was a good idea to always carry a handkerchief. Handkerchiefs had gone out of fashion in my lifetime, most people having let their germaphobia steer them toward Kleenexes instead, but to me having a handkerchief you never used except to offer to a lady in distress was an act of gallantry that never lost its charm, even into the 1990s, when I bit the bullet. So, on coming to Hell, I continued the practice of carrying one. I'd never offered it to anyone before, though. Flo was the first person who seemed worth it to me.

Florence Nightingale was a soggy mess. Her eyes were bleary red and her nose dripped like a basset hound's. None of that mattered, though, as she fell into my arms. She was the most beautiful woman I had ever known.

Flo cried for a long time, her breath coming in and out in jagged gasps. It wasn't long before the handkerchief was soaked, but still she cried. I held her, stroking her hair, rocking her gently in my arms. I hummed a lullaby – 'Too Ra Loo,' I think. Eventually, her sobs lessened, then stopped entirely. Still I held her, not wanting to let go. Flo looked into my eyes and smiled. "Amidst the horrors of Hell," she said softly, "there yet is kindness. It gives me hope."

Not wanting to push my luck, I kissed her forehead and released her.

Florence took my hand and guided me to the chair next to her. "You know what Uphir did?" she asked, still holding my hand.

"Yes." I didn't know what else to say. *How horrible?* Too obvious. It was pretty much par for the course down here in Hell, but I didn't think saying that would provide much comfort to her, either.

She looked at the ceiling, where an asbestos-laced tile, water-stained because of some plumbing leak above it, threatened to pull from its supports and fall to the floor. "Why is this place here?" she whispered.

"The hospital?" I asked, brushing an errant lock of hair from her forehead. I'd never seen her so disheveled, so ... discomposed.

"No,' she said, shaking her head. "All of it: the hospital, the fiery pits, the endless torture and suffering. Why?"

I shrugged. "I guess there have been a lot of bad people on Earth over the years."

She released my hand, flinging her arms wide. "Where? Where are all these bad people? I understand there have been some truly cruel and evil humans in the course of history. Maybe they deserve to be here, though most of them were probably insane. But the people I encounter here do not seem so bad, just miserable. Were you such a bad person in life?" she asked, looking intently at me.

How to answer that one? "I didn't think so. I was arrogant, no doubt, and had a short temper, for sure, but otherwise I thought I was okay. I paid my taxes, helped Mrs. Feenie carry her groceries up the stairs in our condo building." I paused, trying very hard to come up with something else that was nice about me. "I liked dogs, I remember that."

"See?" she exclaimed, as if my liking dogs was the next thing to sainthood. "You were a good person, I'm sure of it, because I know you now. I sense the kindness within you." I blushed, but she continued. "People here weren't evil in life. They were just human, with all the frailties that go with that condition. And so I ask again, why is there a Hell?"

I opened my mouth to respond, then snapped it shut, like a small child who was getting ready to say something that would get him in trouble. "I d ... don't know," I ventured finally. "There appears to be this cosmic rulebook. It seems mostly arbitrary to me, and I don't think it makes a clear distinction between evil and sin ... though maybe it should."

Flo got out of her chair and began pacing the floor. "Ah, sin. Yes. The Bible. I was reading the 'Thou Shalts' and 'Thou Shalt Nots' from the time I was a child. Your description of it as a rulebook seems apt to me. Or a set of instructions. But where is the discussion of goodness, other than in following the rules?"

I scratched my chin in thought. Having her put it this way made a certain amount of sense. I was a simple handyman and this conversation was getting way beyond me, but I wondered if the Bible wasn't put together to serve a practical purpose, laying down rules like a government would create laws, to keep the people in line, to keep them from doing horrible things - to avoid Chaos. But saying that would open another can of worms. Flo was worked up enough as it was, and I didn't want to throw another log on the fire, let alone mix my metaphors, so I responded to her question simply but honestly. "I think goodness is supposed to show in the examples set by the people in the stories. Like Je ... like the J-Man. Pattern your life after Him, and you will be a good person."

Now Flo looked truly angry. "But that's not fair! He was the Son of God! How can we measure up to that standard? Besides, according to Matthew and Mark, even Jesus cursed the fig tree. If He can make a mistake, how can we be expected not to?"

Interesting that Flo was able to invoke the names of the Big Three without getting in trouble, but since she wasn't damned to begin with, she must have had something akin to diplomatic immunity. "Calm down, Flo," I said, rising from my chair and holding her by the arm to stop her ever-faster pacing. "Perhaps it wasn't a mistake. He was probably trying to teach something."

"That may be," she sniffed, holding her head erect. There was fire in her eyes. She was indignant. Good. That was better than the despair I'd been watching for the past hour. "But he still showed his temper. He lost control. How is that any different from a boss snapping at his secretary before he's had his first cup of coffee for the day?"

"And there's the issue of faith," I said, continuing the discussion despite myself. "Faith. Good Works. A religious discussion that's been going on forever. Many believe it's impossible for us to be good enough to get into Heaven on our own. We have to have faith. If we do that, the J-Man will intercede on our behalf."

"Did you have faith?"

I smiled ruefully. "Sort of, though I didn't go to Church much. And I sure believe now, with all the evidence around me."

"So," she concluded, QED, "you believed, but didn't get to Heaven, despite being a basically good person. That doesn't seem fair to me. And do only Christians have a chance for Heaven? What about Buddhists, Hindus, the moral atheist or secular humanist?"

"I don't know, dear Flo, I just don't know. I've only encountered Jews, Christians, and Muslims in Hell. Oh, and the virtuous pagans on Level One." And now Mao. There was also the occasional figure from dead mythologies that Satan, on a whim, had appropriated. A number of exceptions to the rule seemed to exist, but I kept this new insight to myself. It would have just complicated the discussion more than it already was.

"Our Hell is for people from the religions of Abrahamic tradition," I continued. "Well, also atheists and agnostics from predominately Christian, Jewish, and Islamic nations." I imagined briefly that Jews in particular must have been surprised at this version of Gehenna. It was a might longer than twelve months and a lot more about punishment than purification. With an effort, I banished these unsettling musings. "Beezy's told me there are other places for people who have different beliefs. 'There are more things in Heaven and Earth, Florence, than are dreamt of in your philosophy.'"

That made her smile. "Why, Steven, quoting the Bard now?"

"Seemed appropriate for the occasion. All I'm saying is that these cosmological discussions are really beyond our ken." I winced. Pinkerton was rubbing off on me already. "Beyond our ability to understand them."

"I know what 'ken' means, Steve," Flo responded, then plopped wearily back into her chair. It was the first ungraceful movement I'd ever seen her make. The crying, the anger, the lack of grace: they all made her seem more human to me, less an unapproachable paragon of virtue, and all the more beautiful as a result.

I sat down next to her. "Flo, all of this is getting to you. Have you thought about my offer?

She smiled wryly. "You mean, will I go out on a date with you? I don't know, Steve. I don't get out much."

"It would be good for you," I said, taking her hand again. She didn't pull away. "This place, it's going to eat you alive ... or dead," I amended quickly. "Besides, you need a break and I could use your help."

"What? Oh, Steve, I'm sorry. I've been so wrapped up in my pain and anger that I didn't think about what you might need. What's wrong?"

This wasn't exactly how I'd planned the conversation going, but in this instance honesty seemed like the best policy. I told Flo about my whole day, about the Escalator failing, the rebuilding of the Stairway, and Satan's command to find the insurrectionists and stop them.

She looked at me in surprise. "You would help him? The Prince of Darkness himself? Why?"

I held out my empty hands, palms up. I had nothing, except, "He rules Hell, and I'm one of his minions, uh, underlings. Besides, I'm scared shi ... I'm terrified of him."

Flo lifted her head in proud defiance of the Lord of Hell. "Well, I'm not afraid of him."

I smiled, shaking my head. "I don't think you're afraid of anything, Miss Nightingale. Most of us, though, aren't as strong as you. Besides, you never were meant to come here anyway. Satan has no power over you."

"I suppose that's true," she said, thoughtfully, "except to force me to watch the suffering he and his lot cause here. But how can I help, and more importantly, why should I help?"

I told Flo about the alternate measures Team Satan was using to get the damned from Gates Level to Hell. "It's really barbaric, Flo. Those poor souls, they're already terrified, and being flung into the Mouth of Hell is beyond terrifying. It reinforces all the horrors they'd learned about damnation in their lifetimes."

"Oh, that's awful," she said, shuddering. "But how can I help?"

"According to Pinkerton ..."

"Allan Pinkerton?"

"The very same."

"Oh, I know him. Such a pleasant man, though his brogue is so thick you could cut it with a knife. I met him in the 1860s when I advised the Union army on how to organize medical services in the field."

Here I was, trying to get a date with someone who died more than forty years before my birth. Knowing people from all different time periods was sometimes disorienting, but I'd mostly gotten used to it since coming to Hell. "Anyway," I continued, "Pinkerton says the anarchists - that's what he thinks they are, anarchists - like to gather in jazz spots. Some of them will be at Red Square tonight."

"Red Square? I thought we were going to the Red Note."

"Change of plans. Besides, the Miles Davis Sextet is performing at Red Square."

"I love Cool ... well, what little I've heard of it. As I said, I don't get out much."

"So, will you come with me? I could really use an extra set of ears and it would make me look less suspicious, too."

Florence leaned over and kissed my cheek. "Yes, Steve. I was going to say yes all along."

I gaped in astonishment. "You were?"

She looked down demurely. "Yes. I like you, Steve. Very much. You have always been so kind to me and, well ..." she looked me squarely in the eyes and smiled. She was breathtaking. "... I like you."

"You said that," I mumbled, then nearly bit my tongue off. *Stupid, stupid.* "I like you, too," I added, recovering quickly, and prepared myself for the inevitable pie assault. Surprisingly, it didn't happen. I guessed Satan was cutting me a break.

Flo kept smiling at me, eyes locked on mine. I was tempted to plant a big wet one on her, but frankly didn't have the nerve. After a long moment, I stammered, "Go ... go home for a while, Flo. You need to get out of here. Right now I have to check on something before going to my apartment and changing into an outfit more suitable for clubbing. I'll come by your place in a little while and pick you up." With that, I stood and headed for the exit.

"Change?" I hear her say as the lounge door closed behind me. She sounded unsure of herself for perhaps the first time since I'd met her. "What shall I wear?"

Chapter 11

There really is no day or night in Hell, just a perpetual grayness in the sky. There's also no precise finish to a regular workday, no work whistles going off, for example, to signal the end of a shift. Things just usually proceed on and on, without a break in the humdrum of Eternity, until we all sense that we must retreat to our little hovels and prepare for restarting the Humdrum. For many of us, getting up and going to work is part of our damnation (no sick leave, vacation or retirement here), so we have to have a start to the day. Oh, which is always Monday. We don't ever get the weekend, but we do get the Monday after it.

In keeping with this, I felt rather than saw that, for me at least, the 'end of the day' was at hand. Before getting dressed for my night on the town, though, I needed to swing by the Fourth Level and see how Orson and his work crew were getting along.

I gasped when BOOH dropped me at the worksite. Hundreds of workers were moving with absolute efficiency, some carrying wood, others mixing cement, driving trucks, etc. Orson and his team were working very fast. Already, rising half a mile above me was the enclosure for the stairwell. The black monolith, standing against the gray landscape and sky, loomed impressively.

"Coming through!" hollered a brawny worker pushing a wheelbarrow. Funny, he looked gray, too. In fact, there was no color to anything around the worksite at all.

"Crane down!" yelled a familiar voice, as what looked to me like the arm of a cherry picker truck descended to ground level. There was Orson, dressed in a tweed suit, a white beret on his head, and a megaphone in hand. He too was all in gray. "Hey, Steve!" he shouted, getting off the crane.

"Orson," I whispered, looking nervously around me. "What's going on? Why is everything in black and white?"

"Oh," he said casually, "I do my best work in black and white. It just makes more of an artistic statement, don't you think?"

"But ... but this is a construction site," I sputtered, "not a movie."

Orson looked a little hurt. He kicked at the dirt, pouting. "You said I could be the director."

"Well, sure. And you've gotten a lot done since I left, way more than I would have thought possible. But, speaking of possible, how did you get things to be in black and white?"

"Remember," he smiled, looking exceptionally pleased with himself, "I'm the director. I get to do what I want. Beezy came by a while ago to check on us. I said it would go faster in black and white, not having to mess around with getting the colors right. He thought I was nuts but I guess he remembered Satan's blank check. A wave of his hand and, presto, black and white!"

I shook my head. "Well, he is Beelzebub, so I guess he can do what he wants. Anyway, you really are making great progress."

"Thanks. Just a second," he said, waving me to the side. He lifted his megaphone and spoke in a voice I swear had been electronically amplified; it seemed to carry for miles. "Great work, boys! We're over halfway to Level Three. We'll finish the shaft before quitting time." He leaned over to me conspiratorially and whispered, "Whenever that is. The repairs to the Stairway lower levels are complete and I have another crew building another shaft on the Third Level. I haven't been able to check their progress as much - that damn elevator takes forever - but they're a little behind us. Once this shaft is complete, and I get the men started on putting in the risers, I'll shift my attention to the workers on Three. I'll get some laying risers downward. We probably won't get it right when we meet in the middle, but it will be good enough for government work," he said, winking again at me. I wished he would stop that. "The rest will finish building the shaft up to Two and continue on building to Level One. By then, all the Work on Four to Three should be done, and I can move this entire work crew onto finishing the shaft up to Level One. Then, finally, splitting the team again, I'll put some men on One and have them work risers and stairs down, while the other crew works from Two, until we meet in the middle. With luck, we can finish tomorrow."

"You're kidding."

Orson patted me on the back. He was possessed with a frenzied energy I'd never seen in him before. "No, I'm not. We spent the first part of today just getting organized. It's all worked out now, and we can spend the rest of the day and all of tomorrow just knocking out sausage."

"What?"

"Oh," Orson chuckled, "just a metaphor I thought up. We build the casing," he said, indicating the shaft for the stairs, "and then we stuff it. Nothing to it, really. Besides, I have an idea for how to motivate the men."

That sounded suspicious. "What are you up to, Orson?"

He smiled beatifically. "Nothing, really. Just going to up the production values. Come by Level Two in the morning. You'll see."

"Okay." I stared up at the black shaft piercing the ash-colored sky above. It had almost reached the clouds. "Oh, anything from Tesla?"

Orson frowned. "Beezy told me that Tesla and BP still can't find the problem."

"Well, all the more reason to finish here. Orson, thanks for doing this. You're doing a great job."

My assistant flushed. "I'm just glad to be doing something useful again. Something I'm good at."

I nodded. "I know what you mean. At least, I think I do. Not much call for an economist down here."

Orson nodded. "Besides, what would you do? Predict a recession or something?"

"I doubt that. Hell seems to be a pretty healthy franchise. Not much unemployment, for instance. Listen, hate to leave you after just getting here, but I've got a date."

"You're kidding, right? Flo actually said 'yes'?" Probably nothing I could have told Orson would have surprised him more. "How did you pull that off?"

"Not sure frankly, but I've got to boogie on home and get changed. You got it here?"

"You bet, boss," Orson said, stepping back onto the crane. The mechanical arm started to rise. "Give my best to Flo."

"I will."

BOOH scooped me up and headed for the Throat of Hell, dropping me at the trailer. I gave him another treat, then sent him off for the evening. "Thanks again," I told him. "I shouldn't need you anymore tonight. But let's meet up early tomorrow, okay?"

"Skree!" And then he was gone.

I checked my desk for anything urgent. There were fifty new work orders but nothing critical, which was good because there wouldn't have been time to deal with it.

Now to head for home.

Only a few blocks separated my office and my apartment. I tamped down the tape holding the door closed on the trailer and started walking.

Many people down here have apartments. There's not much to them, or much point to them. None of us really sleep at night. That's part of being in Hell. Oh, we have beds and all, but we spend our nights tossing and turning, thinking about the futility of our afterlives, staring at the alarm clock as the minutes and hours swing by, wide awake, dreading the buzz of the alarm, when we have to get up and do it all over again.

Some people don't have apartments, but they don't hate getting up in the morning the way some of us do. Many of Hell's minions just stay in eternal damnation mode all the time. Apparently, for them, agony without abatement is more troubling than getting a night off and dreading the alarm clock. Me, well, I'm just not a morning person, so getting up early is part of my punishment. Therefore I have an apartment.

I was almost there now. My place was a walkup. That wasn't special; everybody who had a place had a walkup. No one got to live on the ground floor. Mine was a sixth floor walkup, which made carrying up the groceries kind of a bitch. Climbing the stairs to my apartment in the Underworld was only slightly more hassle than ascending those to my place in Manhattan, back when I was alive. That one was on the fourth floor. My New York apartment had been rent-controlled, which was a pretty good deal, and I had a view of Riverside Park. In Hell, I paid no rent at all, but I stared at a brick wall with a Toxic Waste symbol painted on it.

After huffing up all six flights, I put my key in the lock and turned it. The doorknob came off in my hand. Déjà vu all over again. I pried the door open with a screwdriver. The roaches were over every surface. They cocked their heads in unison as the door opened, then scrambled out of sight.

My flat would have been familiar to anyone who'd lived in an old building in New York. It was a studio, meaning it was just one room that served, thanks to the Murphy bed hiding behind the gray panel on the right wall, as both living room and bedroom. A small kitchenette hung off to one side, a little round table separating it from the main living space. There was a small bathroom and, hiding in a cubby hole behind the paneling, along with the bed mattress, a miniscule closet for my miniscule wardrobe.

Not much of a place, but you don't need much in Hell. Most people live alone, except those who really want to, like people who had lived with spouses for sixty years in life and now just wanted to be left to themselves. They, naturally, got to live with those spouses for all Eternity, unless they were among the precious few mortals who actually wanted to stay with their mates forever. Those wedding vows - ' 'til death do us part' - that's actually a promise of parole for most people. The rest of them, well, they were just crazy, in my opinion. Certainly, if their marriages had been anything like mine, spending Eternity with your spouse would be part of your punishment.

So we live alone. No live-in lovers, as it's hard to find anyone particularly likeable in Hell, and sex, almost by decree, is unpleasant and dissatisfying. Besides, Satan doesn't want you happy. I think that should be pretty clear by now.

Stripping off my coveralls, I hung them in the closet before beginning my toilette.

Toilette. Hah. That's a good one.

Any kind of bathing in Hell is an unpleasant experience. Most of us get a cold shower with water that isn't very clean. It comes out of the spray head as a yellow fluid, probably because of rusted old pipes, like at work. The liquid has that urine smell, though, so you can't be sure. Still, when you're going on a date, you take a shower beforehand. That's just what you do.

I turned both spigots, including the hot - hope springs eternal, and sometimes you get a blast of hot water when you're not expecting it, though it's usually excruciatingly painful - and stepped in the shower stall. To my amazement, the water was clean and the temperature perfect.

"What the fuck?" I looked around and saw a freshly-laundered washcloth and towel, a new bar of Ivory Soap, and a bottle of Pert Plus. Suspicious, I wetted my hair and worked the shampoo into my scalp. It lathered up just fine and rinsed right out. As an experiment, I even followed the universally-ignored instructions; I repeated the steps. Same thing, and my hair - well, what little there was of it - felt cleaner than it had since my last shower on Earth. Next, I took the washcloth from the rack and got it wet, then worked some Ivory into it. I started scrubbing, scrubbing away the grime of Hell, even cleaning my back, my ears (in and behind), and between my toes.

After rinsing off, I closed the taps and reached for my towel. There wasn't any grease on it; the thing just looked like a clean towel. I patted my body down carefully, figuring this was the trick to catch me, but the old bod just got dry - and stayed clean.

I stepped to the mirror to brush my teeth, blow-dry my fringe of hair and shave. *Curiouser and curiouser*. Again, everything went without a hitch. I didn't cut myself shaving, but got chin, cheeks, and neck as smooth as a baby's butt. And my hair ... did it look a little fuller than usual?

"What is going on?" I said to no one in particular.

In my closet, I rummaged around for any clothes that might be presentable for a night on the town. There wasn't much hanging there, other than my coveralls, a clown suit, some mauve hot pants and a puffy shirt. "No, no, no," I mumbled to myself, flipping through each item, until, at the back of the closet, I came across a tuxedo. I didn't remember that ever being there before. A clean and perfectly-pressed white shirt, in my size, was there as well, along with a black cummerbund and bow tie - the latter fake, which was good, since I'd never gotten the hang of tying a real one. The tie had a neck band that hooked discreetly under the bow, making it easier to mess with and better looking than the real thing. On the floor beneath the ensemble was a pair of classic patent leathers.

This was like having a fairy godmother come to visit, but since this was Hell, the situation was more than suspicious. I pulled open one of the three drawers built into the wall of the closet, the drawer that held my precious few undergarments, and found a clean T-shirt and boxers.

Okay, there was one place where something always went wrong - the sock drawer. In all my afterlife I had never found two socks that matched in that drawer. Such an event was rare enough even in life. Back then, everyone joked about gnomes who stole socks either from the laundry room or the sock drawer. There was no way I'd find a matching pair. Not a chance.

And yet, there they were: jet black, elastic still holding, neatly folded together. The socks looked brand new; certainly I'd never seen them before.

Someone was playing me for a sucker, I was sure of it. Nothing goes right in Hell. Yet there was no denying this was the perfect outfit for my date with Flo. Maybe Satan was being nice to me for all this extra work on these important special projects. It wasn't his style, though, and that made me worry, but that wasn't getting me anywhere, so I just got dressed.

My apartment was actually equipped with a full-length mirror. It wasn't for me to primp before, though. The mirror was mounted to the back of the front door, so that every morning before work I could see how crappy I looked. The glass was yellowed, with a four foot crack, but I could still see myself pretty well. I don't think I had ever looked so good, not even in life.

A trench coat was draped over the back of the sofa. On top of it was the perfect fedora. I didn't recall either of them being there when I came in the apartment. Still suspicious, I slipped on the coat. My fairy godmother again or, more likely, my fairy roach mother.

I heard a chittering come from behind the walls. Ugh. Perhaps that thought was a little too close to the mark.

I started to button the coat but abandoned the notion, tying it closed with the belt. Donning the fedora, I took a final look in the mirror. A rakish tilt to the brim, and my ensemble was complete. "Here's looking at you, kid," I lisped in my best Bogart impression and left the apartment.

The sky was gray, as always, but it seemed to be the gray of dusk, almost a promise of dark to come. The streets were deserted and a wind had picked up. Loose sheets of newspaper blew, like tumbleweeds, down the avenue. The scene was as desolate as an old west ghost town. Lining the road were dingy buildings like my own, dilapidated and mildly grotesque parodies of the brownstone I'd inhabited near Columbia during my lifetime. Graffiti was scrawled on many of the walls. Most of it was obscenity, but then something caught my eye.

Remember Niagara!
Free Hellyons. Forever

Remember Niagara? What did that mean? Was it something like 'Remember the Alamo?' I tried to figure out the sign above the words. A hand with an eye painted on it, with another hand pointing at the eye? There was some hidden meaning here, but I was damned if I could figure it out.

Well, I was damned even if I couldn't. Either way, if you know what I mean. Regardless, this obviously was not a random design, yet what did it signify?

These Free Hellions really were everywhere, I decided. Pinkerton said I just hadn't been paying attention, and he was right. Now that I knew what to look for, I saw Hellion graffiti everywhere, sometimes just with a phrase intended to incite, other times accompanied by the hands and eye logo.

I sighed. Enough worrying. I had a date with an angel.

I'd never been to Flo's place before, but I knew where it was. It was a bit of a hike, not an impossible walk, but I wanted to keep my clothes looking nice, so I decided to take a cab.

I whistled loudly, catching myself just before I yelled for BOOH. I'd already gotten used to having him around.

Usually it took forever to get a cab in Hell, but the driver of a yellow taxi that was just going by on the opposite side of the street heard my whistle and did an immediate U-turn, pulling up to the curb beside me. I opened the rear passenger door. "Oh, hi."

My cabbie was Louis Braille.

"Bonjour, mon ami," Louis said amiably. *"Où aimeriez-vous aller?"*

"Can the French, Louis. It's me, Steve."

"Oh, *pardonnez moi* … I mean, sorry about that, Chief. Where do you want to go?"

"The Victorian Quarter."

"Sûrement … er, certainly. Just tell me when I need to turn, oui?"

All cabbies in Hell are blind. You get used to it.

Louis kept a smile plastered to his face as he pulled away from the curb, but I wasn't fooled. His entire body quivered with nervous anticipation as he careened along the avenue. He looked to be in a perpetual state of high anxiety, always waiting for the next crash, but unable even to see it coming.

Having to navigate the streets of Hell, including its major freeway, the Road to Hell, which, as we all know, is paved with good intentions, without being able to see - what a pisser.

I shook my head. Any damned soul could relate to Louis and his plight. Each of us might have had our unique versions of damnation, but feeling helpless was a common characteristic.

Braille tried to keep the vehicle far to the right of the street, letting it bump periodically against the curb, as a blind man would probe with his walking stick. Because his senses were so refined, his bumps were more like gentle nudges, though he started with every touch of concrete against tire.

Louis had been driving the streets of Hell for a long time. He knew most of the major destinations, so he really didn't need much help from me, though I'd occasionally yell something like, "Slow down!" or "Dump Truck!" or "Holy Shit!" Driving blind: Hell for the cabbie; Hell for the fare. Pretty much like being in a taxi in Manhattan.

With only a few near-misses along the way, Braille got me to the outskirts of the Victorian Quarter. "Thanks, Louis," I said, handing him the fare and a large tip in the scrip Hellions use to pay for services down here. It really had no value at all, but you had to hand a cab driver something. Louis, relieved by having made the drive without incident, smiled beatifically as he dumped the money out the driver's open window onto the already-littered street. "*Rien*. You coming to poker night?"

I smiled. "Wouldn't miss it." Louis never won a hand, since he couldn't see the cards, but that never stopped him from playing. "Later."

I made a turn down Flo's street and immediately found myself in a gaslight district. The road's surface had changed to cobblestone. It looked to me like a poor copy of Victorian London. There was more activity here than on my own street; people were beginning to head out for the evening to engage in some pointless, painful or humiliating activity. Those not walking climbed aboard horse-drawn carriages; Double jeopardy, as both the horses and their drivers were blind.

In Hell, the damned usually were housed in places much like they knew in life, though invariably in a lower-rent district. Holing up in a familiar dwelling was not likely intended as a kindness. In Hell, construction was constant, to keep up with the ever-swelling ranks of the damned, and the architectural styles reflected those being built in the mortal realm at about the same time. As a result, every circle of Hell was comprised of a mishmash of architectures, Victorian shoved up against Tombstonesque or Parisian or modern Turkish. Or, in my case, buildings like those found on the upper west side of Manhattan.

I stepped on the single stone stoop that marked the entrance to Flo's building. There was no need to buzz to have her release the door lock - that technology wasn't in use here - so I turned the knob and let myself in.

Flo's room, according to the directory mounted on the wall just inside the entrance, was on the second floor.

Chapter 12

The stairs had a shabby runner held in place by tarnished brass rods. Some of the rods were loose, and I slipped once while making my way up the stairs. I cursed under my breath but reached the landing without any major mayhem. Flo's door was just a few yards down the hall. I knocked softly.

"Steve?"

"Yes, Flo, it's me."

"I'm not quite ready," she said through the door, "but give me a few seconds, then come in."

I took off my hat, smoothed back my hair and opened the door. Behind it was an apartment decidedly more pleasant than my own. Perhaps the fact that Flo didn't belong in Hell had affected the space around her. Certainly just being near her made anyone in the Netherworld just a little bit better, so it wouldn't have surprised me if her aura - for that was the only word that adequately described the special quality that was Florence Nightingale - warped Hell's reality, and in her own place, her center of power perhaps, beauty was possible.

An antique Persian rug covered a clean wooden floor. Delicate curtains, trimmed in lace, framed the window at the back of the main room. A round table with two chairs was by the window; the tablecloth covering it was clean and freshly pressed. On the wall, perpendicular to and right of the window, were two closed doors, one of them presumably leading to the room to which Flo had retreated, the other maybe to a bathroom. On my left, a small fire burned in the fireplace. Remarkably, the flue seemed to work, unlike every other flue in Hell, which tended to be blocked up. This chimney drew well, for there was barely a hint, and only a pleasant one, of smoke scent. Two worn, but comfortable-looking, chairs sat before the fire, a lamp for reading between them. Bookshelves covered most of the wall at the front of the room. I didn't see many books in Hell, so I went over to take a look. The shelves were filled with medical texts, books on mathematics, and the great works of philosophy and literature.

As I was examining her collection, a door opened behind me. I turned at the sound and gasped.

There stood Flo in a sleek, white, silk satin evening gown, one shoulder bare. Her luxurious black hair was pinned up, showing off her long, elegant neck and the diamond necklace around it. Flo even had on diamond earrings, dangly ones that looked great against her bare neck. (I wondered idly when she'd ever had the need or opportunity to get her ears pierced.) She wore white evening gloves that stretched nearly to her elbow. In one hand she held a silver clutch. Draped over an arm was a full-length white fox cape.

"Do I," she hesitated, "do I look presentable?"

"Heavens, Flo," I whispered, ignoring Hell's rule about invoking anything remotely divine, "you are beyond presentable. You're so beautiful, you glow!"

Flo blushed prettily, making her cheeks match the faint touch of lipstick which was the only makeup she was wearing. "I've never worn anything like this before, but it was the only thing in my armoire tonight. Even the nurse's uniform I had on today disappeared while I was taking my bath."

"So you had a visit from your fairy godmother also," I said, opening my trench coat briefly to reveal the tuxedo.

"You look very handsome, Steve," Flo said.

As she walked toward me, her hips swung gently but noticeably in the tight fabric. She straightened my tie, smiling at me a little uncertainly. "Are you sure I look presentable? I've never worn anything this ... revealing before."

I beamed. "Better than presentable. Much, much better. It's not likely Hell has ever before seen anything as stunning as Florence Nightingale in a white evening gown."

"I wonder about these shoes, though," she grimaced, pulling up the hem of her garment to reveal silver pumps with three inch heels and a very shapely calf. "They're more comfortable than I was expecting, but how can anyone walk in them?"

"Flo, you are the most elegant person I've ever known, living or dead. Just now you practically glided over here. You'll be fine."

"Then would you help me with the cape?" She handed me the fur and turned, presenting me with her glorious back. It was all I could do to keep my hands off her, to keep from kissing the nape of her neck - from which a few wisps of unpinned hair were beckoning - or caressing her bare shoulder. I took a deep breath, summoned all my self-restraint, and slipped the cape over her shoulders. She turned again, flushed.

She was embarrassed. Not only was she beautiful, but she was embarrassed about it. That was very endearing.

As usual, I was grinning like a buffoon around her, so I composed myself and offered my arm. "Shall we go?"

She smiled and slipped a gloved hand around my arm.

We reached the base of the stairs without mishap. "I don't know if I can walk all the way to the club in these shoes."

"Do you think you can get to the end of the street? We should be able to get a cab there. I don't know if the carriages ..."

"Phaetons," she corrected.

"Oh, really? Well, anyway, I don't know if the *phaetons* are allowed to leave your neighborhood."

Florence smiled. "I can walk the block. I'm getting used to ... What is it you usually say? Oh, yes, I remember. I'm getting the hang of these shoes."

We reached the end of the block and, surprise, surprise, a cab was waiting for us.

I am by nature a very suspicious person. I mean, I'm not personally suspicious, not to others, or at least I don't think so, but I am suspicious when the sequence of events is too perfect, especially since I died, after which things pretty consistently started to go downhill. This whole evening was entirely too conveniently arranged, but I was doing the Lord of Hell's work, so I decided for once to turn off my suspiciometer and enjoy things.

The cabbie was unfamiliar to me but he knew the route to Red Square. We arrived there without incident after only a few minutes in the car. Well, there *probably* wasn't an incident, but I was so busy ogling Flo I wouldn't have noticed anyway. For her part, Florence mostly stared down at her hands, caught up in the wonder of gloves that were purely ornamental. She did, though, occasionally glance over at me and smile.

The cab pulled up to Red Square. After paying the fare, I slipped out of my side of the car and hurried to open Flo's door for her.

The club's doorman, a stocky fellow in a long double-breasted coat, complete with brass buttons and a military-style hat, beat me to it. Yet I got there in time to offer her my arm and help her from the cab. The doorman inhaled sharply as Flo stepped onto the curb. She was a vision of white radiance that seemed to illuminate the entire block.

Red Square was located in a brownstone just off one of Level Five's main avenues. The club entrance had an awning of bright scarlet, leading from the curb to the front door. The distance was a mere ten feet, where we found another doorman, similarly attired to the gentleman who'd met us at the curb. The new guy held open the door and we stepped inside.

Red Square was a nightclub in the old style popular during the thirties or forties, more like New York's Copacabana than a discotheque from my own time period. A large stage, capable of holding a big band from the days of Swing, was at the back of the main floor. Between it and the round tables that were already filling up with the evening's customers, was a parquet dance floor large enough to host a high school sock hop.

We checked our outer garments with a homely grandmother type at the coat room. The manager of the club was a devil in the classic fashion - horns, goatee and tail. He sported a bright red suit, his tail sticking out from under the back of his coat. The unruly thing was like a snake; it seemed to have a life of its own, bobbing up and down as he fussed over his seating chart.

The manager glanced up and dropped his pen. All thoughts of his chart forgotten, he hurried over to greet us. I wasn't surprised. You almost never saw a pretty woman in Hell. Flo would have been stunning in a burlap bag, but dressed as she was that evening, she looked like a goddess who had just descended to the floor. I didn't look half-bad myself, but I was an afterthought, just as a tux is really only a black backdrop against which to place a woman and her dress.

Don't think that devils can't appreciate beauty. They love it. Remember, they were angels once, staring for what promised to be Eternity at the glory of Creation and its Creator. This could very well be the reason most devils are so ill-tempered. While they delight in hurt and disfigurement, a part very deep within their souls (yes, devils have souls also, just not as complex as human ones) still yearns for divine beauty.

And that was Flo that evening - a divine beauty.

A table out front, right next to the dance floor and slightly off center stage, had just opened, and the manager escorted us over to it. He pulled back Flo's chair and expertly scooted it back in, scooping her up like he would a sweet dollop of ice cream.

The table hadn't been cleared yet, and the maître d'evil snapped his fingers once. The sound cracked like a whip; the snap could have been heard on the other side of the room. A busboy in white shirt, black slacks, a tie and white apron hurried over to remove the old dishes, replace the table cloth and put down two fresh place settings.

He was one of the uglier men I'd ever encountered, on either side of the grave. His face looked like it was made of putty that had been molded inexpertly into a permanently angry expression. Then the sculptor had taken an awl or something, making a few pits and divots in the complexion to enhance his homeliness. The man's nose was an especially big blob of ill-formed putty. He had black hair, parted in the middle, and ears that were too big by half to belong to the rest of his head. The man looked familiar to me, like someone I knew, but the features weren't quite right. Something about the hair, maybe, was throwing me off. Perhaps if it were combed differently I might figure out who he was, or at least who he reminded me of.

The busboy noticed me staring at him as he worked, and his face folded up on itself, making creases in the skin where I didn't think frown lines could be possible, as if my attention had made him angrier than usual. Soon he finished his work and left, and I dismissed him from my mind.

By the standards of Hell, Red Square was quite the elegant place, but a careful eye could see the frayed linens on the table, the ragged wallpaper, the paint peeling in spots by the entrance to the kitchen, the tarnish on the brass footrest that ran the length of Red Square's fifty-foot bar. Yet, this night, I was in no mood to dwell on the imperfections of the place. Besides, with Flo at my side, noticing much of anything but her was almost impossible.

A waiter came to us bearing a champagne bucket and a bottle of Dom Perignon. "Wait," I said. "We didn't order ..."

"Compliments of the manager," he said, popping the cork. We looked over to the devil near the entrance. He made eye contact with Flo and kissed his fingers. I was vaguely repulsed by his attentions, but Flo nodded with great dignity, like a queen receiving her due. The waiter poured the champagne into two crystal flutes that looked like they were Rosenthal. But that would have been inconceivable. Too perfect.

The champagne, I was sure, could not possibly be Dom Perignon. More likely it was horse urine with bubbles. This was Hell, after all. But the moment was perfect. Here I was, with the most wonderful woman I'd ever known, getting ready to drink something that looked like champagne. Who cared if it tasted like horse piss? I was going to toast her, drink it, and enjoy the experience. We lifted our glasses and clinked them together. "To you, Florence Nightingale," I murmured, mesmerized by her luscious brown eyes. "The most magnificent woman of all time."

She blushed. "No. To you, Steve, my knight in shining armor, who has made my sojourn here bearable."

Now it was my turn to blush. "To us," I whispered.

Flo dimpled prettily. "Yes," she agreed, "to us."

We took our first sip, and I prepared myself for the inevitable disappointment.

Which did not come.

It really was Dom Perignon, and it tasted divine, even better than the sherry I'd shared with Lucifer.

Flo laughed.

"What?" I asked, concerned that she found the moment ridiculous.

"I've never had champagne before. The bubbles, they tickle," she said, putting her hand atop mine.

I was in heaven. Well, I was really in Hell, but you know what I mean.

"What'll ya have?" said a gruff voice. I looked up and saw the strange putty-faced man who had cleared the table earlier.

"I thought you were a busboy."

The man glowered at me and I felt even more sure I'd seen him - or someone who looked very much like him - somewhere before. "We're short-staffed tonight. Now, what'll ya have?"

Flo, who had already perused the menu before the champagne had arrived, ordered *Fettuccini Alfredo*. I quickly ran my eyes over the choices and saw one of my favorite delicacies - at least it had been during my time on Earth.

"Are the sweetbreads good?"

Putty Face frowned at me, twisting his head to one side as if he'd never seen a creature as strange as me. "This is Hell, bub. What do you think?"

I considered the question carefully. Just about everything since I'd come to the Underworld had been uniformly awful, and that argued the sweetbreads would taste like spoiled calamari soaked in linseed oil. But then I'd had that sip of sherry with Lucifer. When that happened, I knew that, Satan permitting, there could be good things going on here. And then just now, we'd had real Dom Perignon. The Lord of Chaos might have allowed the champagne just to pull on our chains, to remind us of what we'd lost, but ... but looking over at Flo, I realized that things sublime, even in Hell, were possible. This evening had gone perfectly so far, and I decided to take a chance.

"I'll have the sweetbreads. And we'll take a bottle of chardonnay to go with our entrees."

"Isn't all of this a lot to drink?" Flo asked after the waiter left. She was hiccupping from the bubbles in the champagne.

"You can't get drunk here. Don't worry," I said, squeezing her hand while feeling atypically optimistic. "It will be fine."

In a few moments, our salads arrived: fresh spring greens, some craisins, roasted pine nuts, and crumbled goat cheese, all topped with a balsamic vinaigrette. Delicious.

As we ate, the band began to set up. In the center of the stage was a white grand piano. The man standing next to it was pianist Bill Evans. He looked longingly at the magnificent instrument before placing the thin black case that was under his arm on the piano bench. He opened the case and pulled out a glockenspiel.

Tonight's group was a sextet, most of the same players who had recorded the best jazz album of all time, 'Kind of Blue.' Other members of the group joined Evans onstage: John Coltrane on kazoo, Julian 'Cannonball' Adderley on slide whistle, Paul Chambers playing bass on a large-bore bit of PVC piping, and Philly Joe Jones, carrying an array of pots and pans that he placed on a table. He also had some long wooden spoons to use for drumsticks.

Philly Joe was a substitution. Jimmy Cobb, who played on the album, wasn't available. Somehow he'd managed to make it into Heaven, so Davis enlisted his original drummer from his first quintet.

Finally, the star of the ensemble entered. Miles Davis carried a decrepit bagpipe that wheezed as he walked; the bag had a leak somewhere. The pipes rested on his left shoulder. He was having a little trouble with the instrument, and it looked to me like an octopus trying to strangle him. Must have embarrassed the hell out of him but you couldn't tell. He was still Miles Davis, the epitome of cool. Besides, his sunglasses hid his eyes; that was usually where embarrassment was the most obvious.

They didn't bother to tune - what was the point? None of the instruments was really tunable anyway, except the slide whistle - and perhaps the PVC pipe, I added mentally. Nothing to do if it was sharp, but if it was flat, Chambers could have sawed off a piece. That trick would only work once, though.

And this was Hell, so no one expected them to play in tune anyway.

Davis spent a few minutes filling the air bladder of his bagpipes, then he did a quick count-off, and the sextet began playing a screwball version of 'So What,' the glockenspiel and PVC pipe setting up the introduction. The group's performance was spirited, if not very musical.

"Did Cool sound like this back on Earth?" Flo asked me. "I've only heard it played this way."

"Well ... sort of. The instrumentation was a little different."

"How?"

I told her about the original album. She had heard early phonographic recordings, probably made by Edison, near the end of her life, but Davis and his crew made 'Kind of Blue' nearly fifty years after her death.

"Trumpet? Miles Davis played trumpet?" she said, disbelieving.

"Yeah, he was a great trumpet player. Not his technique, so much as his ability to interpret a song, to give it his own unique sound."

"Well," she sniffed, "I think the bagpipes are a great improvement, don't you?"

"But he can't play in tune on them."

"How can you tell?"

We continued this banter as the musicians moved from one chart to another and as we polished off the champagne. Miles looked a little winded; I bet those bagpipes took a hell of a lot more air than his trumpet ever did.

Soon our entrees came, and in keeping with the entire evening, the sweetbreads were excellent. The waiter opened the chardonnay and poured us each a glass. "Oh dear," Flo said, her cheeks flushed, "I don't know if I should."

"Why not?"

"Lean over and I'll whisper it to you." When I did, she kissed me on the cheek. "The wine seems to be going to my head." She smiled flirtatiously as she caressed my sleeve.

Yes, something very odd was going on this night. Still, Florence Nightingale had just kissed me on the cheek, so there wasn't much to complain about.

We finished our meal. A few couples had straggled out to the dance floor. I stood up and extended my hand. "Flo, would you care to dance?"

"I haven't danced in almost 200 years, but I'd love to." She took my hand and we stepped onto the dance floor.

The devil manager had just had a short conversation with Davis, who was shaking his head vigorously. The devil pointed at me and Flo, and snapped his fingers. Flames rose from his hand. Appropriately chastised, Miles relented and turned to his band, whispering a few words.

What was that about?

Miles and his ensemble incongruously started up a waltz. That was lucky, because it was one of the few dances I could manage, most of the other classic ballroom moves being beyond me. I held Flo a little closer than was really necessary, but she didn't complain. As we finished the dance, she rested her head on my shoulder briefly before pulling away.

"That was lovely," she breathed as she took my hand in both of hers and we headed back to our table.

We were working on dessert and coffee, crème brûlée and espresso for both of us, when Flo reminded me why we were there. "How are we going to go about finding information on the Hellions?"

Not being a spy by profession, I really hadn't actually considered how we'd do our snooping. "Well ..." I said slowly, "maybe we just keep our ears open and hope someone says something."

Flo cocked her head to one side. "I can't hear anything but the band, can you?"

I confessed that I really couldn't. I wasn't much good at this spy stuff.

"Then there's just one thing to do," she said, motioning to our waiter.

"What's that?"

"Ask someone. Excuse me, sir," she said to Putty Face when he came to our table. "Do you know anything about the Free Hellions?"

"HEEP! Heep heep heep heep heep heep heep heep!" our waiter uttered incoherently, like a hoarse roadrunner on speed, or a man with an uncontrollable case of the hiccups. I perked up. Well, that was interesting. He looked very upset, like Flo had just punched him in the stomach or something.

I'd never thought about the direct approach.

"They seem to be some sort of revolutionaries – anarchists, I think. Have you heard of them?"

The waiter took a handkerchief from his pocket and mopped his brow. "Can't ... can't say I have. Excuse me, miss." Putty Face hurried off.

The man was lying. It was as obvious as Eternity was long. "Excuse me for a minute, Flo," I said, rising. "Enjoy the rest of the set. I'll be back shortly."

Trying not to draw attention to myself, I moved as quickly as possible after the waiter, who had just disappeared into a stairwell. Opening the door to follow, I heard his hurried footsteps clanking on the steel stairs above me. I tried to match the rhythm of his stride, so he wouldn't be able to hear me behind him.

The man left the stairwell on the second floor and I carefully cracked the door to see where he was going. He stepped into a room about halfway down a long hallway. With all the stealth I could muster, I tiptoed along the hallway carpet.

Room 222. I put my ear to the door. The voices inside were muffled, so making out what they were saying would prove difficult. Beside the door was a tray with a half-eaten bowl of Cheerios and a glass of water. I dumped the water into a planter holding a dead weed, placed the open end of the glass against the door and my ear against the base of the glass.

"... and then this dame just up and asks me about the Hellions!" That was our waiter, no doubt.

"Who is she?" asked another voice that sounded so similar to the first one they could have been brothers.

"Has to be Florence Nightingale," the waiter said. "Either that or a succubus. She's a major babe, but she looks a little too innocent to be demon spawn, and I don't know of another beautiful woman in Hell, at least not around here."

"Who's the mug with her?" asked a third voice, not so much like the first two.

"Don't know."

"Well, find out," said the one who appeared to be in charge.

"You ain't the boss of me!" snarled Putty Face. "I'm older than you and ..."

"Oh, yeah?" I heard a loud smack.

"OW! Why you ... I oughta ..."

"You oughta what?" said the leader in a threatening tone.

"Now, boys, we've been together too long to fight like this. OW!"

"Whoop whoop whoop whoop whoop!" There was a fourth person in there, but he was apparently an imbecile, because he didn't seem to be able to speak. "OW!"

"All of ya mugs, shut it," the leader said. "And, you, get downstairs and see what you can find out about Nightingale's companion. Maybe do a little persuadin', get him to 'forget' the Hellions, if ya get my drift."

"Why should I?" Putty Face said, still defiant.

"Because I'll hit you if you don't!" ***SMACK!***

"OW!"

"Besides, you're their waiter, and you need to get back to work, don't you?"

There was a pause in the conversation. "I guess so," Putty Face admitted grudgingly.

The sounds of footsteps came through the glass, so I hurriedly placed it back on the tray and ran toward the far end of the hallway. When 222 opened, I made myself go flat against the door of another room, mostly hiding myself in the outer part of the door jamb. The waiter headed back down the stairs. I found another stairwell at the end of the hallway and descended as well.

I opened the door on the first floor at the opposite end of the room. The waiter had preceded me by a few moments. He looked at my table with alarm then started scanning the room. I was well away from the stairwell, though, before he spotted me. He frowned and headed toward me, but another customer grabbed his arm. By the time Putty Face dispensed with him, I was leaning over Flo's shoulder. "Did you miss me?"

She batted her eyes coquettishly, as if she'd been doing it her whole life. "Very much, dear."

"Ah, listen, Flo, this has been wonderful, but I think it's time for us to leave." I placed some money on the table. It didn't really matter how much the tab was. In Hell, it was the act of paying and tipping that was important. Just like with the cabs.

"Do you think so? Oh," she said, frowning a little. "And I was having so much fun, but you're probably right. I can feel the wine."

"No, you can't," I said absently, helping her to her feet.

She swayed a little. "Yes, I can," she laughed, kissing my cheek again.

I blushed while leading her to the coat room. I retrieved our coats, slipped the cape over Flo's shoulders and donned my trench coat.

As we left the night club, an old man with silver hair jostled me. "Pardon," I mumbled without looking up.

"It's me, ya wee eejit," a voice whispered. A closer look at the old man revealed Pinkerton in disguise.

"Room 222," I mumbled. "Something's going on there. I think it may be the head honchos."

"Really, now? Me thinks I must take a stroll up there, then. Ah'll see you in your office first thing in the mornin'. For now," he said, bowing to the lovely Florence Nightingale, "goodnight." With that, he left us.

A cab was waiting at the curb and we slipped inside. As the taxi pulled away, I saw our waiter standing at the exit to the club, watching us.

With an effort, I put him out of my mind. Flo was sitting very close to me, hanging on my arm. She smelled heavenly. "What's that perfume you have on? I've been meaning to ask all night. It's lovely."

She flushed. "Just a little rose water in my bath."

"Mmm," I said snuggling against her, which she didn't seem much to mind, since she snuggled right back. "Well, you smell wonderful."

In a few minutes, the cabbie had us at the entrance to the Victorian district. I helped Flo out of the car and we strolled, hand-in-hand, down the quiet, lamp-lit road. The walk was all too short, though, and in a few minutes we were on the stoop to her building.

Our eyes met as I took both her hands to say goodnight. "Would you," she hesitated, "would you like to come up?"

My throat went dry. Was she asking me just to come up or, well, to 'come up?'

I wanted to, more than anything, but I was concerned about the happenings at the club. Or maybe that was just an excuse. And I really respected this woman. Not on the first date, not with someone you really care about; that was the old rule from my youth. Or maybe that was an excuse, too. Maybe I was just intimidated by a very beautiful woman. "I ... I'd love to, but could we make it next time? There's something I need to take care of still this evening." That last bit was a fib, but it was the best I could do on short notice.

"Next time?" she asked, actually pouting a little. "Will there be a next time, Steve?"

I took her in my arms. "I hope so. I'd like there to be."

"Me, too," she said with a smile that dazzled me.

There was only one thing to do, so I kissed her, right there on the stoop, for all of Hell to see. What's more, she kissed me back, a long, passionate kiss, with plenty of tongue action on both sides. I felt myself wanting to come up after all.

"Next time," she whispered in my ear.

I swallowed hard, just nodding. I must have looked like an idiot, which was quickly becoming my usual expression around her.

Flo caressed my cheek, gave me another smile that melted my heart, and stepped into her building.

For a minute or two after the door closed, I just stood there, my mouth agape, considering what had happened. I had just kissed Florence Nightingale. And, amazingly, she liked it. She even kissed me back. What's more, she really liked me, maybe even cared for me.

At this point, I expected five demons to appear, carting me off to some deep, dank dungeon of Hell, where I'd be persecuted for a century or two - but it didn't happen. I had kissed her, might even have loved her, and Hell wasn't raking me over the coals for it.

Heading back toward the main road, outside of the Victorian sector, I found myself humming. It could have been 'Singin' in the Rain,' but that would have been way too corny. Besides, while I had the trench coat and fedora, I lacked an umbrella. And it wasn't raining anyway.

Chapter 13

Hell actually seemed beautiful to me that night as I walked home along the main avenue of the Fifth Circle: there was less trash on the road than was common; the smell of sulfur was gone from the air; the screeching sounds of tires, of human souls howling in torment, were curiously absent. Silence reigned everywhere, which suited my mood. I looked to the sky. There were no stars to see, this being the Underworld and all, but the main burn-off fire from the oil refinery was unusually bright that night, and if I squinted a bit, the blaze looked a little like a full moon.

I was three blocks from my apartment, passing across the narrow entrance to a dark alley, when two sets of hands pulled me in.

Three toughs confronted me, the two who had grabbed me and a third who stood patting a baseball bat into his left hand. All three were dressed in white ballerina costumes.

"What's with the tutus?"

The men looked at me sheepishly. Playing tough while dressed like a bunch of girls must have been hard on them. "We just finished performing in 'Swan Lake,' " one mumbled, a heavy-set guy whose head was shaved bald.

"Don't say it like that," commented his near twin. The two reminded me of Tweedledee and Tweedledum. "At least it's show business."

"Shut up," said a voice from the shadows. There was a crash, as what I assumed was a half-full trashcan was kicked over. I heard its lid skittering over the asphalt.

I had a pretty good idea who owned the voice. The man stepped forward into the faint light emitted by the burn-off moon. Yep, it was Putty Face. He had discarded his apron and wore a dark coat, the collar turned up, presumably to add to the tough guy effect, or maybe just to obscure the whiteness of his shirt. "Don't answer his questions. He's supposed to answer ours."

The man turned to me. "Alright, ya mug," he said in his thick New Yorker dialect. "Start talking."

"About what?" I said, with a false sense of bravado. While he couldn't really hurt me or my eternally damned soul, if he decided to do some nasty things to me, the pain would be real. I didn't like pain.

The tough guy looked me up and down. "Well, for starters, what's your name?"

That seemed like a reasonable question and, since I was pretty well known in these circles, especially the Fifth Circle, there was no reason to hide it. "Minion. Steve Minion."

"Oh," said the leader of the ambush committee. "A wise guy, huh? We're all minions here, ya goon, and you know it."

"No, really. My last name is Minion ... *OW!*" I screamed, covering my eyes with a hand. "You poked me in the eyes! Why the hell did you do that? Shit, that hurt!"

"I don't like wisecrackers."

"Wait, boss," said one of the men, one of the two who had grabbed me. In his tutu, he looked like Frosty in a skirt. "I recognize that name. Steve Minion is Hell's Super."

"Hell's what?"

"You know," said the other goon who'd pulled me into the alley. "Hell's Superintendent for plant maintenance, Mr. Fixit, like I was on 'Joey Bishop,' except he does it for all of Hell."

The boss frowned. "That true? Is that who you are?"

"Yeah," I said, blinking over and over, my eyes still smarting. "And who are you guys?"

Putty Face frowned but the other three started laughing.

"I'm Joe," said the first of the underlings who had talked.

"I'm Joe, too," said the second.

"Me, too," said the third, who bore a strong resemblance to his boss.

Then they all started laughing again.

"Very amusing," I said, picking my hat off the alley floor and dusting it off. I shoved it back on my head so hard I almost tore the rim. I was pissed off now. "And what's your name, Mr. Waiter?"

For some reason this set him off. "Why do you want to know my name? Nobody ever remembers my name. It isn't important. I know," he said, with a leer, "call me Joe, just like the others."

Great. I was surrounded by Joes One, Two, Three and Four. How original. "Okay, Joes. What do you want from me?"

Boss Joe leaned so close to me I could smell the garlic on his breath. "We want to know why you're asking around about the Hellions."

"I didn't ask anything about any Hellions. What's a Hellion, anyway? OW! OW!" Boss Joe had punched me in the stomach then, when I bent over from the blow, brought his fist back up quickly, thwocking me in the forehead.

"Don't deny it, creep. You may not have asked, but Nightingale did. Everyone knows Nightingale is a goody two-shoes. She wouldn't be involved in this on her own, so I'm figuring you put her up to it, right?"

That was absolutely right, but admitting it wouldn't help me any. "You leave her alone!" I shouted. Without realizing it, I had doubled my fists.

That's considered a threat in most circles.

"Fine, fine," he said, holding his hands before him in a placating gesture. "I have no beef with Nightingale. Besides, it would draw too much attention if I messed with her. You, on the other hand ..." He cracked his knuckles meaningfully. "You...well, stay out of Hellions business."

"Fine...Joe," I said, in my toughest voice, which, being a former professor, was like me lecturing a freshman on the dangers of plagiarism. In other words, not so tough.

Boss Joe turned his back on me and started to walk away. "Oh," he said over his shoulder, "and just so you don't forget our little conversation, break his legs, boys."

"WHAT?" I screamed, and the three other Joes laid into me with two baseball bats and a rubber chicken. They broke my legs with the bats and they hit me on the head a dozen times with the chicken, apparently just to see it bounce off repeatedly. They laughed as they left me sprawled on the pavement.

I felt like hell, but my legs mended themselves almost before my assailants had left the alley. Glowering at the backs of the departing thugs, I got stiffly to my feet. My trench coat, tuxedo, even my fedora, were ruined. My bones could re-knit themselves just fine. My clothes, though ... not so good.

Still aching, I headed for home. The six flights of stairs up to my apartment were slow going.

* * *

Nighttime is Hell, Take One - Action:

What is night? How do you define it? Is it measured by the setting and rising of the sun, the hours between the instant light fails and is born again? For firemen, policemen, bakers, and others who work odd schedules, night must be curiously shifted. Perhaps for them it starts when their heads hit their pillows and ends when their alarm clocks go off.

Since light levels don't change very much in Hell, workdays and alarm clocks are even more arbitrary in the Netherworld than on Earth. The closest parallel to Hell's version of night in the mortal realm must be what is experienced by the insomniac, who tosses and turns for hours on end, watching the slow forward movement of the clock, knowing there is no rest for the weary, no sleep that provides a blissful break from an unpleasant reality.

For many in Hell, eternal damnation is unremitting, scorching flames without relief, remorse without respite. For those of us in Hades who have a version of night, it is simply a setup for the *ennui* of the day to come. Ishmael and Queequeg, as they cozied up to each other in the first chapter of 'Moby Dick,' realized they couldn't really understand warmth without experiencing a contrast, and so in the toasty confines of their shared bed, they really appreciated heat, because compared to their noses stuck out into the frigid air of their room, the rest of them was doing pretty darn well.

I've said this before, but it bears repeating, because there may be nothing more hellish than Netherworld nights: No one sleeps in Hell, not even those of us, like me, who have the 'night' off. We lie on our lumpy beds, staring at the ceiling, thinking about all of our regrets from a life badly lived, about the nature of damnation, the eternity of Eternity, the misery of our unique experiences in Hell. We stare at the alarm clock, not knowing whether to wish for more time in bed or for the bell to just start ringing so we can get the day going, do something, get it over with, and then come back to this bed that does not promise rest or sleep or dreams before starting the cycle all over again.

That night I was even more conflicted than usual. Nothing done in Hell really made any difference, that was a certainty, and yet here I was worrying about escalators, stairwells, insurrectionists, and women - especially women, or rather, one particular woman.

It was all false hope, a complete setup. Even my problems implied that what I did had some meaning, that whether or not I solved them made any difference. But nothing down here was of any consequence. I knew that and yet continued to worry.

Cut, Nighttime is Hell, Take One

It was the human condition, I decided, crawling out of bed when the alarm clock - in sync with the internal ticker of my eternally damned soul - rang out, screaming that, at least for me, this night was over. I shut the cursed thing off. Humans wanted to hope, all evidence to the contrary. And in Hell, the evidence pointed toward a bad outcome.

Start a new day with hope, only to be disappointed; struggle with problems that look insurmountable, and find out they really are; try to accomplish work that seems significant, and learn it isn't. Love, even though love cannot be had in Hell.

Flo had been on my mind a lot that night. Maybe I should have just gone upstairs with her and banged her for all she was worth, for all I was worth, which didn't seem very much. Except ... except ... I cared too much about her to cynically have taken her that way. Perhaps I was worthless, but Florence certainly wasn't. She may have been the only good person in all of Hell; even if the rest of us belonged here, she didn't. She deserved better.

Skipping my normal morning shower, I pulled on my coveralls. Then a new thought occurred to me. Maybe Flo was a game-changer. The rules of Hell didn't seem to apply to her. Maybe by associating with her I had a chance at something more than the tedium of my eternal punishment. Maybe, just maybe, I could love her and get away with it.

On my nightstand, beside the alarm clock, was a small object - the champagne cork. It was a keepsake from last night's date. On a whim, I picked up the cork and placed it in the pocket next to my heart.

I limped down the stairs. Though completely healed from last night's beating, not to mention my crash landing on Satan's carpet, the memory of the pain was still fresh and I reflexively favored my non-existent wounds.

I knew not to think too much about the previous evening. If Satan happened to be monitoring my thoughts, he'd take away my meager hope. That seemed certain. He'd take Flo from me.

And so I tried to wall off my growing affection for her, seal it in a hidden corner of my mind, in the hope that no one was paying attention. The tactic was a feeble one. After all, Satan could pluck thoughts straight out of my head if he wanted to, yet hiding my thoughts of Flo was the only thing I could think to do.

Parts was open early, so I swung by to check on the status of my orders. "Has the bulb for Hell's sign come in yet?" I asked Dora, who was flicking an ash on the concrete before her office door.

"No, not yet, dearie, but," she added, reluctantly, "the glass and the replacement lock for your door are here."

"Okay, give them to me." I didn't know when there'd be an opportunity to fix the door, but getting things from Dora whenever she admitted to having them was always good policy.

"Sure, Steve," she drawled, taking another drag from her Newport. "Got them right here." She disappeared for a moment but returned quickly, first with the glass, then with the door knob. "I hear you got a little action last night."

"Don't know what you're talking about, Dora," I said, signing for the two items. My face was turning warm; it was probably a bright red.

"Oh, come on, Steve. Word travels fast in Hell. You know that. So," she said, leaning over the counter of her half-door conspiratorially, "is she any good in the sack?"

I looked at Dora in absolute horror. "*What?* I didn't sleep with her."

"Yeah, right." She leered at me but she must have seen something in my eyes, for her expression turned to one of astonishment. "You're telling the truth. You could have popped her cherry, but you didn't."

"Watch your mouth, Dora."

Dora blinked, incredulous. "I'll be damned! You're in love with her." And she broke out laughing. Grumbling, I turned my back on her and left, carrying the glass and knob to my office.

The door to the trailer was already open. The duct tape hung loosely from the doorjamb, flapping in the soft wind that was blowing that morning. The breeze smelled of sulfur, but then it almost always did. Stepping through the opening, I smelled something else: freshly-brewed coffee. Bad coffee, but freshly-brewed. Pinkerton was pouring himself a cup. He had beaten me in.

"Top of the mornin', laddie!" he said, far too cheerily it seemed to me.

"Whatever," I whispered, setting the glass and doorknob in a corner, then leaned briefly against the wall as I was suddenly overcome by exhaustion.

So tired this morning. Can hardly process what anyone's saying to me.

I got the Stupid mug from my desk and went over to the Mr. Coffee. "What did you find out?" I asked, yawning, then took my first sip of the day. *Ugh*. Flo's presence in my life sure hadn't improved the office coffee any. It still tasted like piss, but maybe that was partly the sour taste in my mouth from dealing with Dora.

"You were right about 222. Ah jimmied the lock on an adjacent room and spent an hour listening through the wall to their conversation. Bunch of blatherskites, the lot of them," he said in disgust.

"Pinkerton ..."

"Call me Allan, laddie. Now that we be workin' together."

"Okay, if you'll stop calling me 'laddie.' "

"Righto, boyo." *Boyo? Isn't that Welsh? Whatever.* "Ah mean, Steve." Pinkerton took a flask out of his coat pocket and poured what I suspected was some Scotch into the coffee. "Care for some? Your coffee's terrible, ya know. This might help."

"Doubt it," I mumbled, but let him put a shot in my mug. I was right; it didn't help. Now my coffee tasted like piss mixed with motor oil. "Allan?"

He took a sip of his doctored coffee and winced. Bad coffee mixed with bad Scotch didn't seem to be working for him, either. "Yes, laddie ... er, Steve?"

"I don't own a Scottish to English dictionary. What the hell is a blatherskite?"

He chuckled as he sat down on Orson's stool. "Oo, that's someone who has a lot to say, but says very little. Those boys were big on talk but short on content."

I fell into my desk chair, coffee in hand. As I took another sip, three work orders shot out of the pneumatic tube. "So, they weren't the leaders of the Free Hellions?"

"Ah dinae say that, Steve. Ah just said they dinae have much to say."

"So they are the leaders of the Hellions!"

"Aye. Ah think so, anyways. They just don't seem all that bright to me."

I thought back to the thug talk, the fighting, and the incongruous 'whooping' sounds of the imbecile in the room. "You're probably right about that. What little I heard made me think they were morons, but when has intelligence been the hallmark of a great leader?'

Pinkerton, shrugged. "Sometimes, laddie ... Steve ... but not usually. Still, these fellahs are clearly in charge. And now we know their number. There be three o' them."

"And if that's so, what do they have planned?"

"Ah'm not sure, but tis something big."

"Yeah? So far, I'm unimpressed. What does 'something big' mean anyway?"

"Well, they said the failure with the Escalator was as they'd planned it."

"The damn monkey wrench they threw in the gears wasn't even the cause."

"And what makes you think that?"

"Because both Ford and Edison don't think the monkey wrench was what broke the Escalator. They're smart, despite being major fucks, so I pay attention to what they say. Besides, Tesla believes the problem happened up Gates Side, that the breakdown was electrical, not mechanical."

"So what do you believe?"

I stood up from my chair. This was a tough question. "I believe ..." I threw my cup against the wall. It spilled all of the noxious fluid onto the wall and floor, but the mug itself did not break. "... I believe that none of this makes a rat's ass difference. We're just going through the motions of meaning." The bitterness in my own voice surprised even me. "None of this counts. The Escalator, the Stairs, the insurrectionists. You. Me. Flo. Nothing."

Like I said, I'm not a morning person.

Pinkerton, his curly beard still tinged with gray makeup, looked at me without flinching. Then he nodded. "Maybe," he said in a quiet voice. "Maybe you're right. Maybe we're all just damned souls, doomed to playing Satan's silly games. I don't know, Steve. All I have is me, the small bit of integrity I call my soul. I don't know why I'm in Hell. I don't know why you're in Hell. Hell, I don't know why almost everyone I've ever heard of is here, whether they've been good or bad."

I smiled wryly. "Like Santa Claus's list."

"Aye, Steve, as with Saint Nick's list. It seems to me, though, that precious few have been on the 'good' side of that list and made it through the Pearly Gates."

"You're right," I sniffled, on the verge of tears. Fatigue, stress and the memory of pain were getting to me. Or maybe I was just fed up with it all. "Almost no one makes it into Heaven. I saw Mother Theresa enter one day when I was changing one of those stupid bulbs that keep burning out on Hell's Welcome Sign. I saw John Paul II when he came up. He went through the Pearly Gates, too. I saw a young man, a hemophiliac in life, who had contracted AIDS from a transfusion; he went in. Yet so many other good people, they are here, in Hell, and I don't know why."

Allan scratched his beard in thought. "Nor do I, Steve. But this I do know. The universe, mortality, immortality, life and afterlife are way beyond my ken. All I know to do is be the best person I can, do the best I can do, and let the chips fall where they may."

"Even if that's not enough? Even if it means you're damned for all Eternity?"

At first Pinkerton said nothing, but then he nodded. "What else would you have me do?" he asked finally, looking at me with eyes that glimmered from barely suppressed tears.

We both sat silently. Allan brooded into his cup of very bad joe. I picked my mug off the floor and went to refill it from the Mr. Coffee. Walking by Pinkerton, I patted his shoulder. "Nothing else, Allan," I said softly. "What more can you do? What more can any of us do? We don't call the shots. We're not the Almighty - or Satan."

He nodded. "Besides, laddie, and in this case I use that word with all affection, we humans are hopeful creatures. We are ... how would you say it? Oh, aye, I know. We are hard-wired for hope. That's the reason Hell works so well. We have hope, it is dashed, and Satan gets his jollies. If we didn't believe things could work out, Satan wouldn't have any fun at all, now would he?"

I smiled ruefully. "Oh, we can't have that, can we?"

"Nae, Steve, we cannae. So," he said, stretching. I think he'd had a long night of it. "Ta work?"

"To work," I nodded as I cleared my desk of the work orders that had come in. "What do you have?"

"These, for starters." Pinkerton handed me a stack of flyers. Most of them bore the symbol of the two hands and all-seeing eye. Many of the messages were the same as I'd seen before, 'Remember Niagara,' which tugged at my memory for some reason, and 'Whoop the Devils.' But there were also more ominous phrases, like 'Our Time is Coming,' 'Soon, Brothers and Sisters,' and 'Be Ready.'

I flipped through them quickly and pushed the stack toward Pinkerton, who promptly pushed them back to me. "Keep em. Ah have more an' plenty. All of Hell seems to be littered with these things. Ah tell ya, Steve, the Hellions are preparing for something big. And there must be many more of them than we thought."

I frowned at the pile of leaflets, then pulled one out, and with a thumbtack stuck it to the wall. It was one of the 'Remember Niagara' ones, complete with the hands and eye. The rest went into a drawer in my desk.

Pinkerton took another sip of his Scotch-laced coffee. "About the Escalator. Whether or not the Hellions broke it, they at least tried to, a pretty dangerous act of insurrection when ya consider how important the Escalator is to the workings of Hell. Just look at the problems caused when the beastie failed. The Free Hellions should be taken seriously. They are dangerous."

I snorted. "As dangerous as a bunch of morons can be."

"Which is plenty dangerous. They could have big plans, muck them up and still cause a lot of damage. But back to the Escalator. Whether or not they succeeded, the failure of the Escalator fits their larger plan."

"Which is?"

"Ah dinae know. They didn't say."

"Great. Good work, Sherlock."

Pinkerton frowned at me. "Ah dinae know this Sherlock ..." he said slowly.

I waved my hand, trying to dismiss the comment, which was a cheap shot, I knew. "Fictional character. After your time."

"... but that sounded like sarcasm."

"It was. Sorry about that." I got up and went to the window of my little trailer. Even though it was early, cars and trucks were whizzing by on the street, horns blaring, brakes screeching. At that moment, two trucks collided into each other. There was a popping sound, and a crowd of demons, wearing police uniforms, appeared around the crash site. The demons whipped out tablets and started writing tickets for the hapless drivers of the two vehicles.

Having an office so near a major thoroughfare was unpleasant, and some days - like today - tuning out all the noise was harder than usual. I turned my back on the scene playing out before my window and returned to the desk. "Did you hear anything that might be useful to us?"

"Oh, aye, la ... Steve. The masterminds seemed very pleased that work had commenced on the Stairway, very pleased indeed."

"That's odd. Why should they even care?"

"Dinae know, but it seems to fit in with their other plans. They're going to be meeting tonight at the Red Note, along with some of their top lieutenants. Ah plan to be there and do a bit more eavesdropping. You in?"

"I suppose," I said reluctantly, knowing that Satan would expect me to go. Then I told Pinkerton about the four thugs who'd assaulted me the night before.

"Four against one." He spat on the floor. "Ah hate bullies. Maybe you should go with some protection tonight."

I considered it for a moment. "No, they can't really hurt me. Well, they can hurt me alright, but they can't do any permanent damage. Besides, I'll get Flo to go with me again." That thought brightened my mood perceptibly and I smiled for the first time all morning. "They seem to be wary of tangling with her."

"Aye. That makes sense ta me. She's a free radical in an otherwise orderly system."

"Well, they're anarchists, so what's the difference?"

"The difference, my friend, is they are anarchist-wannabes. They still function, though, within the confines of Hell's laws. Florence, she's completely different. If she wanted to, she could walk out of Hell tomorrow."

"Well, she'd need a key to the Elevator but I get your drift. There is nothing keeping her here."

"And they, though they'd like to think of themselves as anarchists, are subject to the perverse sense of order decreed by the Lord of Chaos. Anyhoo, that they don't want to tangle with Miss Florence Nightingale doesn't surprise me in the least. If nothing else, Satan and his underlings keep a close watch on her. The Hellions must know that."

"So, as long as I'm with her, I'm probably okay. When I'm not, I'll just be careful, not wander deserted streets, take cabs - that sort of thing." I had a sudden flash of inspiration. Perhaps I would wander alone. A plan had just formed in my pea brain, a way to get a little payback for the previous night's manhandling. I wasn't sure it would work but thought it might. After all, we were becoming pretty chummy. Hmm. Why hadn't I thought of it last night? Heat of the moment, probably.

"Why are you grinning, my friend?"

"Oh, nothing, nothing. Listen, I need to call Flo about this evening, then check on some things. See you tonight?"

"Sure, Steve," Allan said, finishing the last of his coffee as he stood. He had a pained look on his face. "Ah have some barrels to make before heading to the club."

As the door closed behind Pinkerton, I pictured him returning to his own version of Hell. The man seemed to thrive on all the skulking around he was doing. The spying, the disguises, peeking through keyholes: they must have provided a wonderful respite from an Eternity of barrel botching.

Me, I could do without the cloak and dagger stuff, though it did give me an excuse to spend time with Flo. With that thought, I went over to the phone. Going to the hospital and seeing her in person would have been preferable, but there was just too much to do. I'd have to make it a phone call.

I rang up the hospital. "Hospital Switchboard," rasped a familiar voice. Then he hung up on me.

I sighed and rang the number again.

"Hospital Switch ..."

Before the operator had time to disconnect the line again, I blurted out, "Uphir, I have a blank check from Satan. Don't hang up on me again or I'll tell him you haven't been cooperating."

The demon hissed. "Minion. What do you want?"

"I want to talk to Flo."

"Well, I don't know where she is, so you can just bite me."

"I doubt you'd taste very good." I heard Uphir choke on the insult and smiled.

Someday, when all this was over, there was going to be a number of devils and demons irritated at me for using Satan's authority to push them around. Uphir would probably be at the top of the list. Screw him. He was a jerk and it felt pretty good putting him in his place. "And don't tell me you don't know where she is," I continued. "You always know where she is, so get her and put her on the line."

Uphir hissed again. "One moment ... *please*." He put me on hold.

After what seemed like fifteen minutes, in which time I could have walked over to the hospital and found her myself, Flo came on the line. "Nightingale here," she said in her work voice, pleasant, but all business. Uphir must have interrupted her from giving comfort to the suffering. I don't think she appreciated it.

"Flo, it's me, Steve."

Her tone changed immediately. "Oh, Steve," Flo said warmly, "It's good to hear from you. You know, a girl doesn't always get called first thing the next morning after a big date."

"I'm sorry for interrupting what you were doing."

"It's fine. I was just trying to help some incoming patients with their insurance paperwork. It can wait a few minutes."

"Good. Listen, I had a wonderful time last night." Up until I had the shit beat out of me. Best not to share that part with her.

"So did I," she responded brightly. "I hope we can get together again soon."

I was grinning at the telephone receiver. Good thing she couldn't see me; I was getting tired of always being caught with a love-struck expression on my face. This way, over the phone, I could at least pretend to be suave. "I'm glad you feel that way, honey." I risked a 'honey' at this point in the conversation, feeling on safe ground after last night's kiss. "Are you up for another date tonight?"

"I'd love it. What time?"

"I'll pick you up at seven, okay?"

(Despite time not really being meaningful in Hell, you're supposed to give your date a time when you'll meet her - that's just how dates are handled, as I'm sure everyone knows - and hope that your clock and her clock will work in synchronicity.)

"Wonderful, darling." *Darling?* She called me 'darling.' My grin got bigger until it threatened to split open my face. "I'll be ready."

"Okay, sweetheart." She didn't gasp over the phone, so I guessed 'sweetheart' was okay, too. "See you tonight."

"I can't wait. Bye, Steve."

"Bye."

This special assignment definitely had its benefits.

Chapter 14

I had no sooner placed the receiver on the hook when the phone rang.

Usually work orders come in through the tubes and it was particularly odd that this one came in over the phone, especially since the caller couldn't, rightfully speaking, well, speak. Instead, all that was coming from the receiver were some odd clacking soundings.

Initially, I was ready to write it off as static from our less-than-optimal phone system. After all, we were still using an analog, Alexander Graham Bell sort of phone network.

We had tried a VoIP system years ago. Voice over Internet Protocol basically meant using the wires of the computer network instead of the old-fashioned ones employed by a traditional phone. There was more to it than that, such as a totally digital signal, but most people didn't care about the details. Anyway, the crappy sound quality couldn't be overcome by all of Hell's IT types, who touted the virtues of an IP-based phone system. Sure, we could pick up our phones and plug them into other network ports, taking our phone numbers with us, but, well, if we couldn't hear, who the fuck cared how easy it was to move the damn phones? So, we went back to a tried-and-true analog system. It sucked, too, but it was a dependable sort of suckiness.

Like I said, on answering the phone, all I heard where a bunch of clicks and clacks. At first, you would have thought I hadn't picked up a phone at all but instead had slipped back in time and gotten the rattlings of an old Morse code receiver. And you wouldn't have been far off.

Fact one: I was using a phone, not a 'straight key' keypad. But fact two: the sounds coming over the earpiece were definitely Morse code.

How and why did I learn such an arcane method of communication, especially since Morse code had been a dying system through most of my life? Well, the reason could have been that I serviced every denizen of Hell, and they communicated in all sorts of ways, from high oratorical utterings, à la the Roman Senate, to hexadecimal codings of computer geeks from the TRASH 80 days, to communications from a period well after my death, when they'd figured out some digital-optical-whatever way of transmitting data for all five senses through the ether. Hell, compared to that, Morse code was child's play.

That could have been the reason, but the truth of the matter was I learned the code as a kid in Boy Scouts. It was either that or wave those stupid flags around. I'd gotten pretty good at it - Morse code, not flag waving - and, for some reason, it stuck with me. In life, I would sit around coffee shops, using a spoon to beat out little Morse code rhythms on my mug just to amuse myself. My tappings drove my ex-wife crazy, which probably contributed to her pursuing ex-wife status.

So I could do Morse code. However, even in Hell there weren't very many people who used it. Samuel Finley Breese Morse himself was a die-hard. He wouldn't even talk to you in English but insisted upon communicating verbally with dot and dash sounds. It was very tiresome, especially when we were playing Twenty Questions at a block party. (He lived on my street). Considering how quickly the telephone came on the heels of his famous code, you'd think he'd have resigned himself to the fact that, like the Pony Express, he'd come up with a very good but ultimately pretty ephemeral idea. (Except with ham radio operators. They still loved it, the pathetic dweebs.) Morse should have just stuck with painting. I always liked his paintings.

Other than Sam, there was hardly anyone who used Morse code. Yet, on hearing clicks (dots) and clacks (dashes) over the phone receiver, I immediately knew who was on the other end of the line.

"Hi, Ronnie. What's up?"

"…. . . - .. . - .. - - - - - .. - - / … - . … - . . - . - . - / .. / …. . - … - . / . - / . - - . . - . - - - - … . - .. . - - / .. / - . . . - .. / - . - - - - - .. - . - . / …. . . - .. . - - . / . - - .. - …. . - . - . -"

"Really? So, what's the problem?"

".. / . - - . - … / .. - . . . - . . - . - . - - .. - . - - . / . - / - . - . - - - .. - . - - . . - .. . / - - - .. - . / - . . . - - / . - .. - - - … - / … - - - .. - . - .. … / . - - . - . . - . - - - … … / - …. . / . - . .. … - . . - . - - .. - - / . - - . - .. / - - - - . . / - - - .. - . / - …. . / .. - .. .. - - - - … / - - . - - - - / . - .. - - . - . .. - . - .. / . - / . - - . - - - - - . - . - .. / . - / …. - - - . - .. . / .. - . / - - - . - - / - … - - - . - - . - . - . -"

"Oh, sorry to hear that. Listen, I'm really swamped. Can it wait a day or two?"

"- . - - - . - . - . - / - . - - - - - .. - / - . - - . - - - . - - / .. - / - . - . . - - . . - - - - . - . - . - . -"

I sighed. "No. I suppose not. Be right there. I'll bring a blank work order with me and you can fill it out, okay?"

"- - - - . - . - - . - - . - . - . - / - …. . - - . - . - … - - .. - - / … - . … - . . - . - . - / - . - - - - - .. - . - - - - - . . - . . / - …. . / - … . … - . - . - . -"

"You're welcome, Ronnie. Be there soon."

Great. Just great. This was the last thing I had time for but Ronnie was a friend of mine. Besides, he rated special attention in Hell.

I stepped out of the trailer and called for BOOH, who scooped me off the pavement and made skyward.

"The dock on the corner of Styx and Acheron, Level 0.5, BOOH. And step on it. Charon needs our help."

Hell didn't generally have half levels, but Charon's realm was a unique, ah, backwater in Hell. For that matter, Charon himself was a bit of an anomaly. While Hell was populated with a multitude of creatures, most of them were devils, demons, or damned souls. Charon, like BOOH, was different. Both were morally neutral, not creatures of evil at all. They just happened to hang around in the same space as Hell, so naturally Satan put them to work.

Charon was very, very old. He'd been around before Christianity was even a twinkle in You-Know-Who's eye. Charon came from Greek mythology. He was the ferryman for the dead, helping them cross over from the land of the living to the other side. Some said he ferried souls across the River Acheron; others said it was the Styx. It was actually the same river and went by both names. I preferred Styx, because 'stygian' sounds way better than 'acheronian.' I mean, what the hell does 'acheronian' mean, anyway? 'Stygian' at least means something.

When the Greek pantheon went out of fashion, Charon got a gold watch and a pension. Being immortal, though, he was way too young to retire. As a result, for a while, he was kind of at loose ends. He needed a job, but all he knew how to do was run a ferry. To tell you the truth, I think Satan felt sorry for him, but if he hired the old guy out of pity, it was a good move. Charon labored tirelessly. He hadn't missed a day of work in over 2,000 years.

Level 0.5, which by the way is more of a spur off the main event than an actual circle, used to be the sole access to the

Underworld, back when it was run by Hades, the Greek God of the Underworld, not to be confused with Hades, one of the many names for Hell itself. When Satan bought the place from that Greek fellow, the Devil started his franchise deep within the metaphysical bowels of the cosmos, building his office in what would come to be known as the Ninth Circle, and consolidated all the virtuous pagans onto the second oldest level of Hell: One.

I have no idea what he did with the unvirtuous pagans. Greek Hades (the place) contained no-goodniks as well as the good guys. The bad folk were kept in a deep portion of the ancient underworld called Tartarus, but that's where Satan wanted to set up shop first, so he gave them the boot. Presumably, since they weren't Christians or Jews, and they weren't virtuous, he felt no obligation to provide them with free room and board.

Sometimes, when I think about this, I wonder what Satan did with the unvirtuous Jews before he bought this particular piece of real estate from an old Greek god. They may have a home now, but the unvirtuous pagans of ancient Hellenic times, well, I guess they're wandering around somewhere, but they sure aren't doing it in Hell.

After the big S took over, he added circle after circle as he needed them, eventually building out Levels Eight through Two. Crossing the Styx continued to be the only access route to Hell for many years; early Christians passed over it, courtesy of the immortal ferryman, before entering Hell. Then we built the Stairway, the Elevator, and eventually the Escalator, and Charon's dance card was no longer as full as it once had been. Most of the damned weren't even aware of him or the Styx as they headed straight down via the Escalator, but those of a more literary bent, especially those who had read Dante or

Virgil or anything about Greek mythology, knew all about Charon. In fact, those familiar with his reputation insisted upon being ferried by him across the river of the dead, where they'd just get on the Escalator - a little below Level One - anyway and head on down. Really stupid, I know. A bloody waste of time, but Charon didn't mind. Neither did Satan. The whole Stygian waters thing, well, it classed up the joint.

The river itself wasn't all that classy, though. The thing was black for a reason: oil, or 'black gold' as they said in the song. 'Texas Tea.' In the late 1960s, when I was still a kid, the Cuyahoga River - polluted beyond belief with oily sludge from the industries and generally crowded conditions around Cleveland and Akron - actually caught fire. And that was just surface oil. Boy, I bet an all-petroleum river like the Styx was a real mess whenever it burned. I'd never seen it happen, but Charon said Satan used to torch the thing occasionally just for kicks, until Peter finally intervened. The river was too close to the Pearly Gates, and the fumes from the blaze would waft all the way up there. Aside from the stench was the pollution. After one of these fires, it would take an angelic work crew a week to scrub the oily soot and grime from the pillars that held the Gates. Reluctantly, after some pressure from Pete's Boss, Satan stopped lighting up the river.

A few damned souls who hadn't heard of Charon the Ferryman, or the River Styx, got a free tour anyway. Satan thought deceased oilmen would be impressed to see a river of oil, and depressed that they'd never be able to cash in on it. "Welcome to Hell. See what you're missing?"

The Styx flowed through a long, wide cavern. The cave's vaulted ceiling and sides were nearly as black as the oil of the river, yet in the pale illumination of Charon's tiny realm, the surface of the tunnel gleamed. It was obsidian - volcanic black glass for those who don't know what obsidian is. The glistening cavern had an eerie beauty not often found in the Netherworld. Oh, Hell had plenty of 'eerie.' It was all over the place, buckets of it in fact. But beauty, that was pretty uncommon down here.

Other than the river, and the cave through which it traveled, there wasn't much more to Level 0.5 than a small patch of ash-covered ground on each end, one on which the damned souls could queue up for their boat ride, the other on which they could disembark for their respective destinations in Hell. Each end had a dock. On the side closer to Heaven, there was a boat house where Charon would occasionally stash his vessel for maintenance.

Oh, there was also a doghouse on that end.

When Satan bought Hell from Hades, he bought a three-headed dog, too. That would be Cerberus. For a while, Satan used the mutt to guard the Gates of Hell, but the silliness of that quickly became apparent. After all, Satan was looking to amass as many damned souls as possible. He didn't want to turn anyone away, except maybe Gilbert Gottfried. (That Aflac duck voice of his can be pretty irritating.) Deciding he didn't need a guard dog, Satan wasn't sure what to do with the critter. He also didn't like buying dog food for the beast. I mean, three mouths to feed: you go through a lot of Alpo with a dog like that. So the Lord of Hell gave Cerberus to Charon as a pet. The two had known one another for a long time and they enjoyed each other's company. That was a good call on Satan's part.

Charon was one of the first denizens of Hell I'd met after my death. He'd put in a work order for me to build a doghouse for Cerberus. This was my first major assignment and I wanted to make a good impression. I worked hard, and despite my lack of aptitude for all things handy, managed to put together a serviceable, if mildly lopsided, house. Charon noted how mightily I'd labored on the thing, and while he might have given me a C for execution, he gave me an A for effort.

And since I knew Morse code, we were able to talk to each other. Charon is a good soul, if indeed he has a soul at all. That's hard to say. He's a bit of a mystery to me, but he's a good guy, soul or not. While I built the doghouse, we got to know each other. That's how I made my first friend in the Netherworld.

BOOH spied Charon before I did. He was tossing a Frisbee for Cerberus and I smiled while watching the three heads fight for control of the disc.

"Hey, Ronnie," I called as we landed. "What's shakin', aside from those bones of yours?"

Charon is a bony white specter. He looks a lot like the Grim Reaper, which isn't surprising since he's Mortimer's little brother. Morty dresses in a black robe, though, while Ronnie prefers his to be charcoal. Being essentially an animated skeleton, he has no tongue, which is why he uses Morse code to talk.

"... - . . - . - . - - / . . - . . . - - . - . - . - - - - . . - - / ... - . ... - . . - . - . - ," Ronnie, clicked and clacked in response. " - - . - - . - - - ... . / - . - - - - - . . - / ... . - - - . . - . - . . - . . / - - . - - - / - - - - . / - .... . / ... - . - - - . . . - . - . - / . . / .... . . - . - . / - - - - . . . - - - - . ... / . - . . . . - ... - . . - . - - . / . . - . / . - - ... - - - . . - - / . - - . / .... - - - . . - . - . . - . - . - "

What he said was: "Very funny, Steve. Maybe you should go on the stage. I hear one's leaving in about an hour."

To this point, I haven't decoded Ronnie's speech, figuring the meaning was clear from the context. But since Morse code can be really tiresome for those who can't decipher it, to make things easier I'll translate from now on.

“Oh, come on,” I said, patting him on the back. “You know I was just kidding.”

Ronnie grinned. Well, Ronnie always grinned, being a skeleton, but I could tell he was smiling. *I know, Steve. I was kidding, too.*

At that moment, Cerberus came rushing up. He pounced on me, licking my face all over. He liked the doghouse I’d built him so long ago and we’d become friends as well. Greeting Cerberus was a little more involved than with other dogs: three heads to pat, three times the drool to contend with.

Hello, BOOH, Ronnie clacked. The two knew each other well.

BOOH flapped up into the air briefly and gave Charon a high five with one clawed foot. Cerberus was also glad to see BOOH, and he came up and sniffed the giant bat’s butt. BOOH rolled his eyes but politely sniffed the dog’s butt in return. Ronnie tossed the Frisbee again and Cerberus galloped off after it.

“So, tell me about the boat. How did it happen?”

Ronnie pulled out a pack of grape chewing gum and offered me some. I declined, politely. He put a big stick in his mouth and began masticating. I never understood why Ronnie liked gum so much, not having taste buds and all, but he never went anywhere without a couple of packs. It was rare that he didn’t have a stick or three in his mouth. The constant chewing made him a little difficult to understand, because you had to parse out the gum clacks from those intended to tap out Morse code, but over the years I’d gotten pretty good at that and hardly noticed anymore.

The whole affair is irritating, really. Things are a little slow right now. With the Escalator broken, taking a ride on the Styx is a bit of a dead end, so I was doing a favor for Belial. He was on a date with some succubus - I didn’t catch her name, but she was pretty attractive, I must say - and he thought a boat ride would be very romantic.

"I thought you'd sworn off the Tunnel of Love gigs."

Ronnie grimaced. (Yes, I can tell the difference.) *I had, but as I said, I was doing Belial a favor. Against my better judgment. Last time, too,* he added with a grumble.

"So what happened?"

The two of them were getting ... how do you put it? ... Oh yes, a little hot and heavy, and, well, you know what happens to a devil's tail when he gets excited.

I snickered. "Stiff as a spear."

Cerberus came back and Ronnie wrestled the Frisbee from him. *Yes. It poked a hole as big as your thumb through the bottom of my boat.* He tossed the Frisbee again and the dog took off.

I didn't offer to throw the disc. All dogs, even infernal ones, didn't know when to quit. You'd never suck me into a game of fetch with Cerberus, but fortunately Ronnie had the patience you'd expect from an immortal who spent most of his existence going back and forth across a river of oil. He seemed to never tire of playing fetch with his dog.

I was still laughing as Charon stuck another piece of gum in his mouth. *I'm glad you're amused by all this. For my own part, I need to get back to work.*

"Sorry, Ronnie," I said, wiping tears from my eyes. "You've got to admit, it's pretty funny."

Not to me, it isn't.

"Okay, okay," I said, trying to placate him. "Show me this hole."

With a single bony finger, Ronnie gestured for me to follow him to the boat house.

His craft was in dry dock, lifted out of the river by two winches (as opposed to two wenches, which might have worked, too, but only if the girls had been really strong). The boat was not a large one; it probably could have held no more than ten people, and that would have been a bit of a squash. The vessel had a high prow and stern, along with a flat bottom. It was much like a Venetian gondola, but instead of having a handsome, burly young Italian ferrying his passengers around to the romantic tones of *'O solo mio,'* this boat's riders had a frightening skeleton pushing them silently across the river with a long pole that reached the river bottom. And instead of music, all they heard was the quiet hiss of the boat as it slid through the Stygian waters, a.k.a. oil, punctuated by the staccato clicks of Ronnie chewing his gum.

"Where's the leak?" I asked, peering at the vessel in the dim light of the boat house.

Here, he said, sticking his forefinger in a hole about a foot behind one of the passenger benches. I tried to picture what position Belial and his girlfriend must have been lying in to place it there and decided that was really more information than I needed or wanted.

Charon removed his finger as I slid under the boat. A little bit of light was coming from the hole. "I've got just the thing to fix this," I said, pulling the champagne cork out of my pocket. I didn't really want to part with the cork, having intended to keep it as a souvenir, but this was a good cause. Besides, I didn't know what else to use, not being exactly a master craftsman. I held the cork to the hole. If I hammered the stopper in there, it would probably stay put. Champagne corks are bigger on top than on the bottom, though the bottom does splay out a bit, which in this case would be a good thing. I thought the cork would stay in the hole more tightly. The pressure of the oil against cork and hull would help as well.

The only problem was the hole looked to be just a tiny bit bigger than the narrowest portion of the cork; some leakage was possible. Then I had an idea. "Say, Ronnie. Give me the gum in your mouth."

Why? I just got it to the right consistency.

"You want your boat fixed, right?"

Well, yes, but I don't see how ...

"Then don't argue. Just give it to me," I said, sticking out my hand. A slimy mass of goo went smack in my palm. "Jeez, Ronnie, you weren't kidding! How did you get it all slobbery like this? It's not like you have a tongue or anything."

How perceptive of you, he said sarcastically. *It just so happens that I'm a creature of magic. I'm more than a one-trick pony, you know. I can do many things far beyond mortal ken.*

"You mean aside from shoving your boat along this river. Like what?" I said, conversationally, as I took the gum and wrapped it around the middle of the cork.

Well, Ronnie hesitated, *well, I can throw a Frisbee. Oh, and I play a mean set of spoons.*

Not very impressive, but Ronnie was really my friend, and I'd kidded him enough already. Besides, I suddenly remembered that he had a bit of an inferiority complex. It probably stemmed from growing up with his more talented older brother. With a small effort, I pretended a little enthusiasm for Ronnie's questionable musical abilities. "Spoons, huh? I'd like to hear you sometime."

Now you're just being patronizing, he pouted.

"No, really." I placed the gum-fortified cork beneath the hole, and with my hammer drove it through the opening. Then I slipped out from under the boat. "Next time I come by, maybe you could play something for me?"

Ronnie helped me to my feet. *I'd be glad to. Do you think it's fixed?* he asked, looking inside the gondola. A nub of the cork stuck through the bottom of the passenger area.

"Almost," I said, pulling an X-ACTO knife from my tool belt and gingerly cutting off the nub. With the excess trimmed away, the cork was completely flush with the rest of the gondola's deck. A small purple ring was all that showed. I used my finger to smear out the gum a little in all directions, thinking it might make for a better seal. "There," I said at last, satisfied that this was one of my better repair jobs. "The gum will be sticky for a while but it should dry out over time."

A little gum on one's shoe never hurt anyone, Ronnie opined. *This looks really quite good, Steve. Thanks.*

"You're welcome. Here, let me help you get the boat back in the river. Oh, and be careful not to bump the bottom of the cork when you're pulling the gondola in and out of the Styx. That might knock it loose."

Warning duly noted. Caveat emptor.

That's Latin for 'Buyer Beware.' You probably knew that, but just in case ...

Together we got Charon's vessel into the river. He climbed in. *The patch doesn't appear to be leaking, but I'd like to put more weight on it to make sure. Climb aboard.*

Even with me in the boat, the cork held, but Ronnie still wasn't satisfied. He whistled for Cerberus, who leapt in the gondola and stuck his three heads out to one side of the craft, all three tongues lolling out of their respective mouths. I guess the dog thought he was going for a ride.

Still holding well, but if we could just test it with a little more weight.

I checked my watch. It wasn't displaying the proper time. This was one of those moments when the hands decided to spin backward. Still, my mental clock told me this was all the time that could be afforded to this assignment. "Well, if it's weight you want, BOOH!"

When the bat settled on the prow, the craft immediately went perpendicular to the river. Charon appeared unfazed; he maintained his balance easily. Cerberus and I, however, were nearly thrown into the drink. The dog's three jaws were clamped down tight onto a railing and I was clutching desperately to a bench. "BOOH! Move toward the center! Quick!" BOOH obliged and the boat returned to its position parallel to the river. "See!" I gasped. "No leaks. If the boat doesn't leak with BOOH on it, no way it's gonna leak with your passengers."

Ronnie nodded. *Good. I am satisfied.*

"Here," I said, giving him a blank work order. "I've gotta go. Just fill this out, sign it as complete and send it over to my office when you get a chance. I'd love to stay and visit longer, but we have to fly."

Sure thing, Steve, said Charon, Ferryman to Hell, taking the paperwork from me. *Thank you for your help.*

"Anything for a friend. Later!" I shouted as BOOH whisked me away.

Chapter 15

We hovered above the River Styx as I gathered my thoughts. Yes, we had to fly, but to where? Gates Level? Check on Orson's progress with the Stairwell? Swing back by the office?

Dangling like a dead squirrel from the claws of my batty friend, I considered all that had to get done. I needed to get my butt in gear, do something decisive. "BOOH! Quick!" I yelled, my voice echoing against the black glass tunnel. "To the library!"

With a screech, BOOH did a loop-the-loop and dove into the Mouth of Hell. We were passing through Level Three before my stomach caught up with us.

Hell's Library, unsurprisingly, is located in the Fifth Circle, along with most of the social services the Devil deems *de rigueur* for his denizens. It's located next to the Department of Mental Health and Mental Retardation, where most of the Underworld's intellectual luminaries are ensconced.

As we descended, I saw Gauss and Newton standing in front of the MHMR building, probably heading inside for a day of basket weaving. The two were having a bit of trouble getting the doors open. This didn't surprise me. The doors to the facility sometimes opened inward and sometimes outward. The way they functioned was totally random, all intended to make the person pulling or pushing on the handle feel really stupid.

After unleashing impressive strings of invective, one in German, the other in English, the two mathematical geniuses plopped to the pavement before the door. Each pulled a stick of chalk from his pocket and started scribbling furiously on the concrete. In seconds, numbers and arcane mathematical symbols began to cover the walkway. They were probably trying to predict which way the doors would act the next time.

As BOOH dropped me to the sidewalk, I considered their chance for success. Not much. Maybe if they'd known something about chaos theory, but Poincaré didn't do the early work on that until thirty years after Gauss's death and more than 150 years after Newton began rotting in Hell. They would have done better continuing to jerk back and forth on the doors, until the building decided to cooperate and let them in, but old habits die hard. Reaching for the Calculus was as natural for them as grabbing my duct tape was for me. Not as cool, though.

The Public Library of Hades was an impressive edifice with Corinthian columns, each painted in a bright primary color, red against blue against green, supporting an ornate frieze into which were carved iconic representations of the Seven Deadly Sins. On each side of the massive front door, where you might expect a couple of regal lion statues, were two iron-hued dragons, real ones, though they were doing their best not to move.

BOOH wended his way to the rooftop of the library. Swallowing once, I screwed up my courage and walked between the two reptilian monsters. They may have been motionless but their raspy breathing was pretty loud. The air between the two bodies was uncomfortably warm and I felt sweat start to form on my brow. Just before reaching the door, I tripped over one of their tails. There was a hiss and the tail jerked back quickly, giving me a hard thwack on the butt in the process. With a quiet groan, I scrambled to my feet and pushed against the library door.

That door, it weighed a ton, taking all my strength to open it enough to slip inside the building. It thudded shut behind me.

"Quiet, ya eejit!" the librarian shouted.

Another Scot, though this one could turn his brogue on and off like a light switch, just to suit his mood. Since I spent a lot of time in Hell's Library, this man was no stranger. Glaring down at me from his perch behind the elevated wooden circulation desk was a wild-eyed, white-bearded ferocity of a man.

"Hey, Andy."

The man behind the desk rolled his eyes. "A thousand times I've told him," he muttered to himself, before glaring at me again. "If you must call me by my first name, then use 'Andrew.' "

Andrew Carnegie was much more impressed with himself than I was; than I was with him, I mean. I don't think I'm particularly impressive either, though I'm basically okay. He, on the other hand, is a bit of a *prima donna*. He's kind of stuck on himself - the great capitalist turned great philanthropist.

"Okay, Andrew," I said, in a voice suitably contrite, though my smile probably undermined any appearance of sincerity. "Sorry."

I'm not really fond of people who have an expanded sense of self-importance, but, as with Orson, I got along pretty well with Carnegie, despite his aforementioned snottiness. He had been a coldblooded businessman in life, like Edison and Ford, but Andrew had a genuine streak of kindness in him. From a very young age he looked at himself as only a steward of those assets he gathered to himself during life. When he finally had enough money - well, maybe a little more than enough - he invented modern philanthropy by giving away most of his great wealth.

And, like me, he liked libraries. He used his money to build a bunch of them, too, though I don't think he ever expected to work in one. But there he was, rubber stamp in hand, pressing out cards with meaningless due dates as rapidly as he could. (All books checked out of Hell's Library were overdue as soon as they left the building, which was probably why the circulation statistics tended to be on the low side.)

Every few seconds Carnegie looked up from his work to inspect, with preternatural attention, every corner of the facility. Periodically, he would release a loud "SHHHHHHHHHHHH!" even though the place was perfectly quiet and I was the only patron in sight.

"Why do you do that, Andy?"

Carnegie turned his gaze back on me. "Do what?" he responded, ignoring the 'Andy.'

"The shushing thing."

"It's a stereotype."

"I know it's a stereotype, so why do you do it?"

Andrew looked pained. "Because if I don't say it regularly, I get a 120 volt shock up my entire spine. Look." He turned so I could see his back. There was a long extension cord running from him to a nearby electric outlet.

Oh boy.

Leaving the head librarian, I turned toward the stacks. The place was in its usual state of disarray: volumes were scattered everywhere, in random fashion, though the senior page, Melvil Dewey, was running through the stacks, trying to order the shelves according to his own Dewey Decimal classification scheme. I'd watched him work many times before. As soon as he put a book in its proper spot, the volume would either pop out onto the floor or shift with others of its kind, as if each book stack was an elaborate tile game. With the possessed volumes deciding on their own where they were going to reside, Dewey's efforts were futile.

There was a little research project I wanted to do, but I wasn't sure where to start. There was a bank of computers on one wall, but all they could access was Facebook, so they were of no use to me. The library had a single machine that could surf the rest of the Web. Since I didn't have a PC at home or the office, I usually used that one to Google something or search Wikipedia. Problem was the computer was broken as often as not, especially when someone really needed to use it. Like today. Too bad, because I wanted to do an image search.

Time to do my research the old-fashioned way. With a sigh, I turned to the antediluvian card catalog, where half a dozen damned souls were filing. I knew from previous experience with the catalog that the card filers were profoundly dyslexic. Their brows were dappled with beads of sweat, and the pain of their concentration, as they tried to place new cards in their proper places within the drawers, was evident in their expressions. They were doomed to fail at this enterprise but they had to keep trying.

I ambled over to the subject portion of the catalog and found a drawer that seemed to have more cards starting with 'I' than any others in the general vicinity. I was looking for 'Iconography,' though perhaps that wasn't even a good heading. It was a start, though, and if 'Iconography' didn't work, I'd try something like 'Symbols.'

I flipped through the first hundred cards. 'Insignificance ... Idiot ... Icarus ...' *No, no, no* ... 'Ignoramus ... Jackass, See Donkeys ...' *Wow, that was out of place!* 'Insolence ... Icky' *Icky? What kind of a stupid heading is that?*

I sped up my flipping, finishing the entire drawer in what felt like a very long time, but was probably just a few minutes. The last card in the drawer said, 'Iconography - see Symbols.'

Well, that wasn't very helpful, since that's what I was going to do anyway. I wandered over to the 'S' drawers, pulling out the one that seemed most likely. There was indeed a card on

'Symbols,' but it was the kind spelled with a 'C,' and I didn't think a loud musical instrument would do me much good. Besides, it said, 'Cymbals - see Iconography.' I dutifully flipped through the rest of the drawer but didn't have any more luck with it than with the 'I' one. After running across a string of headings like 'Sap, "Sissy,' and 'Stupid - see Minion, Steve,' I decided the catalog was just trying to insult me.

In disgust, I slammed the drawer back in place. As on Earth, certain laws applied in Hell. In this case, for every action there was an equal and opposite reaction, especially if it caused trouble. The force of my movement popped another drawer out of its slot and it fell to the floor. In the process, the long metal pin that ran through the bottom of the drawer holding the cards in place came loose and sprang out of its hole, like a jumping jack, or a kid wearing moon shoes.

It should go without saying that every card fell on the floor.

"AGGHH!" screamed all the filers in unison.

"Uh, sorry, sorry," I mumbled, backing away from the mess. Some of the filers were running their fingers through the pile of disheveled cards like teary-eyed misers watching gold slip from their grasps. The others pulled pins out of some drawers and turned in my direction. These brass rods looked like short epées to me, especially since the tips were on the sharp side. As the filers approached, makeshift weapons in hand, I continued to retreat, sure that being skewered with the hardware of a disrespectful card catalog wouldn't be very pleasant.

With a thump, I came to a halt, my back against the wooden end of a bookshelf. At that moment, a hand grabbed me from the side and pulled me between two sets of stacks.

"Quick!" Dewey hissed. "Run this way!"

Well, there was no way I was going to run that way. Dewey was prancing down the aisle like a show horse, his knees going higher than should have been possible. Still, a hasty retreat seemed like a good idea, so I hurried behind him.

A few stacks in, he stopped. "They won't follow us here," he panted. "They get in trouble if they leave the catalog area."

The card catalog was hidden from view. "I didn't mean to knock that drawer out," I said with regret.

Dewey, still panting a bit, nodded. "I know. I saw it. You just have to realize how hard it is on them, trying to get a whole drawer back in order."

"From what I could see, there wasn't a whole lot of order to the cards anyway."

"They do their best," Dewey said as he used a handkerchief to wipe the sweat from his brow.

Melvil Dewey was a balding, bespectacled octogenarian with a good mustache. Since I was a regular at the library, we'd known each other for a long time. Pretty nice guy, though a bit on the anal side. Through the thick lenses of his glasses, he eyed me keenly. "What are you looking for, Steve?"

"I've found an unusual graphic symbol on some flyers scattered around Hell and I'm trying to figure out what it means."

"What does this symbol look like?" Dewey asked.

I described the two hands and eye logo. Dewey took off his glasses and started cleaning them with his sweat-dampened handkerchief. "Oh, yes, the insignia of the Free Hellions. I've noticed it, too. Can't say I'd ever seen it before the Hellions started using it."

"Well, it reminds me of a Freemason symbol, you know, like those on a dollar bill."

The old man nodded. "I can see why you'd think so, but even if you're right, and even if we could find you a book on mystical symbols - 'Signs and Symbols' is the subject heading you should have checked, by the way - you're unlikely to find any information that will help you."

I shrugged. "I thought it was unlikely but worth a shot."

"Maybe, but just remember, doing research in Hell's Library is like doing a patent search."

"Huh? What does that mean?"

"If you find what you are looking for, you won't be able to use it."

"Great." He was right. Why would Hell's library be of any help to me?

Dewey patted me on the shoulder. "It's not totally a lost cause. Like I said, looking for information here is like a patent search. Still, if you don't find what you want, or if you do, you might be able to use a little reverse thinking to draw some conclusions about the logo."

I thought about the twisted logic of Hell and nodded. "Yeah, that sounds about right. But where should I look to not find what I want or to find what I don't want?"

A crafty look came to the old man's eyes. He slipped his glasses back on his face, then gestured for me to lean closer. "I saw a book a few minutes ago that might help."

"Why are you whispering?" I whispered.

"Because if the book in question hears that we want to consult it, it will go into hiding. In order to have any chance of nabbing the volume, we'll have to employ some stealth." He looked at me dubiously. "You wouldn't happen to have a butterfly net on you, would you?"

"Fresh out," I said, showing my empty hands.

"Too bad. Well, we'll just have to do the best we can. The book we want is a few aisles from here, tucked away in the musical instrument section."

"Why would ...? Oh right, cymbals."

The old man nodded. "It's a folio, which means it's a great big fat volume, and it's on the bottom shelf. It's the tallest book there, so it's easy to spot. Now this is what we're going to do. I'll walk ahead of you a few feet. We'll just talk a bit, casually, as if we're discussing the weather. When I get next to the book, I'll lunge for it."

"And then you'll have it?"

"No, you'll have it. The book will try to evade me. Just stay sharp when you watch me make my move and you'll have a fair chance of catching that tricky tome."

"Nice alliteration, Melvil."

"Words are my business. Let's go."

I grabbed his arm. "Wait. Why are you helping me?"

Melvil looked at me as if I were some alien being. "I'm a librarian. We help people."

"Even after you're dead?"

He shrugged. "You never stop being a librarian."

I smiled, recognizing a profound integrity in his response. "Lead the way, Mr. Dewey," I said in my most respectful tone.

As we started to walk, Dewey began speaking in an abnormally loud voice. "I HEAR THE ESCALATOR HAS BROKEN DOWN. TOO BAD ABOUT THAT."

"YES," I agreed, following Dewey as he made a turn up an aisle. "THE WHOLE SITUATION IS CAUSING ME NO END OF TROUBLE."

The old man turned to face me, putting his elbow on one of the shelves and glancing meaningfully at his feet. On the bottom shelf was a large volume, bound in leather and embossed with ornate cymbals ... symbols. I nodded my head slightly.

Dewey quickly dropped to his knees and reached for the volume, but before he could touch it, the book shot from its place on the shelf and began to fly through the air, away from him ...

... and right into my waiting arms.

The volume struggled for a moment, then, realizing it was caught, lay still.

"Thanks, Melvil," I said, holding my catch triumphantly before me. That got me a blast of Hellfire in the face, though no pie. The library had a very strict no-food policy.

"Don't mention it." Just then, apparently in an act of revenge, all the other books on the shelf fell on top of Dewey, burying him beneath their weight. I stooped to help, but his hand broke free of the pile and waved me away. "I'm used to it," his muffled voice sounded from beneath the pile of books. "Just get your research done before anything else happens!"

"Yeah. Sure. Sorry about this."

"Go!" he gasped.

I hurried away from him and found a table, away from the stacks and away from the catalog, where the catalogers were eyeing me in anger. They had picked up all the fallen cards and were trying to put them in order.

Good job, Minion.

Taking a seat, I considered how I'd ruined seven people's days in all of ten minutes. But the only thing to do was make their sacrifice count, and so I began perusing the book.

To my surprise and delight, I found three or four symbols in the book that looked very much like the Free Hellions logo. True, one of them was a CD cover by some rapper, and another a still from a movie called 'Pan's Labyrinth,' but others were definitely mystic symbols. The hand with the eye in the palm was apparently the 'All-Seeing Eye,' like the one on the dollar bill. The book indicated many believed the 'Eye' was in fact Lucifer's own. It was a favorite symbol of the Freemasons and the Illuminati, another mystical order that was patterned after the Freemasons. All evidence pointed to the symbol being of mystical importance.

Which meant it wasn't, if Dewey's logic held. As soon as I released my grip on the volume, it skittered off the table and darted back into the stacks. "Ow!" I heard in the distance.

The book was apparently giving Dewey a little payback. I was sorry my research needs had caused him so much trouble but grateful for his words of advice: "Doing research in Hell's Library is like doing a patent search ..." The Free Hellions logo, according to the book, was definitely a mystic symbol, which meant it wasn't. The logo probably represented something incredibly mundane.

I scooted my chair back and stood. *Shit.* I didn't know what it was, only what it wasn't. Feeling discouraged, I headed slowly toward the exit.

"Steve!"

Lifting my chin from where it hung morosely on my chest, I saw Andrew Carnegie standing between me and the card catalog. The filers had re-armed themselves with the drawer pins and were heading in my direction. "Get out of here! I don't know how long I can hold them off!" In his hand was his electric umbilical cord. He had coiled it into a loop and was using it to beat back the card filers.

I hurried to the exit and pulled open the heavy door. Before it slammed shut behind me, I glanced back. The book stacks were toppling like so many dominoes. In the center of that chaos, no doubt, was a battered Melvil Dewey.

The door slammed behind me. What a mess! And all because I just wanted a little information.

I hurried past the two dragons. Smoke was coming out of their noses and their tails were twitching angrily. Disaster was imminent.

"BOOH!" I yelled at the top of my lungs.

"Skree?"

"Anywhere! Gates Level! Just get me out of here, fast!" I replied desperately. He lifted me into the air just before two blasts of flame blackened the concrete where I'd been standing.

The library seemed to shrink beneath me, as if I were Alice right after she drank the growth potion. I saw Newton and Gauss still struggling with the doors of the MHMR Building. Instinctively, I reached toward them, wanting to help, to throw my hammer through the door glass, anything to, in some small fashion, make up for the carnage I'd just caused in the library. But, in an instant, they were gone from my sight. We had left the Fifth Circle behind us.

Chapter 16

Adding Carnegie to the body count raised my misery-inducing index to eight people, ten if you counted Newton and Gauss. I could at least have helped them if I'd just kept my wits about me, but instead I'd made a cowardly retreat. Admittedly, there were some pissed-off dragons involved, but still ...

Not that helping them really would have mattered. Anything I did was meaningless in Hell; nothing could change its essential nature. Unremitting misery without the possibility of change, that's what the place was all about. Yet, being Satan's little windup toy, I had to keep moving. As BOOH carried me upward, my thoughts turned to the Hellions, the Stairway, the Escalator. There was so much to do, an overwhelming amount, but in the end my actions were going to be completely pointless.

As I pondered the futility and hopelessness of my situation, a familiar knot of anxiety began to squeeze the air from my lungs. It was Hell.

"Ow!" That's when I became aware of BOOH's razor-sharp claws digging into my shoulders. He'd given me a little squeeze to get my attention. Sure it hurt, but beyond all reason I felt some comfort at his touch. BOOH provided me with a certain surety. He wouldn't drop me, and for some inexplicable reason I also knew in my heart that he wanted me safe. It was very weird: BOOH was probably one of the two or three most frightening creatures ever to have existed, and yet I felt safe with him.

As he bore me up to Gates Level, a soft, almost hummingbird-like, whirring came from the preternaturally fast beating of his wings and a deep rumble came from his throat, accompanied by the hissing noise of the wind as it blew over me. All of these were warm sounds, a sort of tuneless serenade, as if BOOH were trying to make me feel better. Without volition, I reached up and stroked his leg, his foot, the claws on his toes. He rumbled again and I recognized the sound; it was his purr.

For some reason, I started crying. The infamous Bat out of Hell was carrying me up to the cosmic DMZ, and as he was doing it, he was both keeping me safe and calming me down. I didn't know how he was comforting me, or why he was doing it, but I was grateful beyond measure.

When we reached Gates Level, BOOH was moving slowly, almost like a zeppelin floating across the sky, coming to moor at its landing port. As he set me on the ground, oh so very gently, I gave his leg a final stroke. Rather than his normal *'Skree,'* BOOH let out a soft 'Urm.' I didn't know what it meant but guessed it was some form of bat intimacy.

For a long moment after BOOH released me I stood very still. Above me, the giant bat hovered for a moment before flying back into the Mouth of Hell. He probably had lots of responsibilities. I couldn't possibly have fathomed how many demands he had on him.

BOOH may have been just about the scariest critter I'd ever seen in my life or afterlife, but he had already demonstrated himself to be a constant, dependable presence. Integrity manifests itself in different ways, but BOOH seemed to have it, more than almost anyone - human, animal, demon or saint - I'd ever encountered. And his caring meant more to me than I could say.

Wiping my eyes on my sleeve, I composed myself. The crowds around the Mouth had been greatly diminished since my last visit, enough so, in fact, that the D&D Squad had been reduced to a mere handful of demons, and third-class ones by the look of them. As a new soul was damned, a single demon would almost casually shove him or her into the yawning chasm of the Netherworld.

It all worked efficiently enough. There was really no need for an Escalator or even a Stairway, but still, the brutality of the fall was too much. We needed to either get the Escalator back online or finish the Stairway. Both, probably. We needed a backup, a failsafe mechanism so that we were never again put in the position of having to rely on 'the old ways' of getting a soul down to Hell.

Over by the Escalator, Edison and Tesla were sitting on the cloud cover, elbows propped on knees, heads propped on hands. They both looked pretty discouraged. "Hey, guys," I said cheerily though not feeling all that chipper myself, "how's it going?"

"Not well," Tesla muttered. "We are along no farther than yesterday."

"He's right," Edison grumbled, though it must have pained him to agree with anything Tesla said. "We still can't find the problem." He looked up and scowled at St. Peter who was standing officiously at his podium and trying very hard to ignore the three of us. "We need Heaven's cooperation to trace the line. Apparently the electricity is shared up here, but the power plant is on the other side of the Gates. We need to get into Heaven in order to fix the Escalator, but Peter won't allow it."

Tesla spat in disgust. "*Nema*. No. We need divine intervention but do not have much chance of getting it."

Great. I was going to have to negotiate with Mr. Holier-than-Thou. To be fair, he was holier than I was, holier than just about anybody, but he didn't have to rub my nose in it. "Well, let me take a crack at him and see what I can do."

Both men shrugged and went back to staring into space. Screwing up my courage - and my manners - I headed toward Heaven's Concierge.

Peter made a point of not looking at me.

I cleared my throat. "Ah, excuse me, St. Peter, sir."

Peter exhaled hugely and, with great reluctance, turned to me. "Minion. What do you want?"

A scream of terror echoed from the Mouth of Hell as some poor sap began his plummet into the Netherworld. "The same thing you do, holy one, uh, sir: to get the Escalator moving again, so we can stop this fear fest."

St. Peter turned a page of the heavy tome in front of him and made a note with a quill pen. "Then do it and leave me alone."

"Sir, I would if I could, you know that. My best men are working on this, but the line needs to be traced from the other side of the Pearly Gates."

"Yes, Tesla and Edison already said that. That's impossible. The damned cannot step through the Gates of Paradise."

"Then give me a break here," I said, exasperated. "I mean, please give me a break. Surely you must have electricians in Heaven who could work with my team."

He nodded grudgingly. "We have a few but they would be out of practice. Nothing breaks in Heaven."

"Really?" I said, genuinely surprised, though I don't know why. Heaven would naturally be pretty low maintenance. "Well, would it be possible to get some of them to work on their side, my guys working on this side, in order to find the cause of the power loss and fix it?"

St. Peter considered it for a moment. "What you propose is highly irregular."

"I know, but ..."

"The request would have to be made formally," he continued, interrupting me, "in writing. And Satan or one of his high-ranking officers would have to present it to me in person."

"Oh," I said, a little deflated. Who knew how much trouble that might be? "Okay. I guess I can do that. Thank you sir, your, uh, worshipfulness." I bowed myself out of St. Peter's presence. Since he didn't like me anyway, I thought staying as respectful as possible was my best strategy.

When I got back to Tesla and Edison, they were playing Rock, Paper, Scissors. From all the grumbling on Edison's end, he was probably losing more than he was winning. They scrambled off the celestial firmament at my approach.

"Listen, guys. We may have a chance of getting some heavenly cooperation, but somebody with major clout down below will have to make a formal request to the higher powers up here. I'm going down to see Beelzebub. You can't do anything more here until I get this set up, so for now you might as well head back to your regular jobs."

Edison's eyes were as big as saucers as I whistled for BOOH. "Oh, relax, BP. BOOH's my ride, not yours. You can take the Elevator along with Tesla." Edison sighed in relief and the two of them headed for the shaft.

BOOH whisked me down to Beezy's compound in two shakes ... make that eight. The bazaar was its usual bustle of activity, but Beezy wasn't in his office. A fog of flies flew toward me hopefully, but when they saw I wasn't their master, they returned, somewhat forlornly it seemed to me, to the desk, settling on some rotting cheese. I slipped out of his office through the revolving door, trying to figure out who was going to help me if Beelzebub turned out to be unavailable. I sure didn't want to go back to Satan; he'd been very specific about not wanting to see my face again until all my special projects were finished.

A scream went up from the bazaar, and then another and another, until merchants and customers alike were all howling in terror. I looked around to see what had frightened them.

In the distance, a monstrous sandstorm flowed across the desert. The supernatural rapidity with which it moved was indeed frightening, especially since it was heading our way. There wasn't even time to call for BOOH to get me out of there, yet I wasn't really worried. The bat, perched atop Beezy's office, looked at the whirling sand with disinterest, which made me think there might be more sound than fury to this storm.

It was still impressive, though, as it twirled and twirled, gobbling up the landscape, sucking up sand and motes of dust in its frenzy, growing ever larger. Finally it reached the bazaar, where it halted. The fury of the spinning continued for a moment, then stopped abruptly. In place of the storm, a giant creature of sand stood before me, like a gargantuan genie of a child's tale. Arms extended, it looked as if it was going to lift the entire bazaar, like a plate, in its hands.

There was a rush of wind, like a giant sigh, and the genie began to disintegrate until, in its place, stood Beelzebub.

BOOH took a glance at Beezy and yawned.

The Lord of the Flies cracked his knuckles a couple of times, then spotted me and walked over. "Minion? What do you need?"

"Some help with St. Peter," I answered. "What's up with the sandstorm? I thought that was Azazel's gig."

He frowned. "It is, though I can out-sandstorm him any day of the week. Today, though, well, sometimes I just have to get away from the damn flies," he said, going through the revolving door. As if summoned, the winged nasties rocketed from their perches on the cheese and swarmed their lord and master. "Yes, babies," Beezy said sarcastically, "Daddy's home."

He settled in his desk chair and picked up the flyswatter. "What kind of help, specifically, do you need with Pete?"

I explained about wanting to trace the line from the power plant behind the Pearly Gates to the Escalator. "He's not being very cooperative."

"Naturally he isn't," Beezy said, as he swatted three bugs at once. "Not bad, huh?" showing me his handiwork. "My record is ten with one blow. With the flyswatter, I mean." He looked at me fiercely. "I could kill them all instantly with will alone."

"Yeah, uh, great. Now, about St. Peter: he says he can allow some electricians from Heaven's end to help us, but only if he receives the request in writing and delivered in person by someone high up in Hell's hierarchy." I looked at him hopefully.

"And you want me to do it, huh?"

"Well, uh, yes. I mean," adding quickly, "there's not anyone much higher than you down here." He's high up, down under. A little confusing but Beezy knew what I meant.

"Except for Satan. Why don't you ask him?" he said, smiling evilly at me.

"He," I began uncertainly, "he told me not to bother Him again until all this mess was cleared up. He also told me to work through you, and since you're my boss and all, well ..."

"Never mind, Minion. I was just pulling your chain. It's what I do, you know," he added.

"Yes, sir." It was indeed what he did, almost every day of my non-existence.

Beelzebub scratched his forked beard with his flyswatter. "Okay, I'll do it, but I can't today. I have a confab with the other Princes of Hell." I nodded in understanding. The top devils had a weekly poker game and Hell would freeze over before any of them missed it. Soon they'd all gather round in some stinking fire pit to drink and cheat each other at cards. The boys were likely to go all night; they usually did.

"Tomorrow morning should be early enough, I guess."

"I won't make it until the afternoon. I'll probably sleep in."

Devils don't need sleep, but they can do anything they feel like doing, so what was I going to say? "Okay. I mean, yes, sir. Tesla and Edison will be ready to work from the Escalator end starting around one, if that's okay with you."

"Fine," he said, standing. "Now get out."

"Yessir!" When Beezy tells you to leave, you don't mess around. "Oh, sir, would it help if I drafted the request for you?"

Beelzebub snorted. "It's already done," he said, pointing at his outbox. Sure enough, there was the memo, on fine parchment, with Hell's letterhead and all. It even had Beezy's Arabic named scrawled on it.

"How did you do that?"

Beezy chortled. "I'm the Lord of the Flies, human. There isn't much I can't do. Now, what did I tell you to do?"

"Yes, boss. Getting out right now."

I had just reached the revolving door when he stopped me. "Wait. How's the work going on the Stairway?"

"Very well, sir. I'm on my way there now. At the rate they're moving, they'll finish sometime tomorrow." Orson had said 'tomorrow' yesterday, which meant 'today' today, but being an experienced maintenance man, I knew to hedge my bets. Since Beezy had visited the site shortly before my own visit, though, he knew about as much as me. I hoped he was just asking out of habit. He liked to micromanage that way.

Fortunately, he was. "Acceptable," he said, belching loudly. I could smell his breath from ten feet away. Not good. "And what of the Free Hellions? Any progress on that front?"

"Yes, boss. I had my first encounter with them last night." And every bone in my body still ached from the experience. "Pinkerton and I are beginning to put together the pieces of the conspiracy." At least, I felt we were. The three leaders, the four thugs, the posters, the image of the hands and eye, Niagara - they fit together somehow. The answers would come, I was sure of it. Whether or not we figured things out before there was more trouble was less certain, but Beezy didn't need to know that. "Pinkerton and I - oh, and Flo too, she was very helpful last night - we'll meet again this evening. With a bit more information, we should be able to identify the prime movers soon and shut down their whole operation."

"Good, good. Now get out of here. I'm late, so scram," he said, waving his flyswatter at me. The gesture flung my body ten paces, crashing it against the revolving door. The door whirled me around two or three times, then spat me out on the sand outside. I got off the ground and dusted off my coveralls.

What a nice guy, my boss.

An explosion momentarily deafened me and knocked me back on my ass. BOOH dropped from the roof, settling beside me, as the wooden building shattered. The top of Beezy's office split open and a vast mushroom cloud filled the sky. A voice bellowed from the heart of the cloud, "Party! PAR-TY!" The cloud dissipated and Beelzebub was gone.

I noticed, though, that the building was already re-knitting itself. This probably wasn't the first time the Lord of the Flies had manifested himself as a thermonuclear explosion.

BOOH used one of his claws to pick me off the ground. "Thanks," I said, and once again brushed the dirt from my clothes. "He sure seems to like the dramatic entrances and exits, doesn't he?"

BOOH rolled his eyes. I decided he was singularly unimpressed by the Lord of the Flies.

I laughed. “You said it, buddy. Hey, let’s go see how Orson is getting along.”

Chapter 17

We found Orson right where he said he'd be, on Level Two, where they were just getting ready to break ground on the Stairway shaft that would run up to the First Circle of Hell. He was walking around the dig, mumbling to himself. I could see the black shaft of the Stairway that ran from Two down to Three just poking through the dirt. Workers, like so many ants, were swarming down the shaft with piles of treads in their arms that they were carrying down to install.

"How's it going, Orson?"

"Huh?" Orson seemed distracted. "Okay, I guess. The shafts from Four to Three and Three to Two are done. We're starting to lay the treads now, as you can see. Two other crews are doing the same on Three and Four as we speak." Orson frowned. "We ran into a little difficulty getting through the bases of the second and third Circles, though. All the old concrete from the old stairwells needed to be blasted away. It slowed us up a bit. I," he hesitated. "I don't think we'll be able to finish until tomorrow morning."

Rookie. Good thing I'd fudged Orson's estimate when I reported to Beezy. I was pretty sure my assistant had low-balled the amount of time he'd need. It helped to know his history as a director. Always late, always over budget. Well, usually anyway. Besides, in Hell you had to be especially wary of Murphy's Law: 'If anything can go wrong, it will.' Murphy's Law applied in Hell more than anywhere else in all universes, all realities, both life and afterlife, with the possible exception of Haiti. Better to plan for the worst-case scenario in Hell, since that's usually what you got here. "Not to worry," I told him. "You've made an incredible amount of progress, though this black and white effect still strikes me as kinda weird."

"You get used to it after a while," he said, a bit vaguely.

"What's wrong?"

"Huh? Oh, nothing. I'm just waiting for the music."

"The what?"

"Ah," he said, spying a truck that had just driven onto the worksite. "Here they come now." He turned to me. "The music. A little something to class up the production and motivate the workers."

The truck, a ten foot U-Haul that had seen better days, or decades, pulled up before us. The driver got out. He looked to be a young man in his mid-to-late thirties, with dark, thinning but wavy hair that he wore combed back and heavily greased. He was pretty good looking, though his nose was a tad large for his face - not that I should talk. He seemed familiar.

"Steve," Orson said, indicating the man. "Meet George. George Gershwin. Oh," he added, indicating the old man in glasses who came around from the other side of the truck, "and his brother, Ira."

Both men wore bright red coveralls, which meant they must have normally worked for Ukobach, tending the fires of Hell. Ira sported a boater atop his pate. A round of handshakes was in order and we dutifully made them.

"Did you get it?" Orson asked.

"Yeah," George said. "It's a piece of shit, but that stupid demon almost wouldn't let us have it. Said he played it all the time in his honky-tonk band. He only gave it up when I said we had a blank check from Satan." George looked a little uneasily at Orson. "You weren't kidding, right? You do have a blank check, don't you?"

"He doesn't but I do. Which demon are you talking about?" I asked, mildly curious.

"Whizzer."

"Ah, yes, he's a fun one." Contrary to his name, Whizzer was not the demon of urinary tract infections but the demon of noise. He delighted in nothing more than creating sounds that clashed, those with onomatopoeic names such as *crash, crunch, hiss, clank, grrrr, bam,* and *eeeeeeeeeeee*. He used to be a nobody, actually kind of a loser among Hell's minions, until he inspired the little boy of squeaking chalk fame, and for this he was promoted by Satan to Demon First Class. It went to his head and he started meddling in, of all things, music. Whizzer went on to be the demonic muse of some of the more annoying composers out there, like Arnold Schoenberg and Charles Ives, especially Ives, to whom he gave the idea of tuning every note on a piano a quarter tone off from standard pitch then playing it against another piano tuned to standard pitch. The resulting 'Three Quarter Tone Piano Pieces' became something of a horrific classic, though to most of humanity it sounded like cats being tortured. *Ugh.* For that musical abomination alone, Ives was consigned to the Eighth Circle of Hell, just one ring higher than Chalk-Screech Boy. I hear Whizzer got a medal for pairing up Ives with quarter tones.

Writing music for an out-of-tune piano - *brother*, but what would you expect from an insurance salesman? That's what Ives did for a living, since nobody was actually willing to pay him for his music. To say he was not particularly successful at composition during his lifetime was an understatement, but at least he was practical about it in that he heeded an old but good piece of advice: 'That's nice, dear, but don't quit your day job.'

George went to the back of the U-Haul and released the latch. Nothing happened, so he gave a mighty heave on the nylon strap. It broke in his hand, yet there was still no movement on the door front. After George finished an impressive string of curses, which were equally ineffective at raising the door, the four of us got our fingers under the lip of metal and shoved upward. The door really didn't want to cooperate, but after a few minutes we got it raised.

The ramp wasn't much easier to get out, but another five minutes of huffing and puffing had it in place. We were ready to take out the piano.

Now pianos are heavy things. It's possible for two people to move one, but it ain't easy, especially without a piano dolly, which, judging by the lone contents of the truck, i.e. one chartreuse upright honky-tonk piano, George and Ira didn't have. "How did you get the thing loaded in the first place?" I asked.

Ira answered. "Once we finally convinced Whizzer - boy, what a suck-up he is - that we were doing Satan's will, he fell all over himself helping us. Got two demons, strong bastards too, to lift the piano into the truck. They didn't even use the ramp."

I whistled. That was maybe six hundred pounds of dead weight, not that dead was any particular problem in the underworld. Picking up a piano was fine for demons, but how were we going to manage it? I eyed the green monstrosity critically and saw four tiny wheels beneath it, each no bigger than a quarter. The ramp was one of those typical U-Haul jobs - a regular, uneven surface designed to give humans traction. That was great, unless you were trying to roll something heavy with very tiny wheels down it. Then you'd get ...

Bumpity, bumpity

"Damn it, it's stuck."

Bumpity

"Stuck again."

Bump.

... if you were lucky.

I shook my head. "Another example of Hell on wheels."

"You said it," Ira grumbled. "I think we're going to need some help."

Orson motioned to a couple of thickly muscled guys who, in typical construction worker fashion, were leaning against things, smoking and watching other people work. Reluctantly they put out their cigarettes and came over to assist.

Bumpity, bumpity

"Damn it, it's stuck."

Bumpity

"Stuck again."

Bumpity

"Watch out, it's starting to ... ***Aghh!***"

Once a piano starts to fall over, especially at a height, and most especially if you're not a super-strong demon, it's best to just let it crash to the ground, which is what it did. Miraculously, though, the wood didn't shatter into a zillion pieces. The piano just lay there on its side, a big, glowing green turtle of an instrument that couldn't right itself.

Orson cursed. "Come on, guys, let's get it back upright and see if it still plays."

"Are you kidding?" George sneered. "I tried a few notes on that crap box before the demons loaded it on the truck. That fall could have only improved things."

"Yuck, yuck, how droll," Ira grumbled. "You know, Georgie, you were never as clever as you thought you were."

"Shut up, both of you," Orson grunted, "and lift."

The six of us got the thing back on its wheels, though the effort left us groaning and gasping for breath. "Do you think," Ira wheezed, "do you think we could just perform from here?"

Orson eyed the distance between the worksite and the piano. I think he really had wanted it closer, but the prospect of moving the green monster some more didn't appeal to him either. He shrugged. "Whatever. Just get playing."

They hadn't brought a bench with them, so Orson had one of the workers pile some cinderblocks on top of each other. George Gershwin, pianist and composer extraordinaire, settled down gingerly on the cinderblocks. It didn't look like a very comfortable perch, but he didn't complain. I think he was saving all his grumblings for the way the piano sounded. Experimentally he played a few chords, and I winced. The piano seemed very purposefully out of tune. Most pianos, those of any quality anyway, will slowly go flat, but the strings will stay roughly in relative tune with each other. Not this thing. Some keys played the same note, others were a quarter tone off, some were on pitch. It was all pretty random, which meant it was deliberate. On top of it all, the piano had that tinny quality that is a hallmark of crappy old uprights that you hear in, well, honky-tonks and low-end bars.

"Just as I thought," George concluded, "the fall actually improved the sound."

"You're kidding," I said in disbelief.

"No," Ira responded. "Georgie's right. It sounded even worse before."

Orson interrupted impatiently. "Never mind about that. I need you two to get started. We've got a staircase to build. Now remember, guys, only one song. That's all I got authorization for. Just the chorus. No verses. And nothing fancy, George. No jazzy intros or anything like that."

"So now you're telling me how to play the piece?" The artist was clearly offended.

"I'm sorry but I had a hard enough time talking Beezy into this as it was. Play the tune as if it were in a book of classic show melodies for easy piano."

"Arghh!"

"Hey. Look at it this way: at least you're both performing again."

"Yeah, great," Ira grumbled.

"So," said George with a false sweetness, "how would you like me to start?"

Orson frowned. He didn't appear to like George's attitude. Orson thought for a moment, then smiled wickedly. "How about a rousing, *dump da da dump dump dum*?"

"Peasant. Fine. Ira, you ready?"

Ira took his place at the side of the piano, removed his boater and placed it over his heart. The two of them were a gaudy sight with their red coveralls against the iridescent green of the piano. Ira cleared his throat. "Hit it, Georgie."

"*Dump da da dump dump dum*," played George. And Ira began to sing:

I'll build a stairway to Paradise
With a new step ev'ry daaay.

Oh, no. "Orson, you've got to be kidding."

He shrugged. "I didn't really have much choice. It was either this or 'Stairway to Heaven,' and I don't like Led Zeppelin."

With a shrug of my own, I turned back to the Gershwins. As the brothers performed against the black and white landscape, the red slowly leached from their garments until they were as gray as the surroundings. The piano, though, was another matter. "Hmmm," I hmmmed. "Piano's still green."

Orson nodded. "Yeah, I noticed it, too. Wonder why it didn't change to some shade of gray when it came on the scene."

A final shrug was required and I complied. "Demon piano. That's my best explanation."

"Guess so, though I would have thought a Beezy command would trump a crap box demon piano any day. Oh well, you can't have everything, I suppose."

All morning long I helped Orson as his gopher, and it felt good, for both of us I think, to switch our usual roles. The music, even as out of tune as the piano was and as weak as old Ira's voice was, did seem to motivate the workers. They moved more purposefully within the surreal black and white construction site, and the shaft for the stairwell rose at an impressive pace.

We'd been at it for quite a while, long enough for George and Ira to perform 'I'll Build a Stairway to Paradise' at least 500 times, when Orson called me over. He had a big grin on his face as he motioned with his head toward our musicians. "George is ready to crack."

I looked. Ira was manfully singing the lyrics, though he was sounding a bit hoarse, but George looked like he was about to go crazy. His eyes were darting rapidly left and right, and there was an agitated quality to his face. His fingers were punching the keys harder and harder, as if he were reaching a frenzy.

"Wait for it," Orson said. "Wait for it … there!"

Abruptly George's hands shot up the keyboard. His fingers moved at blinding speed as he turned the song into the final cadenza of 'Rhapsody in Blue.' Ira, not knowing how to put his lyrics against that many notes, stumbled to a halt.

Orson looked at his wristwatch. "Three, two, one, blastoff!"

Thunder crackled in the dull gray clouds, the sky split open, and a blast of Hellfire knocked George off his makeshift piano bench.

Orson broke into a hearty laugh. "Beelzebub was right," he gasped, tears running from his eyes as he continued to chortle. "Beezy knew little boy George would go bonkers after a few hours of the same song and try to slip something else into the performance."

"You don't like him very much, do you? Why?"

"Oh," Orson sniggered, "I just don't like his attitude. Ira's okay but his little brother has always seemed like a jerk to me."

I shook my head. Why should we be so hard on each other? Death, at least in Hell, was not exactly a bed of roses. We should be cutting each other a little slack. With that thought, I reddened, remembering my own treatment of Edison and Ford. "Maybe ... maybe he's just bitter over having died so young. After all, he didn't even make it to 40."

"Maybe," Orson acknowledged reluctantly, "but you weren't all that much older than George when you got creamed, and you don't act that way."

I shrugged. "I was never as talented as George, or Ira, or you for that matter. You lived to be 70 and Ira, 83, so you both had many years of creativity. George was just reaching the top of his game when he died, and maybe he just feels cheated out of his destiny."

"What was that saying ...?" Orson asked. "Oh, yeah, I remember. 'Life's a bitch and then you die.' "

"Swell."

"And I still don't like him. Hey, Georgie!" Orson yelled. Ira was helping his little brother, who seemed a bit dazed, to his feet. "I warned you," Orson continued. "Now get back to work."

George nodded wearily and took his place back on the cinderblocks.

"Dump da da dump dump dum ..."

I'll build a stairway to Paradise
With a new step ev'ry daaay.

We worked all day without stopping, and the black shaft rose higher and higher, until it disappeared into the cloud cover. I squinted. "How much higher does it need to be to reach the First Circle?"

"Who knows?" Orson shrugged. "Building stairs in Hell isn't an exact science, you know, but I figure we've reached over halfway. I'll keep the gang working all night if necessary. We'll finish the shaft, but we won't get all the risers and treads in place. Still, we shouldn't have any problem knocking them out in the morning."

"Well, just remember Murphy's Law."

My assistant beamed. "The big question mark is the time it takes to break through the old concrete at the base of the Circles. I've had a crew working on that all day and I just got a call that they're almost through."

"Fool me once, shame on you. Fool me twice ..."

"Exactly. I'm not going to make the same mistake again, not for all the Murphys in Hell."

"Sounds like you have a plan. Also sounds like you have a phone. Where is it?"

Orson gestured at a small storage shed he'd popped in and out of several times during the course of the day. "In my makeshift office."

"Good. I need to call Tesla and Edison and tell them what time to meet me Topside tomorrow." I looked around at the workers. As usual, Orson had them operating at peak efficiency. He really didn't need my help. "And then I have to leave. There's a little more snooping to do."

"And another date, too, huh?"

I blushed. "Yeah."

Orson put his hand on my arm. "Well, enjoy it while you can."

"What do you mean?"

"Oh, come on, Steve, you know exactly what I mean. This is Hell, man. Satan doesn't want us to be happy. We're supposed to be suffering."

"Well, you too," I said defensively. "When this stairwell is finished, you'll have to go back to being my assistant."

The shaft cast a shadow over us, as if a sun had just gone behind the Stairway's monolithic superstructure. There was no sun in Hell, just like there wasn't a moon, but Satan had a flare for the dramatic and I guess a shadow fit the mood. "I know," Orson whispered. "And so, even though I'm trying to finish the Stairway as quickly as possible, I'm savoring every moment. That's all I'm saying, Steve. It won't last between you and Flo. It can't, so savor it."

I nodded reluctantly. He was right. As soon as Satan was finished with me, things would explode. I didn't know how but it would be spectacular. My teeth hurt just thinking about it.

Yet Orson was also right about the savoring part, so that's exactly what I was going to do: enjoy every delectable moment with Flo.

I made my calls, then signaled for BOOH. It was time to dress for the evening, time to let Orson get back to directing his last production.

Chapter 18

There wasn't any need to stop by the office, so I headed straight to my apartment. While unlocking the door to the studio, I heard the scrambling sounds of the roaches as they scurried out of sight. When I got inside, not one of the nasty critters was to be seen, and for a moment I pretended that this was not a vermin-infested place I only went to because I had nowhere else to go. "Ah, it's good to be home!" I said, though my voice lacked conviction.

I heard a faint laugh.

Whatever.

My tuxedo had been pretty thoroughly trashed last night, but by morning it had disappeared anyway, so I wasn't worried about what to wear, figuring the Lord [of Hell] would provide.

I stepped into the shower for a repeat of the previous night's experience. The water temperature was just the way I liked it, the Ivory Soap was on its little ceramic shelf waiting for me, and the bottle of Pert Plus was nearby. Humming, I lathered up.

I stayed in the shower for a very long while, enjoying the experience. Until everything fell apart, I was going to follow Orson's advice: *savor, savor*.

Finally my fingers and toes started to shrivel up. With great reluctance, I turned off the taps and toweled off.

It didn't take long in the closet for me to find the white dinner jacket, freshly-pressed shirt, black tux slacks and new bowtie. Someone had even polished my shoes. I pulled open my drawers: clean underwear, clean socks ... oh, and something else. My socks were wrapped around a long black case. Curious, I opened it and found a double string of pearls, pearl earrings and a pearl ring. The odds were pretty good that they weren't intended for me, so I slipped the box into the inside pocket of my jacket.

Instead of a trench coat draped over my sofa, tonight there was an overcoat. It was charcoal gray and made of cashmere. I slipped it on, admiring the cut, the way it draped dramatically from my shoulders to my calves. The evening might end up being too hot for the coat, but I didn't much care. It looked really snazzy.

No hat, though, not this night, which was just fine by me. The coat looked better without one and I was never really much of a hat guy anyway. Having a little more time than the previous evening, I decided to walk to Flo's place, reaching her apartment right at seven. I gave her door the old 'shave and a haircut' treatment.

"Come in."

Flo was standing in the middle of her main room in a black cocktail dress. It fit very tightly, showing her generous curves. The top evoked the classic peasant dress: bare shoulders, a slight bit of translucent finery forming very short, ruffled sleeves, though the neckline plunged to reveal her ample and lovely décolletage.

She wore her hair down tonight and it cascaded over her shoulders in dark, gentle waves. I whistled. "I didn't think you could possibly look more beautiful than you did last night, but I was wrong."

Flo glided over and gave me a kiss. "Thank you, but it's not quite right. I don't have any jewelry to wear. The diamond necklace and the other dress were both gone this morning."

"I think this is where I come in." Reaching in my coat pocket, I retrieved the box, opening it to reveal the necklace, earrings and ring.

"Oh, glorious," she breathed, slipping the ring on a finger of her right hand and putting on the earrings. "Would you help me with the necklace?" she asked, putting her back to me as she pulled her hair out of my way.

"My pleasure." I draped the pearls around her and fastened the white gold clasp, then gave her neck a quick kiss. "Here, let's have a look."

She turned and graced me with the full-on view. The necklace looked great with the gown, and I told her so.

"I have something for you as well," she said, walking over to her coffee table and picking up an oblong white box. In a replay of my own motions, she opened the box and showed me the contents. Inside was a white silk scarf. "Here." She removed the scarf, tossing the empty box on the sofa in what seemed to me an uncharacteristically casual act for Flo. "Let me fix this." Flo draped the scarf around my neck, letting the two ends dangle loosely on my chest, then turned up the collar of my overcoat. "Very elegant," she purred.

"You should talk, my love." *Did I say that?* For a moment, I glanced nervously around the room, half-expecting a horde of demons to descend upon me. But nothing happened, except for the delighted smile that illuminated Flo's face.

I helped her slip a black fur stole over her shoulders and we headed out.

I really liked the Victorian sector where Flo lived and I said so as we walked to where we could get a cab. "Yes, it's nice enough tonight, but usually it looks like a bad imitation of a Dickens novel: you know, old ladies selling apples or matches on the corner, poor people huddled around a too-small fire, trying desperately to get warm."

"Did you know Dickens?" I asked as we strolled along.

"I met him once at some social function. He didn't seem to be a very happy man."

"Well, he didn't have a very happy life. He was born poor - most of his family went to debtor's prison. He was practically a child slave, working in Victorian London. And his marriage wasn't very happy."

Flo looked thoughtful. "My observation in life was that most marriages weren't. It's one reason I never married."

"That sounds very cynical. It's unlike you." Though, reflecting on my own failed marriage, I knew her perspective was not without merit. Still, I had met some happily married people in my time. "Do you ..." I began hesitantly, not knowing why this conversation was making me uncomfortable, "do you think eternal love is impossible?"

The woman stopped her glide across the cobblestone street. Her hair had fallen over one eye, obscuring half of her face, but she pulled it back to look at me. I was surprised, considering the seriousness of the conversation, to see a bright smile on her face. "I used to, but recent events are making me reconsider my position."

We began walking again, casually, but my heart hammered against my ribcage for the next block. Flo reached over and slipped her arm around mine. The hammering grew louder.

The cab waiting for us had Louis Braille behind the driver's wheel. "Flo," I said as we climbed inside, "Florence Nightingale, this is Louis Braille, a friend of mine. Do you know him?"

"Only of him," she said. "M. Braille, I am a great admirer of your work."

"*Mademoiselle*, I am honored. I strive my best to be a good cabbie."

"I meant your reading and writing system for the blind."

"Oh."

"Louis," I interrupted, "could you drive us to the Red Note?"

"*Bien sûr, mon ami*. Sure thing."

We traveled along for a few blocks, Flo and I holding hands, Louis bumping the occasional curb to get a reference point. Suddenly he cleared his throat. "*Merci bien, mademoiselle*. Thank you for your kind words about my Braille system. I had almost forgotten. It seems so long ago."

Flo placed a gentle hand on Louis shoulder. "Yes, I know. An Eternity."

"Indeed, indeed," he murmured. I saw the glistening tear fall from a sightless eye to his cheek.

"What you did gave millions of blind people the chance to live richer, more productive lives," Flo said softly in her special way that gave comfort to anyone who heard her. "Your system was brilliant, effective and a Godsend."

Tears were streaming down Louis's face now, as he cried silently, the cathartic mourning of a good person who had never understood why he'd been damned in the first place. I wondered once again what it took to make it to Heaven but knew the answer was beyond me. Heaven seemed unachievable. Hell, however, was pretty easy to manage.

"Louis," I said softly, "we're here."

"Ah? So soon?" he said, stopping the car. He took his fare and, as was his custom, immediately dumped it out the driver's side window. "Enjoy your evening, my friends."

"A nice man," Flo said as we watched the cab drive off with another fare.

"Yes, he is." I kissed her cheek with great tenderness.

"What was that for?" she asked in surprise.

"For being you. You were very kind to him. Your kindness, it's one of the things I love most about you."

"There are others?"

I smiled and took her by the arm, leading her toward the entrance to the Red Note. "Don't get me started. The list is long."

The Red Note was a very different sort of place than the club we'd visited the previous evening. While Red Square could have been a set for an Astaire and Rogers movie, the Red Note was a more intimate venue. The room was paneled in dark wood, like walnut or mahogany. The carpeted floor was a little worse-for-wear because of the stains from wine and food spilled over it, yet the muted lights camouflaged these flaws. All of the lighting was soft, except for the spots for the stage, the bar lights and the sconces along the walls.

As we finished checking our coats, Pinkerton came into the club. I wouldn't have recognized him except for those piercing eyes of his. He had shaved off his beard, leaving only a pencil-thin mustache. Allan was dressed much as I had been the night before, in trench coat and fedora, the image of the hardboiled detective. Though he had died forty years before the genre had been invented, he adapted to the look nicely. Only when he opened his mouth did the illusion vanish.

"Ah dinae thocht ya'd beat me heer." Hardboiled detective with a Scottish brogue.

"Good to see you, too," I whispered. "We're going to get a table. Keep an eye on me tonight, will you? I have a feeling we're going to see a certain familiar someone, and when that happens, I'll point him out to you."

"You mean that heigbanger ... uh, nut case ... whose boys roughed you up?"

"That would be the one."

"Aye, that will work. In the meanwhile, Ah'll stay by the bar and see what Ah can learn there."

The whole exchange had taken but a few moments, yet I felt conspicuous the whole time. Fortunately, nobody really noticed me, for all eyes were on my date. As I stepped to her side, fifty male faces deflated.

I tried not to smirk. *Sorry, boys. The woman is mine.*

At least for now, said a cynical little voice in the back of my brain.

I shook my head and resurrected my new mantra: *savor.*

There was a nice table-for-two near the stage, slightly right of center. I pulled out a chair for Flo, then seated myself. A waiter came up promptly to take our drink order. "What would you like, dear?" I asked my date, marveling in the miracle that I actually had a date. "More champagne?"

"Not tonight. I think I would like to try a ... what are they called? ... oh, yes, a martini."

"Really?" I was surprised. In life, Florence Nightingale had been associated with the Temperance Movement. Last night had surprised me, when she so willingly indulged in the champagne and chardonnay, and especially because they seemed to have some effect on her, unlike on other inhabitants of Hell. I had written all of that off to the fact that Flo didn't really belong in the Underworld, and being something of an anomaly here, the normal rules did not apply to her. Still, a *martini?* "That's a pretty strong drink, dear. Are you sure?"

"Oh, yes," she said with a triumphant smile. "I think I can hold my liquor quite well, don't you?"

"I, uh, guess. So, what kind do you want? Maybe a vodka martini?"

Flo frowned. "Sir, remember that I am a British subject."

"Oh. Right." I chuckled and turned to the waiter. "A martini, no make that two, with Tanqueray gin, very dry, straight up, with olives. Oh, and stir and strain them, don't shake them."

"You're a picky sod, aren't you?" said our waiter, an unpleasant chap who reminded me of Noel Coward in a bad suit. Hell, it was possible he was Noel Coward in a bad suit.

I smiled sweetly at him. "The drinks, please?"

Our waiter left grumbling and wended his way toward the bar. He said something to the barkeep, who looked up at me and frowned.

It was Putty Face.

Well, that hadn't taken long. The Hellions must have met in nightclubs because Putty Face worked in them. He could provide the leaders with access to back rooms for their meetings, all the while keeping a lookout for troublemakers. Like me.

Pinkerton had just gotten himself a pint of something. He sat on his stool, back to the bar, as if casually looking over the room. He caught my eyes immediately. With a slight gesture of my head, I indicated the bartender. Unfortunately, there were three other people I could have been pointing to, including the waiter. Pinkerton looked at me again and I made the same gesture, which no longer seemed as subtle - or as precise - to me as it had earlier. Allan scratched the back of his head in thought, then his eyes lit up. He pointed to his beer, took a sip, then indicated the two customers to his left. I sighed and shook my head, no. He placed his pint on the bar and made a gesture like writing in a tablet. Again I shook my head. No, not the waiter.

Good grief. I might as well have just gone up to him and said, "The bad guy is the bartender." It would have been more subtle than this.

Finally Pinkerton figured it out. He pantomimed a man making a pour into a pint glass, then, pointing at Putty Face, looked at me expectantly.

I nodded, sighing softly to myself.

Pinkerton actually gave me the A-OK signal. Putty Face glanced in Allan's direction.

The world's greatest spy had clearly lost some of his edge over the years. Oh well. Anyone could get out of practice.

"What are you doing?" Flo said.

"Trying to communicate something secret to our friend, Mr. Pinkerton, over there by the bar."

"Oh?" she said, turning around. She had not seen Pinkerton when we'd come in. "Where?"

"Don't look!" I hissed. "I mean, please don't look. We aren't supposed to know each other."

"Oh!" she said and leaned over conspiratorially. "More cloak and dagger intrigue?"

"Yes, but not very covert. Whatever. My part is over now. Allan will take it from here and we can just enjoy ourselves this evening."

"Wonderful!" she said. "Oh, look, here come our drinks."

Flo and I clinked glasses. When she took her first sip, her eyes opened wide.

"Too much?"

"No," she said, slowly taking another taste. "No. I just wasn't expecting it to be so strong. It's actually quite good, in a stiff upper lip sort of way, if you know what I mean."

"Why, Flo, did you just make a joke?" I said, amused.

She giggled. "I suppose I did."

The martinis were, in fact, perfect: dry, with the subtle flavor of aromatics that characterizes a good gin. I'd say this about Putty Face - he sure knew how to make a drink.

Savor.

As we sipped our martinis, we flipped through the menu, chatting as we considered the food options. Neither one of us wanted anything too heavy, so we decided to make our dinner off of appetizers. We ordered raw oysters, which we thought would go very well with the martinis, and some shrimp.

After about 30 minutes, Thelonius Monk came onstage. He was all by himself this evening. Around his neck was a child's accordion. At most it could not have had more than two octaves for him to work with, and the shoulder straps were so short the instrument rested almost on his clavicle rather than the middle of the torso, as was proper. Still, for a jazz pianist consigned to Hell, Monk could have done a lot worse than an accordion, even a child's version. At least it had a familiar keyboard for the right hand.

In my lifetime, I had heard blues played on accordion, but never jazz, so I was interested to see what Monk could do. As he began to play, other limitations of his instrument became apparent. Like the bagpipes Miles had played the previous night, the bellows of Monk's accordion had a leak somewhere and every note was accompanied by a slight hissing sound, like a tea kettle that had lost its whistle but tried to make up for it with a noisy exhalation of steam. Surprisingly, most of the reeds were in tune, which was damn lucky since, as with nearly all instruments in Hell, the accordion couldn't be tuned. However, arbitrary notes wouldn't sound at all. This must have been frustrating to a master performer like Monk, who would begin a complicated run up the keyboard, only to have holes poked in his riff by noteless hisses.

Monk began with 'Round Midnight' and moved quickly to 'Blue Monk.' All in all, Thelonius Monk, playing solo on his kid's accordion, produced a more satisfying set than Miles and his gang the night before.

I looked over at Flo. She was a little flushed, which only made her look all the more fetching. "Feeling the martini, Flo?"

"A little, yes, but would you order me another, please?" she asked, finishing the last drop.

"You sure?"

She grinned. Flo looked deep into my eyes as she used lush lips to pull an olive off the toothpick on which it had been impaled. "Yes. It makes me feel all warm and toasty." She took a deep breath of satisfaction and I stared in admiration at her swelling chest.

Flagging down our waiter, we ordered another round. They were as good as the first two. I stretched mine out, wanting to enjoy every drop of the gin's potent clarity. In the middle of our drinks, Monk finished his set. It was a heroic performance, and though the other guests at the Red Note just sat at their tables like the dead things they were, Flo and I gave him a standing ovation. Monk looked at us in surprise. He was clearly pleased by the attention, though. He even came by our table briefly.

"Great set!" I said, shaking his hand.

"Indeed," Flo agreed, then blushed prettily when Monk actually bent to kiss her hand.

"Thank you. Thank you very much. I don't often get people paying much attention to my playing anymore."

"I was a great admirer of yours in my lifetime. I had all your records." The lights on the stage had just been turned off; it now looked like a very empty and lonely place. "Too bad they won't let you play piano."

Monk winced. "I guess it could be worse. I could be playing bagpipes, like Miles."

"Or glockenspiel!" Flo chimed in.

"Oh, have you heard the sextet?"

"Yeah, just last night."

"Well, I guess I'd rather stick with my accordion than play glockenspiel." Monk looked around suddenly, his face assuming a hunted look. "I hope I didn't say that too loud."

Flo touched his arm delicately. "Don't worry," she whispered, "You didn't, and your secret is safe with us."

Monk seemed relieved. He shook my hand once more, bowed to Flo in the manner of a fine English gentleman, and excused himself. As we sat back down, I happened to glance toward the bar. Both Putty Face and Pinkerton were gone.

I shrugged and popped the last olive from the martini into my mouth. "Would you like to stay for his next set?"

Florence gave me a doe-eyed look. "No," she said slowly. "I'm ready to leave."

We got our coats and headed outside.

In minutes, the cab that had been waiting outside the club had whisked us to the entrance of the Victorian sector. We walked slowly, hand-in-hand. I didn't want the evening to end.

Apparently, neither did Flo. "Would you like to come up for a while?" she said shyly - though not as shyly as last night, I noticed - as we reached her apartment building.

Now it was my turn to blush. "I'd love to." I held the door open for her and we stepped inside.

Flo unlocked the door to her apartment and turned on the light. The main room was so warm, so comfortable. It really was the most pleasant space I'd seen in all my time in Hell. While I took off my overcoat, Flo removed her stole and draped it over the sofa. She took my coat from me and placed it on top of her own. She turned and I saw the look in her eyes. Anticipation. Desire.

I don't even recall taking a step toward her, but we were in each other's arms, as if we'd been drawn together magically. Her kisses, tentative at first, grew more passionate.

"I ... I love you, Flo," I said, stroking her back.

"Lower, darling."

"I LOVE YOU," I said in my deepest voice.

She giggled. "No, I meant ..." and she placed my hand on her derriere.

"Oh." I rubbed her backside and squeezed it. She moaned, pressing her body hard into mine. I kissed her lips, cheeks, neck and the soft chest that was now heaving with excitement. I felt myself rising to the occasion.

Flo broke our embrace and took me by the hand, leading me toward her bedroom.

"Sweetheart, are you sure? You've had a bit to drink tonight." And she obviously could feel it, even though I couldn't.

She kissed me again. "Very sure." And that was that.

The clothes flew off fairly quickly, though I had a little trouble with the zipper on her dress and the hooks on her cantilevered bra. In my own defense, I was a bit out of practice. For her part, Flo practically ripped the clothes off me. Except for the socks. Socks and pantyhose: they're always hard and can take a bit of the edge off a passionate moment. Still, in a few seconds even those were off and we were lying on Flo's bed, flesh-to-flesh.

That night, I confirmed to myself that Florence Nightingale had in fact gone to her grave a virgin.

* * *

Flo nibbled on my ear as I idly caressed her. She was so beautiful, so perfect. "Again," she whispered.

Now, we had made love three times already. I should have been too tired to pop, being dead and all, but the stirrings began again as if I were a young buck of eighteen. Flo climbed on top of me and began a gentle rhythm. She trembled and screamed, began moving again and screamed once more.

I'd never known a woman to have so many orgasms. Still, over two centuries of abstinence would probably do that to anybody.

The sex was good. It was really, really good, unbelievably so. I'd tried having sex only a couple of times before in Hell; neither instance had been satisfying. But this, this was the greatest sex I'd ever had on either mortal or immortal plane.

After she had climaxed a fourth time in as many minutes, Flo gently slid off me. She began kissing my chest, my stomach. Then she went lower.

I thought I was going to see stars. "Where," I gasped, "where did you learn how to do that?"

"Mmmm? In a book. Mmmmm!"

Oh, god. Savor, savor, savor ...

"CUT!"

The room suddenly filled with light.

In the corner of Flo's bedroom, next to her armoire, stood two devils. One of them wore a beret, the other was working a video camera. The tails of both devils were sticking straight up behind them, like spears. I was both horrified and repulsed.

"Great! Great stuff, kids!" said the devil in the beret. "We got it all in the can."

"Yeah, I can't wait to get this footage back to the editing room," the second devil said, folding up the camera's tripod and swinging the gear onto one shoulder.

"What, what are you going to do with that?" Flo gasped, hurriedly using the sheet as a screen between her and the devils.

"Why," the director said with an evil smirk, "we're going to make you a star!"

I slipped out from under Flo as quickly as possible. Devils or no, I had to get that camera away from them.

"Oh, please," said the director. "Don't bother to show us out. We know our way." With a puff of smoke and an odor of brimstone, they were gone.

I looked at the now empty spot in the corner of Flo's bedroom. I was afraid to turn around.

"I ... I think you should leave, Steve."

I turned back to the bed. Flo had completely covered herself with the sheet. Even her head was under the fabric.

"But, Flo ...!"

"Please," said her muffled voice. "Go. Now."

"But I love you!"

I found myself on the carpet beside the bed, welts from the coconut cream pie already taking shape on my face. The smell of brimstone was so thick that I was coughing.

Flo had peeked out briefly when the pie and Hellfire had knocked me to the floor, but the sheet quickly went back over her head. "Please leave."

Feeling about as miserable as possible, I gathered up my clothes from where they lay in a pile, intermingled with Flo's own. I carried my garments into the living room, closing the bedroom door behind me. After dressing and slipping on my overcoat, I picked up the stole that had graced Flo's neck that evening and held it to my face. I could still smell her scent. Reluctantly, I put the fur back on the couch.

The silk scarf was nowhere to be found. With a sigh, I left, closing the door quietly on my way out.

Chapter 19

I was in a black mood as I shuffled along the cobblestones of the Victorian sector. The old ladies Flo had told me about, the ones who sold wormy apples and matches that didn't light worth a crap, were back on the streets. The gangs of paupers had returned and they gathered in misery around fires burning in metal drums, trying to get warm on a night that had suddenly turned very cold in a lot of ways.

"Enjoy it while it lasts," Orson had said. He had been right. This was Hell. People aren't supposed to be happy in Hell.

Yet, I mused, kicking a rock along the street, for a while I had been happy. For an hour or two we had experienced joyous perfection - here, in Satan's Dominion. I should have been satisfied.

But I wasn't. I wanted more: to spend every minute with Flo, make love to her night after night, marry her.

Marry her? My laugh was bitter. Where did I think I was, anyway? People didn't get married in Hell, not unless they were terrified of commitment. There were some poor schmoes who had spent their lifetimes avoiding marriage. Upon being consigned to Hell, they were immediately wedded to the homeliest, most irritating spouses that could be found for them in the Netherworld. And they weren't married for life; they were joined for Eternity.

Committing to another person had never scared me. In life, I had wanted to be married. My divorce was emotionally difficult, a great personal failure for me. And up to the day of my murder, I had hoped to find that certain special someone.

Well, I had. It had only taken my dying and going to Hell to find her. And now she was gone.

She would never make love to me again after this fiasco. Hell, I'd be lucky if she'd even let me see her again.

Turning the corner onto the main avenue, sadness, bitterness and anger threatened to overwhelm me. I was particularly furious at Satan and his manipulations, for this had to have all been a setup from the beginning - get the two of us together, make everything perfect, let us fall in love, then humiliate us. Especially humiliate Flo, the one person in all of Hell who didn't deserve to be here in the first place.

Was the whole point of this entire escapade the seduction of Florence Nightingale, and had I been the unwitting dope who had been Satan's instrument for her downfall?

Walking back toward my section of Five, I passed a cinema. On the marquee, in blazing neon, a new movie was being advertised: "NOW PLAYING: Flo Does The Super, Starring Florence Nightingale (with Steve Minion)."

In my mind, I heard Satan's quiet, demonic laugh.

Fuck!

My anger almost made me forget about the alley. Were the four of them such numbskulls as to try and ambush me in the same spot?

I hoped so.

As I stepped by the opening to the alleyway, the same pudgy hands pulled me into the shadows.

The three thugs were wearing black, tight-fitting slacks tonight, no shirts, and at least in the case of the two fatsoes, their guts hung over the fabric of their trousers - or were they danskins? The trio looked like rejects from an Alvin Ailey production. One of them, one of the fat Joes, looked to have been in a fight recently. The left side of his face was purple with bruises.

He and the other big guy pinned me to the wall, while the smaller Joe watched over me with his baseball bat. In a repeat of last night's performance, Putty Face emerged from the shadows. "I thought I told you to stay away from the Hellions! Why, I oughta ..." His hand pulled back, as if he were going to strike me.

I jerked one arm free and reflexively put my hand in front of my face, palm flat, fingers straight and rigid, thumb to my nose. The motion blocked Putty Face, who had tried to poke me in the eyes again.

"Oh, a wise guy, huh?" he said, frowning at me. "Okay, boys, work him over really good. Don't be gentle with him like last night."

"Wait!" I cried.

"What?" said Putty Face, with a leer. "You ready to squeal?"

"No." I whistled once. "BOOH!"

The four of them laughed. "Boo?" said their leader, still chortling. "What? Did you think that would scare me?"

A breeze kicked up, the result of the rapid flapping of wings above us. "No, but this will. Gentlemen," I said, smiling and pointing upward, "I'd like you to meet a friend of mine."

The screams were truly satisfying.

I watched for a while as BOOH picked them up and dropped them from a height again and again. This was my first opportunity to see the Bat out of Hell feed on a human host. You'd think the sight would have disgusted me, but in light of the circumstances I was entertained.

How cute. BOOH was playing with his food.

After about fifteen minutes, I called a halt to the proceedings. "Gee, guys, this has been swell, but I'm afraid I have to run. Oh, and if you ever try to hassle me again, you'll get even worse," I ended savagely.

I waved my thanks to BOOH. He did a truly terrifying ***"SKREE!"*** undoubtedly for the benefit of the four bloodied thugs lying on the alley pavement, and took off.

I left the scene, whistling. Happiness might not have been within my grasp, but payback felt pretty good. Yet there was something in the experience tugging at my memory. I wasn't ready to head to my apartment just yet, so I went to the office.

My mind needed to work subliminally on the mystery of the Hellions. More importantly, I had to take it away from musing on my relationship with Flo. Since generally the best way for me to shut down the old brain was to do something with my hands, I fixed the office door. Installing the new doorknob was easy: just pop out the old and plop in the new. The glass was a little harder. I had to remove the duct tape, remove the wooden molding that had held the old glass in place, put in the replacement, and re-secure the molding with some finishing nails and a small hammer. I almost broke the glass again; in fact, truth be told, it did break along one edge, but the molding hid my mistake. There was no need to resort to duct tape for this job. Caulk was the better choice. Never having been very good with it, though, I squirted some of the goop out with the gun and used my finger to smooth it into the cracks between the molding and the rest of the door. The completed repair didn't look too bad, all in all, especially after I used a putty knife to scrape off the excess caulk from glass and wood. A better than average fixit job for me - that made two in a row, counting Ronnie's boat - and I signed off on the completed work order with a little bit of satisfaction.

Once done, I put on a pot of coffee. At the moment, going back to the studio didn't have much appeal to me. Perhaps staying up 'all night,' whatever the hell that meant, was the thing to do. And I'd drink as much coffee as I felt like. Whether it was good or bad didn't much matter, as long as it was hot.

The Mr. Coffee provided that for me, and despite the nasty taste of badly burnt diner coffee, I was satisfied. Sitting at my desk with a full mug, I stared at the Hellions flyer that was pinned to the office wall.

Remember Niagara!
Free Hellyons. Forever

Damn, there was something familiar about it. Two hands, one seeming to block the other. In the palm of the second hand was an eye, an all-seeing eye.

And then there was Niagara. *Why Niagara?* I wondered, sucking on the dark brew in the shank of the night. Niagara was in western New York. That's where Niagara Falls was. I remembered going there as a kid on vacation, riding in that boat, The Maid of the Mist.

Niagara Falls.

And then I grinned. I had it. It all made sense. I knew who the Hellions, or at least who their leaders, were.

At that moment, there was a knock on my office door. The knob turned, and Pinkerton's face, slightly bruised on one side, poked into the room. "Ah saw the licht," he said, "and figgered you were here. Care to visit a spell?"

"What happened to you?" I asked. "It looks like someone took a lead pipe to your face."

"A baseball bat, laddie," he said, and for once I didn't correct him. "And it warn't in the Conservatory but in the kitchen of the Red Note."

"I looked for you at the club but you'd disappeared," I said, squinting at Allan's face while wetting a rag to place against his bruises.

"You dinae need to do that," he protested. "They will be gone by morning, ya ken."

"Yes, I ken," I said with some amusement, despite the hole in my heart. "But indulge me."

Pinkerton nodded as he sat on Orson's stool. "Fine by me. The wet cloth feels good. Thank you."

"So," I asked, sitting back in my chair, "what happened?"

"Oh, this? Nothing. It actually happened after Ah'd finished my snooping. A bare-chested fat man in long black underwear hit me with a baseball bat."

"That would have been one of the Joes. I've run into them before."

"Well," Pinkerton said with satisfaction, "I gave as good as I got. I clubbed him back with an iron skillet, then got out of there."

"Yeah, I saw your handiwork a little while ago, and he looks worse than you. No, don't worry. They didn't lay a glove on me." I smiled dangerously, but waved away the question in Pinkerton's eyes. "Mainly, I'm glad you got out without getting hurt too badly. But out of where?"

"The secret meeting. See, while you and Florence were starting on your second round, the ugly one slipped away from the bar, and Ah tailed him. By the by, how was your evening?"

"Don't want to talk about it."

"But ..."

"Stop or I'll hit you."

"Oh," he said knowingly. "That bad, eh?"

"You have no idea. Please continue."

"Ah followed him through the kitchen to a door in back. Some stairs led down to the cellar where they keep food stuffs for the restaurant." He shuddered. "Ah'm glad Ah didn't eat anything up at the club. Really repulsive conditions. Roaches were all over the place, even on the eyesters."

"The what?"

"Eyesters. Eyesters. Ya ken, those things served raw on half a shell."

"You mean *oysters*."

"Aye, that's what Ah said. Eyesters."

A wave of nausea came over me. "That's what I thought you meant."

"Anyhoo, there was a back room down there where a bunch of fellas was gathered. Ah recognized a passel o' them. Lenin, Trotsky and Marx were near the front. Ah also saw a fella in a white suit, with white hair and whiskers. Ah think it was Mark Twain."

"That would fit," I said, thinking about Twain's strident atheism. "Anyone else you knew?"

"Aye, knew or recognized from portraits Ah have seen in museums. 'Twas a motley group: politicians, generals, emperors; a large number of Russian, European and South American dictators, Ah believe, though most lived after my time; and then some of the oddest looking humans Ah have ever run across."

That piqued my interest. "Odd? In what way?"

"In lots of ways. Physically, mostly, though there were others who had just strange ticks and mannerisms. Ah think many of them were putting on an act, like circus clowns. Oh, speaking of clowns, there were a number of them there, which was funny to me. They were all wandering around spraying seltzer in each other's faces. No pies, though," he said with some regret.

"I think Satan has the monopoly on pie throwing in Hell," I said, feeling the sting of the welts that had not quite faded on my face.

"You are right there, Ah be sure. There was a gent in a tall stovepipe hat, sorta like what the President, that's President Lincoln, used to wear. He was a fat one, with a red face, as if he'd been drinking too much, and a big nose, like a daffodil bulb. People with crazy hair, crazy beards, crazy mustaches. Ah swear there were as many of these oddball types in the room as people who had lived their lives as revolutionaries."

"How did you see all this without getting caught?"

He shrugged. "Ah'd like to tell you it was because Ah employed great stealth but really the group didn't seem very concerned about privacy. The door was wide open and Ah just stayed outside the room, in the shadows to one side. Ah could hear everything."

"The meeting didn't begin until your ugly friend showed up. He started with a rousing speech about freedom, which seemed sort of out of place in Hell."

"Well, they call themselves the Free Hellions, after all. And," I added as an afterthought, "their leaders, including Putty Face …"

"Putty Face?"

"That's what I call the bartender. I didn't know his real name, but his face looks …"

"Like it was made from putty. Aye, Ah get's it."

"Speaking of the mysterious three," I said, with a twinkle in my eye that caught Pinkerton's attention, "were they there?"

"Aye, but they were behind a curtain ... well, really a sheet thrown over a line of rope so no one could see their faces. Ah told you their identities are kept strictly on the qt. Why are you smiling? That is a smile, isn't it? Kind of a grisly one, though."

Pinkerton was right. It was a smile, but it was coming from a man who had little to smile about.

"You know something?"

"Tell you in a minute. So, if they were behind a curtain, how did you know they were really there?"

"Cuz Ah saw their shadows on the sheet. Periodically your Putty Face would stick his head behind the partition and ask a question, and Ah could hear angry whispers in response. They seem to be a violent bunch, their leaders."

"That's an understatement," I mumbled.

"What?"

"Nothing. What did you learn?"

"That it's all about the Stairway. The Hellions are looking forward to its completion with much anticipation."

"What are they planning?" I asked, curious.

"Ah'll tell you, if you'll tell me who they are. Ah can see you've figured out that much of the mystery."

I tore the Hellions' flyer from the wall and tossed it down on my desk in front of Pinkerton. "I have." Sitting back down in my desk chair, I proceeded to tell Allan how I'd puzzled out the identity of the leaders and then everything I knew about them. "They always had enormous potential for violence, as you yourself figured out. You may very well be right. These guys could be the greatest anarchists who ever lived."

"Then Satan was right to be concerned."

"Maybe," I agreed, though reluctantly. "It kind of depends on what they're planning."

"Well," Pinkerton said, leaning over to speak to me quietly, "they're going to make a run on the Stairway and escape Hell."

"What?" I almost burst out laughing, the idea seemed so absurd to me. "And they actually think Satan, the Duke of Hell, Lord of the Underworld, and one of the most powerful beings in all the universes ..."

"He'd say second most powerful."

"Well, if you count the Big Three up there as one, I guess he'd be right, though didn't Michael beat him once in a fair fight?"

"Oh, you mean the Mont Saint-Michel incident. Aye, Michael supposedly defeated Satan and threw him in the sea, but Beezy always said the fight was rigged."

I snorted. "Sounds like Underworld propaganda to me, but anyway, there aren't many more powerful than Satan, and certainly not these three cretins and their underlings."

Pinkerton reached for his beard, then remembered he had shaved it off, so he moved to the thin mustache that remained. With thumb and forefinger, he flattened down the hair again and again. I'd noticed this phenomenon before with other men of the hirsute persuasion. Stroking their beards or mustaches seemed to help them think. Maybe they were squeezing blood out of their faces, hoping it would go to their brains and help them perform better.

"Aye, certainly not, but there appear to be a lot of these Hellions, and there's strength in numbers. Think we should let Satan know?"

My mind, which just moments before had been working with such clarity, felt all muddled now, and I struggled to remember Satan's exact words to me. Oh, yeah. "I don't want to see you again until you've accomplished all three of your tasks." And the final task was finding and stopping the Free Hellions. Satan would probably deal with them also but he wanted me to stop them.

I put my head in my hands. Why me? But the answer was in my occupation: Mr. Fixit. It was my job. Even if Satan handled the punishment part, I had to do the stopping on my own.

"No, not yet. Satan was very specific with my instructions. He wants me to handle it."

Pinkerton looked at me skeptically. "And how is one person going to stop a horde of angry damned souls?"

"Good question. I'm sure not going to do it with duct tape." I went to the window of our trailer. The bleak night-that-was-never-quite-night of Hell bathed everything in shadow. Outside was the faint outline of a pile of bricks left over from a patio Orson and I had built for Asmodeus a while ago. The bricks gave me an idea. "Allan, I have a plan, but I'm going to need your help. And Orson's."

I picked up the phone and called the construction site. The phone rang a long time. While it was ringing, I considered the possibility of the line being bugged but put the worry from my mind. I didn't think the Hellions could pull it off, and if the line was indeed tapped, it would be by Ernestine, the demon of the Telephone, and she worked for my side.

My side: the thought made me ill. I was on Satan's side. Great. And here I was plotting against lost souls, just like mine, damned for all Eternity, who were desperately trying to escape a fate I wasn't sure all of them deserved.

But it was my job. Besides, if they actually succeeded in escaping from Hell, chaos would ensue, and not the kind that Satan would appreciate, I was pretty sure.

After fifteen rings, Orson picked up. "What is it, Steve?" he asked when he heard my voice. "I'm kind of busy here."

"Sorry. Listen, Pinkerton and I have figured it out." Hurriedly, I explained about the Hellions' escape plan.

Orson whistled. "Those guys must have stones as big as bowling balls to try something like this. Satan will fry them!"

"Maybe, but that will come later. We're going to be the ones to stop them. This is what I want you to do ..." In a few words, I described what was needed. "Can you manage it?"

"Sure. It might slow things up here for an hour or two, but no more. I'll get it done."

"Thanks," I replied tightly and hung up. My love life might have been in the toilet but at least other things were falling into place. I turned to Allan. "And this is your part in the plan ..."

"That's all?" he replied, after I explained what he needed to do.

"Yes, but it has to be on my signal," I said, handing him a key to the Elevator, which he pocketed in his trench coat. "You've got the signal, right?"

"Aye, but Ah dinae understand it."

"You wouldn't. It's after your time. Just listen for it."

"Aye, Steve. Okay," he amended. "So I'll see you around one?"

"Yes, it can't happen any earlier."

"We're taking a big chance trying to handle this on our own, boyo."

"Boyo. You've called me boyo before, but isn't that Welsh or something?" I looked at Pinkerton with suspicion. "Come to think of it, your whole Scottish schtick seems kind of inconsistent to me. I could have sworn 'eejit' was Irish, not Scottish."

Allan grinned. When he spoke again, it was in perfect, uninflected English. "Yes, but it's colorful, isn't it?"

"You do this for effect?" Sounded kind of exhausting to me.

"Sure. I spent most of my life in the States. And my friends down here, the few I have, anyway, like you, well, they're all Yanks. It's hard to keep a Scottish brogue for Eternity. Hell, I've even forgotten what little Gaelic I knew."

"So, 'blatherskite' and all that is just so much blarney, huh?"

"No, that one's real. But I've forgotten more than I remember."

"We're getting off point here." I was ready to wrap things up. Pulling out a piece of paper, I wrote a quick note and stuffed it up the pneumatic tube. "I'm going to try to handle this by myself, because that's what Satan told me to do, but there's no point being stupid about this. I just let Beezy know what's going on."

"Good idea. Conforms to the letter of your instructions but lets one of the big guns know in case things get out of hand."

"Yeah. He's also likely to be up Gates Side when this all goes down, helping me with my Escalator problem. If they get by me, I'd like to see them get by Beezy - or Peter."

"Aye. I mean, yeah. And I'll have a ringside seat." Pinkerton got up. "Think I'll go home for a while, then."

"*Home*," I said fuzzily. I was suddenly possessed with a great weariness. "You have a *home*?"

"Just a room off my workshop, but it's mine. You?"

"Yeah, I have a place, too." Not nice, like Flo's. The thought was bitter. She had a real home but then she was a real person; I was just one of the damned and 'my place' more of a holding tank.

Still, I wanted to get out of my evening clothes. And now I felt the need to get away from my office, be by myself for a spell.

Pinkerton and I left at the same time and, for a while at least, went our separate ways.

Chapter 20

Nighttime is Hell, Take Two - Action:

"We're born alone, we live alone, we die alone." Orson said that to me once - I think he had been quoting himself from life - but he was right.

I was lying in bed, twisted up in my bed sheets, watching each painful minute of the alarm clock tick by, waiting for Hell's version of night to come to an end.

There was something else Orson had told me, probably another self-quote: "Only through our love and friendship can we create the illusion for the moment that we're not alone." The thought sent a sudden muscle spasm through the length of my back, squeezing the air from my lungs. The pain wasn't really physical, but spiritual, just minor torment for a soul holding a long-term lease in Hell.

I usually had that pain when thinking back on my life, and this was no exception. There were many people who had populated my forty-some mortal years on Earth: parents, a couple of siblings, grandparents, aunts, uncles, cousins, nieces, nephews. Childhood friends. Adult friends. Students and colleagues. A wife, who eventually became an ex-wife. True, my marriage hadn't produced any children, but other than that, I'd had the typical menagerie of human companions everyone else had.

But did that make me any less alone in life? No. Like Orson said, aloneness was the reality; togetherness was the illusion. For my whole life, I, like everyone else, had lived in the solitary confinement of my own skull - the trappings of family, friends and colleagues were simply that: trappings, window dressing.

Humans were called social creatures but, writhing on my bed in the depths of Hell, I knew the truth.

There is no joining of mind to mind. Humans aren't ants; we aren't bees. There is no communal intelligence. We talk but we don't really hear each other. We are not a community, no matter how we pretend otherwise. A million people are simply a million social isolates, each one imprisoned within his or her own brain pan, in which a very private Hell plays out.

We are alone. We are always alone.

Great. If we hadn't puzzled out this simple truth in our miserable lifetimes, we got an Eternity in Hell to work through it.

I sat up in a frenzy. From my sweat-soaked body, I tore away the bed sheet and threw it to the floor. Out of the darkness came the chittering of roaches as they swarmed over the new soft thing that now lay on shabby carpet, sampled the dampness the fabric had leeched from a desperate, lost and defeated soul. I squeezed my temples between my palms; a migraine was forming, and it promised to be a whopper. My back and my breast burned with an agonizing pain.

Tonight I finally understood what all those poems had really been about. As an undergraduate, I'd made fun of the English majors, those moony-eyed sillies who were moved to tears by love poems, like Elizabeth Barrett Browning's 'How do I Love You' or Shakespeare's Love Sonnets. Now I knew, though, that they weren't love poems at all, but the desperate cries of tortured souls, yearning for respite from their loneliness.

The first line of Shakespeare's Sonnet 116 came to me now, unbidden:

Let me not to the marriage of true minds
Admit impediments.

The marriage of minds? What a crock, this joining, two becoming one. It contradicted everything I knew.

Yet ... here at last in Hell, tonight with Flo, maybe I'd achieved it. Yes, for a brief while we were one. There was consolation in the thought. Even if I never saw Flo again, I had experienced love, the joining of souls. For an instant I had escaped Hell and gained Paradise.

And then it was ruined, made into a cheap little porn film for Satan and his pals to laugh over.

Fuck!

The light from the fire at the oil refinery shone through the cracked glass of my studio. The illumination was enough for anyone who cared to see that I was now crying uncontrollably.

Hell is being alone. Heaven is release from that loneliness.

Satan could humiliate me over and over; my punishment was eternal. Why, I did not know, but I now understood that, while Hell might be the preservation of man's essential separateness, it was possible to experience more. Even if I would never feel it again, I had once.

No, damn it! I'm not giving up yet.

I turned on the light by my bed and got up, moving to a small desk in the corner of the room. The roaches scattered and the room was empty, except for me and my thoughts. Buck naked, I sat down in the desk chair, pulled out paper and a pen, and began to write.

My Darling Flo,

Tonight, being with you, I realized what Paradise was. I knew Heaven in your arms.

Forget about the devils. Forget about their tawdry schemes, their puerile little movie. They are only envious of what we have and are trying to drive us apart. All that's important is that we stay together.

I thought I knew what love was, but I didn't. I do now. I love you, dearest Flo. And I know that you love me.

Yours through Eternity,

Steve

I read through my note. It sure wasn't Shakespeare. Seemed to me like there should have been more adjectives involved; I should have taken some creative writing courses in college. Oh, well, at least it was heart-felt.

I'd take the note to her at the hospital the next morning, first thing, before the insanity of the day began. Flo always got to work early, even earlier than me. She'd see that we were meant to be together, that we would be together, no matter what obstacles Hell put between us.

I stretched out on the mattress and waited for the alarm clock to signal the start of day.

Cut, Nighttime is Hell, Take Two

My hand was on the alarm the moment it sounded. I headed for the shower. My soap and shampoo were gone, and the water was yellow-brown again, but old habits die hard, so I hopped in the stall. The freezing water took my breath away and no twisting of the hot water knob made any difference. I finished quickly. Whatever you say about a shower in Hell, it wakes a soul up.

I shaved, nicking myself, like most every morning. Pulling my coveralls out of the closet, I noted without surprise that the dinner suit and overcoat were gone.

Big deal. You can have them, Roachy Godmother. I have Flo.

I went over to the desk and found an envelope for my love note. I wrote Flo's name on the outside in a large, bold hand. Or so I thought. "Good grief," I muttered, looking at the envelope again. It looked like a thirteen-year old girl had written on it. The letters were all curly. I had even made hearts out of the dots above the 'I's in Nightingale. Shaking my head, I picked up the note to read it once more before sealing the envelope.

> *Hey Toots,*
>
> *Tonight, you were great in the sack. Tonight, that is. Don't know if it would be the same tomorrow.*
>
> *I'll never forget about the devils. Good thing they got it all recorded. That way everybody can watch you and me play hide the salami over and over again.*
>
> *I didn't know you could do that thing with your mouth. I do now. You're great at it, babe. And I know you enjoyed things from your end - a lot, if all that moaning meant anything. Or maybe you were just faking it, eh? Hey, you know what a mistress is? Halfway between a mister and a mattress. Ha-ha-ha!*

We should try it again, sometime, but not too soon. I mean, after all, we're stuck here through Eternity, and spending time with you might get old real fast.

Steve

I tore the letter into a hundred pieces. Even a simple love note they had to pervert.

Very well. I'll tell her myself.

Slamming the apartment door behind me, I headed to the hospital.

Things were unusually quiet that morning. The waiting room was all but empty. The few patients who were there were leaning over in their hospital gowns to make their butts into good targets for Uphir, who was idly throwing darts at them.

"Where's Flo?" I asked him gruffly, being in no mood to deal with the demon physician.

"Oh, hey, Steve!" Uphir said with a big smile. "Flo? Oh, she's come and gone already."

"What? That's not like her."

Uphir shrugged. "I know, I know. Can't understand it, but she took one look at the morning paper and went back home."

"The paper? Where? Show me."

The demon normally had a trigger temper but this morning he was all cooperation. He found the paper on one of the chairs in the waiting room and handed it to me. "I guess something in it upset her," he said, looking innocently up at the ceiling.

The newspaper was open to the entertainment section. The featured article was a review of 'Flo Does The Super.'

Crap.

As I read through the review, I could feel my face turn red.

Flo's First Film Shows Great Promise
a review of 'Flo Does The Super'

Bifrons, Demon of Science and the Arts
(UPI: Underworld Press International)

Who would have thought it? Our own Florence Nightingale, well, technically not our own, but ours by her own choice, has proven herself the next Marilyn Chambers, queen of pornographic cinema.

Miss Nightingale, where did you get that sinfully great body? Your knockers alone would make a demon swoon. Yes, the whole package is a luscious feast for the eyes. And boy does she know how to use that package!

In 'Flo Does The Super,' Miss Nightingale demonstrates a rare talent for sexual calisthenics. Costarring Hell's Super, Steve Minion, she does it every which way you could imagine. Though Minion has ample airtime, he actually has a rather, ahem, small part. Still, he enthusiastically tries to keep up with Nightingale in her first dirty dance.

Yet it is Miss Nightingale herself who commands the picture. On top, on the bottom, sideways, you name it. The climax of the movie (no pun intended) demonstrates a breathtaking command of, well, I won't give away the ending, but let me say I have just coined a new word: 'Floratio.'

> *I have it on good authority that this titillating masterpiece will soon be playing in every movie house in every circle of Hell. Satan himself has ordered a personal copy for his private theater down on Nine. So, take it from me: Run, don't walk, to the nearest cinema and see 'Flo Does The Super.' I promise you won't be disappointed.*

Oh, no.

"Personally," Uphir said with a leer, "I don't think the review gives you nearly enough credit, even if your part is small."

I threw the paper to the floor. "Up yours, Uphir."

"No, thanks," he said, laughing so hard bloody tears streaked his face. "Your part is too small!"

I hurried out of the hospital, Uphir still laughing hysterically behind me. I had to get to Flo, had to make this right somehow.

Running had never been one of my strong sports and I was wheezing when her apartment building came in sight. With a last burst of energy, I took the stairs two at a time to the second floor.

Knock, knock.

No one answered. I knocked again.

"Go away," said a tearful voice from inside.

"Flo, honey, it's me - Steve."

"You especially go away. I don't want to see you. You betrayed me."

"*What?* No, no, NO! Satan scammed me as much as he did you."

"Did not."

"Did, too," I said, gasping.

"Why does your voice sound so funny?"

"I ran here from the hospital and am a little out of breath. Also, I'm talking through a door. Let me in, please."

"No."

"Come on. This is childish."

"Childish? You seduced me and you think it's childish that I'm upset? Oh, Steve," she said, misery dripping from her words, "how could you? You've made me worthy of Hell, just as Satan wanted."

"What?" I couldn't believe my ears. "First off, I didn't seduce you. The feelings were mutual. You know they were."

"I don't know anything anymore," Flo said in a small voice. "All I know is I am a laughingstock. What's worse, I have sinned and now truly belong in Hell. I am damned for all Eternity, just like you."

Oh no. I understood the humiliation but hadn't considered she'd see our lovemaking as sinful. "Flo, you have it all wrong." Damn, I wished she'd open the stupid door. "Sin is for the mortal realm. You're dead. You can't sin in Hell. It's irrelevant here, impossible."

"It is?" she sniffed.

"Yes, of course. Now, let me in, please."

"No."

I slammed my head against the door in frustration and I heard her jump back. She must have been standing right next to it. A few doors along the hallway opened and several of the other occupants in the building peered out at me. One, an old man with a severe case of gout, scowled and shook his cane at me. I pointed at the back of my coveralls, where the HOTI acronym was prominently displayed, and waved him and the others away. The doors banged closed in rapid succession.

I took a breath and let it out slowly. Feeling a little calmer, I tried again. "Flo, why won't you let me in?"

"Because, whether you're right or not ..."

"I am. You could walk into Heaven right now, I'm sure." Well, I wasn't completely sure, but I was pretty sure.

"I'm still angry with you."

"But I didn't do anything wrong."

"Whether intentional or not, you embarrassed me, helped humiliate me. People won't respect me anymore." She sniffled. "How can I ever show my face in the hospital again?"

"Flo, just be who you have always been. This will blow over and you will be able to go back to succoring those in need."

"Succor?" she said suspiciously. "Is that supposed to be a play on words?"

"How?"

"Well," she paused. "You know. Suck."

"What? No, no. I meant giving comfort! Please let me in."

"No."

Argghh. "Flo, I have to get to work."

"Good. Go away."

"Sweetheart," I said desperately, "you know how I feel about you."

Flo was quiet for a moment. "I don't know. I don't know anything right now. I just need my privacy."

"When can I see you?"

"I don't know," she said again. "I'll contact you. Please, if you care for me the way you say you do, leave now."

And what could be said to that? So I left.

My heart felt like an anvil in my chest that I carried on my slow walk to the office. There was nothing to do about my situation with Flo, not at the moment, nothing to do about the Escalator until Beezy could gain Heaven's cooperation in tracing the bad circuit. I couldn't really even help with the Stairway. Orson had that under control. My showdown with the Hellions was hours away, so I had some time to kill. For the first time since my sojourn in Hell began, I punched in late.

So what?

I went to make the coffee.

As I started on my first cup, a splat from the pneumatic tube signaled an incoming work order. From long habit, I picked it up. "Fix the damn PA system," was all it said, but it was signed Beelzebub, Lord of the Flies. With a sigh, I got to work.

It took a few hours but I finally found a loose wire running from the main switch. After tightening it, Beezy's voice boomed over the PA system. "It's about time."

"You're welcome," I muttered, sending the work order back to him by tube. "Sign please."

The paperwork came back almost before I finished saying please. "Don't be smart with me, Minion."

"I wouldn't dream of it."

"Did Welles finish the extra job?"

I sat down at my desk and took another sip of coffee. "Don't know. Haven't called him yet."

Siren-like noises came over the PA system, like the sounds of a KGB raid or the alarms that went off after a Stalag breakout in 'Hogan's Heroes.' "Minion!"

"Fine," I said, grabbing the phone and dialing Orson. For some reason I wasn't in the mood to be pleasant to my boss this morning. For some reason. Go figure.

Surprisingly, Orson caught it on the second ring. "Hi, Steve. Yes, it's done, and the stairs are, too, or nearly so. We'll be finished shortly. By noon at the latest. I can stall, though, so they're not open until exactly one."

"Actually, as I think about it, noon might be better."

"Why?"

"Two miles of stairs. How long do you think it would take you to climb them?"

"Me? As fat as I am? Probably an eternity. But I see what you mean. No way they can get to Topside before one."

"Right, and they should be pretty tuckered even so. Thanks, Orson. Thanks for everything. Oh, any sounds from down below?"

"Yeah. People have been hanging around entrances to the Stairway all night. Most of the stairs below Level Two are completely full. Like they thought we wouldn't notice." He snorted. "They must think we're complete idiots."

"Either that or they are."

Orson laughed. "Or we all are."

I chuckled for the first time that morning. It felt good. "You said it. Listen, Beezy's on the horn, so I've gotta go. Just time the completion of the Stairs as we've discussed, and Pinkerton and I will handle the rest. Oh, you and your crew should get off the Stairway as soon as it's finished. Those steps are likely to be more crowded than Macy's on Black Friday."

"Okay. Bye, Steve."

"Bye." I had held down the PA transmit button while on the line with Orson. "Get all that, Fat Boy?"

"How dare you?"

"Oh, man, Beelzebub, oh great Lord of the Flies," I said, with a bucket load of insincerity. It was like I had a death wish today, though, already being dead, that was pretty much impossible. Yet every part of me felt the rebel. "Forgive me, great Beelzebub. I got you and Orson confused for a sec. An honest mistake."

"Your sarcasm is worse than your insolence, Minion. Yes I heard it. Are you sure you and Pinkerton can handle this?"

I considered the question carefully, even though, at the moment, I didn't give a flying fuck about any of my plans. "Yes, I think so, but having you up Topside at the same time will be good. If I can't hold back the masses, you'll be there."

An evil chuckle came over the PA's speaker. "I almost hope they get by you. Blasting through a few thousand insurrectionists sounds like fun."

"Yeah, well the way I feel right now, I agree, so let me have my shot at them first, okay?"

"That's fine by me. I'd like to see if one human soul can put down ten thousand others. I haven't witnessed something like that since Samson, the showoff. Should be entertaining. Oh," Beezy said casually, "by the way, loved the movie."

I smacked my forehead. "Jeez, has everyone seen it?"

"Are you kidding? It's already out on Blu-ray. I've watched it on my big screen five times, in 3D, though I hate those damn glasses. Still, it's better than in the theater, because I can stop the action anytime I want and ..."

I'd had enough of this. I started jiggling the recently-tightened wire. "Beezy, sorry. I'm having a hard time hearing you. What was that? I think the PA's failing again. SEE YOU AT ONE!" I shouted then yanked out the wire. The PA system went dead.

There. I'll fix it later.

The pneumatic tube spat out another work order. "Fix the damn PA system - Beelzebub."

I'll fix it later.

I sat in my office, staring at the walls and sipping coffee until about Noon. Then I stood up and stretched, grabbed a couple of iced-down blood bags and stepped outside. With a whistle and a shout, I called for BOOH.

He was as prompt as usual, but instead of hovering above me, he dropped down on the pavement at my side. "Hey, BOOH," I said fondly, scratching him behind the ears. "We've got a few minutes before you need to whisk me Topside, but I thought you might like to have these." I held both bags up in my hands. BOOH licked his lips in a way that, two days earlier, would have given me the heebie-jeebies. Now I just thought it was cute.

I tossed him the bags. He caught one in each claw and settled down on the concrete to enjoy his snack.

"Steve! Oh, Steve!" shouted a voice. Dora was calling to me from the Parts building. I walked across the street to see what she wanted.

The old blonde hag took a drag from her menthol cigarette before she spoke. "I have that special order for you." Dora reached to a shelf out of sight and pulled out a bullhorn. "IT WORKS, TOO!" she said, demonstrating.

After my ears stopped ringing, I took the item from her.

Good. I probably could have managed without it, but this would make things easier.

"Oh, by the way, the bulb for the sign at Hell's gate just came in, too."

"Oh, great," I said, not really meaning it. "I'm heading to Gates Level in a few minutes. Might as well take care of the sign while up there."

"Sign here," she indicated on her form. I scrawled my John Hancock, and she handed me the bulb. It was about the size of a block of ice. Fortunately, it didn't weigh nearly as much as that; I could lift it easily.

Chapter 21

By the time I had gotten back to the trailer with the bulb and the bullhorn, BOOH had finished his snacks. I sat down next to him as he was licking the last drops of blood from the second donor bag.

"You know, BOOH, one way or another, today is going to see the end of my special assignment. After that, I don't think Satan will let you ferry me around Hell anymore."

BOOH shrugged. Well, it looked like a shrug to me.

"I just wanted to say, uh," I cleared my throat, "well, it's been an honor working with you."

BOOH raised his bulk off the pavement and balanced awkwardly on one foot; the other one he stuck out in my direction. It took me a second to understand what he was doing. I smiled.

He wanted to shake. I took his clawed foot in both hands and held it firmly. He squeezed back, no doubt a gentle pressure for him, but still one that nearly broke my fingers. I ignored the pain. "Thanks, BOOH. Thanks for everything."

We would have looked ridiculous if there had been anyone around who could have seen, especially if they'd noticed me tearing up. "Okay, pal," I said, letting his foot go before he completely lost his balance and fell over. "Are you ready to wrap this up?"

"Urm."

I held the bullhorn in my left hand and tucked the light bulb under the same arm. It was a little awkward but I needed my other arm for the grand gesture. With my right index finger I pointed dramatically to the sky. "Then let's fly, partner!"

"Skree!" The two of us shot upward.

As the wind flowed against my cheeks, I was once again exhilarated. It was a heady feeling rocketing through the skies of the Netherworld with BOOH, slipping through ring after ring of Hell. We were off to stop the hordes of Hell, or at least some of them, from breaking free. I remembered a Western song that had played on the radio my entire life. Two lines in particular seemed to fit our current circumstances:

... You will ride
Tryin' to catch the devil's herd,
across these endless skies

The song was called 'Ghost Riders in the Sky'

Hmm. 'Ghost Rider' was a promising superhero name. I was dead, after all, so it fit. But like Batman, Ghost Rider had already been taken. At least BatRider wasn't under copyright protection.

In seconds, Ghost Rider or BatRider, or just 'Little Steve Minion and his Gargantuan Friend,' shot out of the Mouth of Hell. We circled a couple of times above the throng of souls waiting to be judged. BOOH must have sensed I was in a theatrical mood and was making sure our entrance had a lot of flair.

Then we shot to the ground and he released me. I landed without a stumble, even holding the light bulb and bullhorn. A perfect ten.

"Very nice," a voice behind me said. It was St. Peter. "You've certainly got the landing down."

"Thanks ... I guess." Peter had never paid me a compliment, so he was probably just being sarcastic.

"So am I going to have a visitor from Hell soon?"

Yeah. In fact, a lot more than he was expecting. But what I said was, "Yes, St. Peter. Lord Beelzebub will be here shortly with a written request."

The saint scratched his long, white beard. "Beezy, huh? Haven't seen that old coot in a while. He's high enough in the organization, so that should do it."

Gates Level seemed especially crowded to me. "Lots of new souls here today. More than usual." It made me a bit nervous, knowing the chaos that was about to go down. Extra souls up here could cause even more confusion when the shit hit the fan.

"Yes, well, last night was Friday back on Earth. We usually get a bumper crop on Saturday morning, what with all the car wrecks from drunken driving, people dying from drug overdoses, cases of domestic violence and other acts of mortal stupidity. The whole weekend in fact is like this, especially Monday morning. You'd be amazed how many people commit suicide rather than face another Monday morning."

"Do tell," I mumbled absently.

"Well, I've spent long enough chatting with you, Minion, unless you have some news to share."

There was plenty of news but all I said was, "The Stairway is finished and will open shortly. You won't need to watch devils shoving damned souls into the Mouth of Hell anymore." *And pretty soon,* I added mentally, *you might very well be overrun by thousands of Hell's minions, all bent on escaping the damnation to which you had helped consign them. Best of luck with that.*

"Well, that's good." He looked at the package under my arm. "And I see you have a replacement bulb for your sign. That's good, too. It looks stupid with that bug light in it."

I turned to go.

"Minion, wait a second. I wanted to ask you something."

"Yes, sir?"

"What is that thing above the Stairway entrance that BOOH has just landed on?" BOOH was settling right where he could get the best view. I waved to him.

"Oh, that," I said, trying to appear nonchalant. "We're just trying to dress up the new Entrance to Hell."

"It doesn't look very good to me."

"We're just getting started," I responded, with a gleam in my eye. "You'll see."

"Whatever," St. Peter muttered as he walked back to his podium and began processing some more dead souls.

I looked at the bulb in my hand and decided to install it while waiting for the action to begin. Except ... no ladder. Damn.

I was puzzling over how to get the bulb up to the sign when Tesla, Edison and Pinkerton came out of the Elevator. I glanced at my wristwatch, generally a pretty useless device. However, because it was a Casio, when it served Hell's purposes, the thing kept pretty good time. My watch was showing 12:55. That seemed about right.

No time to install the bulb, anyway. The show was about to begin.

Pinkerton gave me a wave then walked over to the entrance to Hell's Stairway. The other two came over to me. "Wasn't that Allan Pinkerton who rode up with us?" Edison asked.

"Yes, what of it?"

"What's he doing here?"

"None of your business. Good morning, Nicky," I said pleasantly to Tesla. "Beezy should be here shortly and you ought to be able to get to work. Meanwhile, could you hold onto this light bulb for me?"

"Da, Steve." Tesla walked over to the Escalator and sat down.

Edison hadn't left. He looked at me in irritation. "Why are you nice to him but treat me like shit?"

"Don't talk like that up here," I said automatically. "It's because I like him. I don't like you."

"Why, Minion? What did I ever do you? I died decades before you were even born."

You disappointed a child who once thought you were a hero.

But instead of saying that, I pointed at Tesla. "He's one reason. I don't like the way you treated him in life."

Edison sniffed. "That was business. Besides, what's it to you?"

"It offends my sense of fair play."

"Oh, what a baby you are."

"And I don't like how you and Ford are always telling me how to run my department."

"That's because you suck at it!" he snapped.

"Of course I do, you moron!" I snapped back, and Edison looked as if I'd hit him, probably not because of my tone but because I'd just called the Wizard of Menlo Park a moron. "This is Hell. This is my damnation. I'm supposed to be bad at my job. If I were good at it, like either you or Ford would be, I wouldn't have the job. Good grief, Tommy," I said, surprised at myself for actually calling him by his first name, "you've been in Hell sixty years longer than I have and you still don't get how the system works?"

"Oh," muttered Edison, reddening. "Oh, right. I'd never have been given your job. I would have liked it too much."

"Right. Now run along and play with Tesla. Beezy will be here soon."

Edison trudged over to Tesla and sat down next to him. In a few moments, they were playing Rock, Paper, Scissors again.

BOOM!

An explosion shook Gates Level, and a mushroom cloud rose out of the Mouth of Hell. Beelzebub stepped out of the cloud and onto the celestial firmament.

"See here, Beelzebub!" St. Peter exclaimed, rushing up to him. "I don't appreciate you stinking up the place with your brimstone. Besides, there are some souls here destined for Heaven and you're scaring them."

"Bite me, Pete," Beezy grumbled, then handed the saint an extravagantly embroidered envelope.

Peter went over to his desk and with a letter opener shaped like a tiny sword slit open the envelope. He read it through. "Yes, everything seems in order."

I walked up to my boss. "Bureaucrat," the Lord of the Flies muttered, then turned to me. "Are you ready?"

"Yes, sir. Me and Pinkerton both," I added, pointing to the Scotsman stationed next to the Stairway. "I'm going to head down the stairs now."

Beelzebub looked at me skeptically. "You'll be trampled."

I gulped. "Maybe, but maybe not. Anyway, if they get by me, you'll be here to stop them."

"Me and Peter both," he said, echoing my bad grammar back to me. "I may not like that supercilious saint but he can break heads with the best of them, if need be. Still," Beezy said, winking at me, "let's keep all this from him ... until the last minute. Sort of a surprise, if you get my drift."

I grinned. "That was my thought, too."

Beezy chuckled. "You know, Minion, maybe Satan is right. Maybe we should make you a lesser demon. You've certainly got the talent."

A rare compliment. "Thanks, boss, but you know, my eternal damnation and all."

He slapped me convivially on the back. "Right you are, boy! Now, get down the stairs and do your thing."

"Yes, sir," I replied, getting off the floor where his gesture of camaraderie had knocked me. "Oh, could you get the boys on both ends of the fence tracing the wire? We might as well get something done while we're waiting."

He looked at me, amused, and nodded.

I headed toward the Stairway, bullhorn in hand. What had he found so funny? Devils. Go figure.

Pinkerton nodded at me as I began my descent. He'd be ready; Allan was the kind of person you could count on. I went down about fifty steps and stopped.

I didn't have to wait long. Within minutes, there was an echoing rumble, the sound of thousands of feet pounding rapidly against the stairs. The noise grew, becoming a great thundering that overwhelmed me, making me feel like birdshot rattling in a tin can. They'd be running on adrenaline by now. Exhausted, but so close.

My heart was hammering in my chest. "Show time," I said to myself.

When the noise grew to a torrent of sound, a black mop of hair showed as it made the turn on the landing beneath me. Right behind were a bald pate and another head with an enormous mass of wiry curls. The three men looked up and I finally saw them: the leaders of the Free Hellions, the greatest anarchists who had ever lived.

Moe, Larry and Curly: The Three Stooges. I'd been right.

It had all clicked last night, after I blocked the eye gouge Putty Face had tried to give me. On returning to my office and spending some time staring at the logo on the Free Hellions flyer, I had been sure of it.

It wasn't some mystical symbol, like what you'd find on a dollar bill, just something imminently practical. (After all, I wasn't dealing with Freemasons; I was dealing with idiots.) The rigid, extended hand protected you from getting poked in the eyes, which was a signature bit of physical humor the Stooges routinely employed in their two-reelers.

I held the bullhorn to my mouth. "STOP! STAY WHERE YOU ARE!"

Boy, I was glad I'd brought the thing. Otherwise, twenty thousand footsteps (do the math) would have completely drowned out my voice. I startled them and the Stooges halted in surprise. The four people behind them, Shemp and the three Joes, couldn't stop their momentum, but knocked Moe, Larry and Curly over, landing on top of them.

Shemp Howard, Putty Face, older brother to Moe and Curly, in fact, sort of a Moe look-alike, though a mite uglier. I'd heard that in life he'd been a really nice guy, sort of a gentle soul. But even though he'd been a Stooge before his baby brother came on the scene, and after, when Curly's health failed at a relatively young age, Shemp had never been the star of the act. Curly had, and so when people thought of the Three Stooges, it was always with Curly in the third slot.

I wondered, standing there and staring down at the Stooges - and the Hellions that were beginning to stack up behind them, like passengers trying to go through the turnstiles of a busy subway station - if Shemp had begun to resent his second-tier status. Perhaps resentment had turned to anger, which was the only way I'd ever seen Putty Face - angry. As for the three Joes - Joe Palmer, Joe Besser, and Joe DeRita (Curly Joe) - each had substituted for Shemp or Curly at various times after the two had been incapacitated or died.

The seven lying on the landing disentangled themselves from each other and stood. They approached me now, Moe at the fore, as always. Moe Howard, the leader of the Stooges for almost fifty years on Earth, maintained his authority over them even after death. He approached me now with the angry frown that was so familiar to me. It was a bit intimidating but I held my ground.

Like lightning, my free hand went to my nose, deflecting the eye poke.

"Oh, a wise guy, eh?"

"Moe," I said, standing on the same step with him, "you can't do this. Nobody escapes from Hell."

"We'll see about that. Now move aside."

The remaining stooges, all six of them, followed by Marx, Lenin and Trotsky, who had just made the turn in the landing, came up behind Moe. I tried once more to reason with him. "Even if you get through, where will you go? They won't let you into Heaven."

Moe looked back at his two brothers and Larry. "We know that. We're going back to Earth."

"Earth?"

"Yeah," Larry said. "We're going to start up the act again."

"Whoop whoop whoop!" Curly opined.

Shemp was more direct. "What do you think we are - stupid?"

"Well, yes," I confessed. "At least you are if you go any farther."

Moe shoved me roughly against the wall. "Get out of our way." Then Moe Howard, his face exalted, as if he had reached the end of a quest, continued to climb the stairs, the other leaders of the insurrection following in his wake.

The remainder of the Hellions had stayed back, its vanguard stopped on the landing below. They began to surge forward now. I only had seconds to act before being overcome.

I put the bullhorn to my mouth. "MOE! IF YOU MAKE IT BACK TO EARTH, DON'T FORGET TO VISIT NIAGARA FALLS!"

"Niagara Falls!" Moe screamed, pivoting on one heel. His eyes locked onto mine, and he moved toward me, as if he'd lost control of his motions, his goal, so close, forgotten for the moment.

The old Niagara Falls bit: many comedians had claimed to have written this classic bit of shtick, and still more had performed it, but to me the Three Stooges immortalized it.

"Slowly I turned ... step by step ... inch by inch ..."

At that moment Pinkerton pulled the cord and a mountain of brick and rubble fell, sealing off the Stairway.

Moe, shaken out of his compulsion by the noise of the manmade avalanche, turned to see the blocked exit. "What ... what did you do?" he said in a daze.

"I," I began through the bullhorn then, realizing it was overkill, lowered it. "I stopped you. You're not supposed to leave Hell, Moe. None of us is."

Moe Howard, leader of the Three Stooges, Leader of the Free Hellions, stared at me, wide-eyed, a lost child in an afterlife far beyond his understanding. And then he began to cry.

Shemp, Curly, and Larry - a brother to Moe in all but blood - rushed to him, wrapping their arms around the devastated man, trying to comfort him.

I felt like a heel.

Bright red light flooded the Stairway and the smell of sulfur filled the air. We all looked up. Beelzebub, Prince of Hell, Lord of the Flies, stood at the top of the stairs. He snapped his fingers and my body collapsed in upon itself, like a baby black hole. ***POP!*** it went, and then ***POP!*** again. I found myself standing next to Beezy. "Nicely done," he whispered to me. "My turn now."

"CURSED HUMANS, YOU DARE QUESTION YOUR PLACE IN THE AFTERLIFE? WHO ARE YOU TO DEFY HELL? YOU ARE DAMNED, ALL OF YOU. NOW BEGONE!"

Beezy filled his lungs, and with a single puff of air blew all the Hellions down the Stairway, back to where they belonged. I don't know exactly where they ended up but most likely each soul stopped precisely at the Level of Hell to which it had been consigned. Such was the power of Beelzebub.

And there were probably devils and demons waiting to greet them.

Now I felt sick to my stomach.

"Well, that was fun, wasn't it?" Beezy put a hand on my shoulder and pushed me toward the rubble. I went ***POP! POP!*** again and found myself before St. Peter's desk.

"What in the name of all Heaven was that about?" he said.

Beezy winced. "Do you have to use that word? Anyway, some of the damned were trying to make a break from Hell, using the new Stairway. I stopped them," he looked over at me, "with a little help from Minion here. Everything's fine for now," he said casually, "but we're going to have to put some security measures in place to see it doesn't happen again."

"What do you have in mind?"

"Oh, nothing much. Minion, while I'm talking with St. Peter, why don't you get BOOH to help you install the new bulb?"

"Uh, sure." I glanced back briefly toward the Stairway entrance, which was covered in several tons of debris. BOOH, who temporarily must have been dislodged from his perch, was settled back on the rubble. Standing near the Elevator, waiting to ride down, was Pinkerton. He gave me a thumbs-up as he lifted the Elevator door then disappeared inside.

I walked over to the Escalator. Tesla was on his feet, looking worried. Even Edison seemed a little concerned.

"What happened?" they asked. Briefly, I told them. "How about you? Any luck with the Escalator?"

Nicky shook his head. "So far, nothing."

"Well, Beelzebub told me to put in the bulb. Nicky, let me have it. Oh, BOOH! Can you give me a hand here?"

BOOH flew lazily over to me. I told him what I needed to do and he obligingly lifted me up to the level of the insect repellent bulb. I pulled off the duct tape, took out the bulb, pulled out the piece of aluminum foil, inserted the replacement bulb and closed the casing. The sign lit up in full:

THROUGH ME YOU PASS INTO THE CITY OF WOE.
THROUGH ME YOU PASS INTO ETERNAL PAIN.
THROUGH ME GO THE PEOPLE LOST FOREVER.
ABANDON ALL HOPE YE WHO ENTER HERE.

And then the Escalator started to move.

BOOH deposited me lightly on the ground. I stared at the moving steps in disbelief, too stunned for the moment to speak.

Tesla was stroking his chin. "The Escalator is wired through the Sign."

Edison turned on me. "You numbskull!" he shouted. "It was your shoddy work all the time. You're the reason the Escalator broke!"

He was right. It had all been my fault.

A stream of obscene invective flowed from Edison's mouth. There was only one thing to do, so I pushed him into the Mouth of Hell.

His screams must have been heard all over the Underworld as he plunged six levels back to the Mines.

Chapter 22

"Bwahahahahahaha!" Beezy laughed, coming up to me. Tesla nodded deferentially toward the Lord of the Flies then fled to the Elevator. "I bet you enjoyed that."

"A bit. He was getting on my nerves. You knew all along, didn't you?" I asked, pointing at the sign.

"No comment." He looked around in satisfaction. "Well, looks like we wrapped everything up. I guess you should head on down and make your report to Satan."

"Right." I looked up at BOOH. "One more time?"

BOOH swooped down, snatched me by the shoulders, and hurtled down, down through the Mouth of Hell, down through the Nine Circles, and placed me on the carpet before Bruce the Bedeviled's desk. Then the Bat out of Hell went to his perch next to the Elevator.

Bruce looked up at me in annoyance. "I don't think you have an appointment."

I glared at him. "Look at your damn book! Bet you I do."

"No, you don't, I ... oh, well, apparently you do." He grumbled. "I wish He wouldn't do that."

The door to Satan's office flew open and I stepped inside. Satan was at his desk. He was in 'man in black' mode. I saw my own reflection in his dark sunglasses.

Before Satan's desk was a simple office chair, in black, with a leatherette cushion. Satan gestured toward the seat.

It beat the folding chair, and it was less pretentious, and in some ways more honest-seeming to me than the wingback before the fireplace. I settled down in the seat and waited.

For a long moment Satan sat quietly, looking at me. I didn't say anything, not out of fear or respect, but simply out of weariness. Well, perhaps a little resentment, and maybe some stubbornness, but mostly I felt the snot had just been beaten out of me. There was little in me left to give.

The Duke of Hell continued to stare at me. I stared back at him. For the first time, there in the presence of my lord and master, my gaze didn't waver. I just sat there, not blinking, giving as good as I got. Finally the Devil exhaled softly. "You want some explanations, I suppose?"

I shifted in my seat. "That would be appreciated."

"You realize I could just throw you out of here. I'm Satan, you know, and you're just a minion, Minion. I don't owe you a thing."

"I recognize that but I thought you might like to gloat or something."

Satan's lips curled slightly. "Cute. And I do like to gloat." He paused a moment longer, then sighed in exasperation. "Fine, Minion. Yes, I used you, just like I use everyone here. So what?"

By leaning forward, my elbows could reach the edge of Satan's desk, so I put them there, propping my head up with my hands. "So nothing." I knew that kind of tone could get me in trouble. I didn't care. Furthermore, I knew that he knew that I didn't care. And he knew that I knew that he knew that I didn't care.

Ad infinitum. Just like looking at your own reflection in a mirror, with another mirror placed behind you. Back and forth, back and forth, forever. For Eternity.

Damnation. I didn't even feel like throwing an exclamation point after the curse.

Satan smiled. "You know, Minion ... Steve, I actually kind of like you. As much as I like any of you poor human saps. Or anyone for that matter," he added on reflection. I wondered if he liked Beelzebub.

"Not really," he said, answering my unspoken question. "Oh, he's very good at what he does, and he's as close to being a friend of mine as is anyone anywhere, but I don't much like him. So, it being established that I don't particularly like anyone very much, even my best friend, my saying I kind of like you puts you in a very exclusive club."

This startled me. "Why, sir?"

The Lord of Hell shrugged. "I don't really know. You have a sort of integrity about you and, believe it or not, I respect integrity. That surprises you, I see," he said, lowering his glasses to reveal his ruby-colored eyes.

That didn't faze me either. No matter what Satan did, I was simply too whipped to be intimidated. But he was right about me being surprised. "Why do you like integrity?"

"Because it's rare, and it's refined, like that amontillado we shared. God has integrity, and even though we are locked in this useless, pointless, eternal struggle, I respect Him. Oh, you thought I didn't?"

"Well, you've been at each other's throats for an eternity, so I just assumed ..."

"Well, you assumed wrong. I respect Him. I respect you, a little. And I respect Nightingale."

"It was a nasty thing to do to her."

Satan chuckled. "It was, wasn't it?"

"She didn't deserve that."

"No, I suppose she didn't, but it was necessary."

"Why, sir?"

"Because, Minion, she has no business here!" Satan slammed his hand on his desk and, for the first time since I entered the room, showed some real emotion. "She has no right to be in Hell. How dare she just saunter down here on her own? What if everybody did that?"

"I doubt that many saints would be particularly enthused about coming to Hell."

"She's not a saint, not officially, anyway. I'm just saying that she set a precedent by coming down here without invitation. If she can deny Heaven and come to do good in Hell," at this point Satan almost spat on his own carpet, "then any do-goodnik can. And I can't have it."

"So you humiliated her?"

"Damn right I did!" Satan groused. "Maybe she'll take the hint and get the hell out of Hell."

I smiled for the first time since entering Satan's office. "Not likely, sir. You don't know her like I do."

"No," he said with a leer. "I don't know her Biblically, as you do, if you know what I mean."

"Ha-ha, sir."

A cold wind blew at my back. "Watch it, Minion. Don't forget your place."

I stood up to go. "Sorry, sir, but I'm just tired of the whole thing and, well, frankly I just don't give a damn."

"Rhett Butler. 'Gone with the Wind,' right?"

"Yes, sir. I guess," and I headed toward the door.

"Oh, sit down." Satan waved his hand at me, and the cold wind I'd felt a second ago picked me up and deposited me back in the guest chair.

I sat still for a moment, staring at the Lord of Hell. I was furious with Satan for what he had done to Flo, too furious at that moment to be afraid of him, yet my anger paralyzed my normally facile tongue. Finally, I found my voice. "You know she thinks she now deserves Hell, don't you? She thinks in having sex with me she's sinned and is eternally damned."

Satan's mouth hung open. I swear it was astonishment, which made me wonder just how omniscient he really was, but he closed it quickly and grinned. "That was a nice added benefit."

"Ha! Caught you by surprise, didn't it?"

The arms of my chair twisted around, grabbing my wrists and sinking metal teeth into them. I didn't care. "Go ahead, torture me. I'm dead, damned. What more can you do?" I said bitterly.

"A lot more than you can imagine," Satan said quietly as the chair released me, "but it's no fun if you're not scared."

"I'm too tired to be scared. Just answer me this. She isn't damned, is she? I told her that sin was for the mortal realm only, that sin doesn't exist in the afterlife."

"You did? I'm impressed. Not everyone gets that little subtlety, but you're right. Once you're dead, you're judged as either damned or saved. Nothing you do in the afterlife is of any consequence, morally speaking, that is. Nightingale's soul is as pure as the day she died."

"So, she could go to Heaven anytime she wants?" I looked at him hopefully.

Satan frowned but nodded. "Yes, that's true. See, Minion, even I have my own sense of integrity."

I shuddered as I exhaled. So, the one innocent in all of this had not been hurt. What a relief.

"I'm glad you feel better," Satan commented, sarcasm dripping from his voice.

"I just wished you hadn't used me to set her up."

"Who else? She liked you; you liked her. If she was going to climb in the sack with anyone, it would have been you."

Some consolation, I supposed. Not much, but some.

"Now that we've got that behind us, why don't you give me your report?"

"I doubt much of it is a surprise, since you probably manipulated just about everything that happened."

"Again, Minion, you impress me. You see things much more clearly than most humans do. Yes, I had a hand in everything that happened, but I'd like your interpretation of the events. Come on. I indulged you about Nightingale, so why don't you indulge me?"

"Fair enough." I got out of my chair and started to pace like the detective in a parlor mystery who is surrounded by all the chief suspects, except that in my case everything pointed to Satan. "First, the Escalator. The Hellions tried to sabotage it with the monkey wrench, but only a bunch of morons would use such a lame method to break the thing."

"True," Satan agreed, "but it was funny at least. What you would have expected from the Stooges. By the way, how did you figure out their identity?"

I shrugged. "After my evening at Red Square, I knew there were three of them - or four, if you count Shemp - and I heard their conversation. What with Curly's "whoop whoop whoops" and Shemp's "heep heep heeps," not to mention Moe's random acts of cruelty, I started to recognize something in their M.O." I was glad for all those Saturday mornings as a boy watching the comedy team on TV. My mom hated the Stooges but I adored them.

It's a guy thing.

"When Shemp tried to poke me in the eyes a second time in as many nights, I automatically protected myself the same way the Stooges did when I used to watch them on television. Then I thought of their mystic sign, the Niagara reference, and it all came back to me. Stopping them on the Stairway was easy. I just arranged to have Orson prepare a barrier at the top of the Stairway, and placed Pinkerton there to pull the rope that released the debris that would block their exit. All he had to do was await the signal."

"And what was that?"

I bit a loose nail. "Oh, he was to wait until he heard me yell 'Niagara Falls' over the bullhorn. Moe never could resist that bit."

"Clever." The Devil chuckled.

"My turn," I said, sitting back down. "You knew it was them all along, didn't you?"

Satan examined his own pedicure. His nails were very pointy and considerably longer than my own. "Why, sure."

"You told me earlier you didn't know who was behind the conspiracy."

"I lied," he said with a shrug. "I am the Prince of Lies, you know."

I nodded, processing the obvious. "That's true, but why, then, did we go through all of this? The whole escapade seems pretty pointless, really."

"Hope, Minion," he responded simply. "It's a basic human need. In this case it was false hope, but hope nonetheless. This is all part of the pain of damnation. People have to hope, then see that hope dashed to the ground, before they can truly suffer."

"So," I said with sudden understanding, "you must have been helping the Hellions from the beginning."

Satan tapped impatiently on his desktop with a pencil. "Of course, of course. I paid for the flyers, got my devils to paint that graffiti all over the place. Get humans all pumped up, give them an idea to gather around and then defeat them utterly. It's great fun, not to mention my job."

"What about the Stairway?"

"Oh, I've thought we needed a backup to the Escalator for quite a while. The stairs had fallen into disrepair and this seemed like a quick way to get things back in place."

"But," I protested, "Beezy had me tearing them down."

"Yeah, well, sometimes the old fart doesn't check with me first. He just goes off half-cocked. I want the Stairway retained and maintained. Still," he added with a grin, "the attempted jailbreak shows we need some added security."

"Like what?"

"Well, normally we don't need the Stairway. It's only if the Escalator breaks again that we'd need it. I'm already having Orson's men remove the treads between Gates Level and the First Circle."

"What?" I said, confused. "But that was the only part of the Stairway in good repair before this all started."

Satan started to chuckle. "I know. Peter had it built himself. In fact, he was the only one who ever used it." Satan's giggles turned into belly laughs.

"What's so funny?" I thought for a second. "Wait. This was all about getting back at St. Peter?"

"Yes," Satan gasped, still laughing. "He's been using the stairs to go play golf down on Level One, but he never pays his green fees. I got tired of it."

I scratched my head, puzzled. "So he can't play golf down on Level One. Big deal. Can't he just play in Heaven?"

"Of course he can, but it won't be the same for old Petey, now that he's played on a real course. It's the only thing we do better than Heaven."

"Beg pardon?"

"Build golf courses. Remember the old saying: 'Golf is a beautiful walk spoiled by a small white ball.' It's the perfect game for Hell."

"I see," I responded stiffly. "So, all of this effort - the Escalator, the Stairs, defeating the Hellions - just to take away Peter's golf privileges?"

"Well, mostly. That and crush the hopes of ten thousand damned souls who thought, for a little while, that escape from Hell was possible. And let's not forget the humiliation of Florence Nightingale."

"Great. Just great," I said as I started to go.

"Wait!" Satan said, still laughing. "We haven't really discussed the Escalator."

"That one I already figured out. I broke it myself."

"Yep, all by yourself. Good job."

My hands twitched at my sides. I actually wanted to strangle the son of a bitch.

Satan looked at me and smiled. I could see his long canines and shuddered. Not a good idea.

"Anything else, Minion?"

My hands slowly stopped twitching and I reached to the inside pocket of my coveralls. I pulled out the work order for the broken Escalator. "Sign here, please."

"Gladly." Satan hummed as he penned his sigil to the paper. The Lord of Chaos held the signed work order just out of my reach. "Trade you for the blank check. You don't need it now."

I nodded, reaching to my pocket. The check ignited when it touched Satan's palm. He handed me the work order, then brushed the ash from his hand. The exchange complete, I headed for the door.

"Minion, take the Elevator. You can't use BOOH anymore."

"I figured that. Oh, and Lord Satan ...?"

"What, Minion?"

"Fuck you." And I left.

The Lord of Hell was still howling with laughter as I punched the button to call the Elevator. I looked up at BOOH, who was eyeing me from his perch.

"If you're ever in my neck of the woods, stop by," I whispered. "I'll keep some of those donor bags on ice for you."

BOOH didn't seem to move an inch. Then I looked again.

He winked at me.

The doors of the Elevator opened. I stepped inside, a wan smile on my lips.

Epilogue

The handle came off in my hand as I turned the knob. With a sigh, I reached to my tool belt, grabbed my hammer and threw it through the glass. Then I reached into the hole I'd made and opened the door with the inside knob.

I stepped over the glass and walked to the time clock. It showed two minutes to seven. I punched in, then checked the stamp: It read 7:16.

"Minion!" a voiced screeched over the PA system, which crackled and sputtered as if it would fail momentarily.

"Late again," I mumbled.

"Late again!"

I stooped to retrieve my hammer, knowing I would now cut myself on a shard of glass. "Damn!" I said by reflex, then sucked the blood from my finger.

How many times had this scene been repeated?

"Damn straight!" the invisible speaker agreed. "If you're late again, there, well ..."

"There'll be Hell to pay," I mumbled on cue.

"Damn straight!" Then a piercing screech that all but broke my eardrums cut off Beezy's voice. The PA system I'd fixed yesterday after returning from Satan's office died again.

I went over to the ancient Mr. Coffee, poured out the remaining coffee, and used the now-empty carafe to refill the appliance with the requisite amount of rust-yellowed water. I emptied the old grounds from yesterday's filter and put in some new ones, set the filter and carafe back in place, and got the thing going again.

Three work orders emerged from the pneumatic tube, landing with a splat in my inbox. I didn't bother to look at them. I knew what they were for.

Same old, same old.

As I filled my mug and sat down, Orson, predictably, opened the door. "Really, Steve, can't you find a better way to get inside when the doorknob breaks? Hey! What's this?"

Wearily I looked at my assistant. He had an envelope in his hand. "Where did that come from?" I asked.

"Under the broken glass." He handed it to me. "It's addressed to you."

For a moment, I felt off-balance. This wasn't how my morning went. This was not routine. I looked at the handwriting on the envelope, the elegant cursive - the writing of which was a skill almost forgotten in my lifetime, with the advent of computers and word processors - was instantly recognizable.

I tore open the envelope.

Dearest Steven,

I hardly know how to begin this letter except to admit to you my confusion over what has happened to me - to us - these past few days. I am filled with emotions, with passions that I never knew before in either my life or afterlife.

I think this is what love is like, yet I mistrust my feelings, for I know the insidious touch of the Dark Angel. I believe his hand has been directing all of this.

How could I not? The elegance of the clothing that miraculously appeared in both of our homes, the perfection of our two evenings together are ample evidence.

I had never before experienced intimacy as I did with you, but I believe it was special, wonderful, more than, I blush to write, mere passion. And yet I am humiliated. You are humiliated. The appearance of two devils in the privacy of my bedchamber, making a sordid video of an intimate moment between, yes I shall say it, between two lovers, was more than I thought I could bear. And then Satan and his vile creatures made the video public for all in Hell to see.

I am undone. I am overwhelmed. I no longer know who I am, what I believe. I shall go to work today - I have already steeled myself against the lurid jests which surely shall come - yet I hope to persevere, and in doing so help ease the suffering that continues unceasing at the hospital.

For now, I cannot see you, I cannot speak with you. Please, I ask that you stay away from the hospital, and from me. I need time, time to relearn what it means to be Florence Nightingale, time to determine if I really do love you or if I was just some pawn in one of Lucifer's schemes. Mayhap both are true, but I must figure this out for myself. And so I ask you to stay away from me. I beg you.

Will we see each other again? I am not sure. I just know that, for now, you must leave me to myself and my work. These words can only be painful for you to read. Please understand that the last thing I want is to hurt you, yet I see no other viable course before me.

Steve, dear Steve, maybe this letter's final words will offer some consolation. That night, that wonderful/horrible night, Satan made a mistake, and through his error I was given ample evidence of your love for me.

The proof was in the pudding.

Yours,

Florence

"Steve," Orson said quietly. "Is everything okay?"

"No, not really." I reread her last lines. "Orson, what's a cream pie made of?"

"Huh? What do you mean?"

Orson had to see the tears on my cheeks when I looked up at him. "Like the cream filling in those pies I get socked with when my emotions get the better of me. It can't really be cream, can it? Cream is a liquid."

"Well, no," he agreed, tugging on his goatee. "The filling in those pies is really more of a pudding."

"Thought so." I folded up Flo's letter, stuffed it back in the envelope and put them in the inner pocket of my coveralls, next to my heart. Through the window of the trailer I could spy the twin monoliths of the Giant Toaster. She was over there, somewhere, trying to ignore the ridicule of Uphir and his kind, calming the fears of the damned, easing their suffering. She was being Flo, holding onto her Flo-ness, like a drowning woman might to a life preserver.

I would give her time. As long as she needed. And if that meant Eternity, I would give her that, too. At least she knew I loved her, and she had ended the note with a special word: "yours."

"We just got another work order," Orson said, seeking to distract me. "Another bulb's burned out in the Sign."

At that moment the large gas jet on the roof of the oil refinery ignited. The fiery radiance made all the windows in the hospital gleam, as if every light switch in the place had just been turned on.

Despite my tears, I smiled, remembering the word that lit up when BOOH and I installed the bulb yesterday.

HOPE

An extract from the sequel to 'Hell's Super'

A Cold Day In Hell

(Circles in Hell, Book Two)

"Don't let go!"

"I'm not letting go!"

"For Go ... for Heav ... oh, shit ... just DON'T let go!"

"I'm NOT letting go!"

I was letting go.

Not by choice, mind you, but the only thing keeping Orson's nearly four hundred ectoplasmic pounds from falling thousands of feet, to be impaled on one of the jagged toe bones of Mount Erebus, was the tenuous grip we each had on the other's wrist. My arm felt as if it was being pulled from its socket, and my fingers were beginning to slip.

My situation was only slightly less precarious than Orson's. A quickly-made lasso of duct tape was fastened to my ankle, a lasso I'd just barely managed to toss over a stony outcropping twenty feet above me; it held me upside down, suspended in midair. Periodically I'd crash into the sheer cliff off of which Orson and I had slipped moments before. Each time I hit, my nose would slam against the rock, and the delicate cartilage in my schnozzle would snap. "Ow! Ow!" I said every few seconds.

"Steve! Do something! You know what will happen if I fall."

Well, actually, I didn't. Falling anywhere else in Hell would just result in a lot of pain, and a passel of broken bones that would knit themselves back together in short order. But this was Mt. Erebus, and the normal laws of the Underworld didn't apply here, according to Satan.

Of course, he is the Prince of Lies. Not the most dependable person to take advice from. Still, he might be telling the truth this time.

My recently-healed nose hit the stones again, breaking once more. It didn't seem to be mending as quickly as it would under normal circumstances, although perhaps being whacked with such regular frequency didn't allow enough time for a proper nose job. Since I didn't know for sure what the Erebus Zone did to Hell's normal laws, I could only assume the worst (which was generally a smart attitude toward things down here), i.e., that Orson's immortal soul was in danger, that a fall to the base of the mountain would snuff it out.

With my free hand, I grabbed for a roll of duct tape. If I could just make a few loops around our two wrists, the tape could hold us until we figured out how to get out of this fix.

Our fingers slipped again. Despite the numbing cold, our hands and wrists were beginning to sweat. Bad luck that. It was hard enough to dispense tape one-handed without having to deal with sweaty palms. But I had to save Orson somehow, and we had to get back on the mountain, make it to the top, finish the job. If we didn't, all Hell would freeze over.

And that would be a very bad thing.

Chapter 1

I looked in disgust at the giant boulder, split neatly in two, as if someone had taken a meat cleaver to it. "How the hell did you manage this?"

A heavily-muscled guy, wearing an ancient crown, stood before me and Orson, my assistant. "I tell you, Steve, I haven't a clue. I was just doing what I always do, you know, roll the rock up the hill, watch it roll back down, roll the rock up, watch it go down, up, down, up ... "

"Yeah, yeah, we get it," Orson said, cutting him off. "The old Sisyphean thing."

The brawny royal frowned, as if we'd just offended him. "Hey! It's what I do." He slapped his chest. "It's who I am."

Which was true. We were talking to the original Sisyphus.

"Anyway, I'd just gotten my bolder to the top of the hill and was standing there, watching it roll down as I always do. When the thing reached the bottom, it just," he looked embarrassed, "well it just split in two."

"You didn't hit anything with it, did you?"

"No, no," Sisyphus said impatiently. "Besides, if I had, the boulder would have flattened it." Sisyphus looked crestfallen. "I've had it all these years, and now, look at it. Ruined, just ruined!"

All these years was right. Sisyphus - whom Satan had picked up from Hades, the Greek god, along with a few other colorful individuals that had lent some class to the place, characters like Charon, Cerberus and Prometheus, at the time the big devil-may-care had bought Hell from his Greco-Roman predecessor - had been shoving that damn boulder up the hill for over three millennia. Both hill and boulder looked a little worse for wear.

Sisyphus, though, was in great shape. They say weight training does wonders, and Sisyphus could have put Charles Atlas to shame. Maybe even Atlas himself.

"Do you still have the owner's manual?"

"I have it here somewhere." King Sisyphus patted down the pockets of his tunic - when he had found time to have pockets sewn into the garment I'll never know - and pulled out a dog-eared pamphlet, entitled "Care and Use of Your Boulder (Model BB1000).

"Oh," I commented, "a BackBreaker 1000. Good choice."

"Thanks," Sisyphus replied. "It's served me well. Never had a lick of trouble in all these years, until now," he said, slightly deflated.

I flipped to the index, found the page I wanted, and turned to it. "How many miles do you think you have on your rock?" I asked, as I read the fine print.

Sisyphus scratched his beard in thought. "Dunno. Ten million?"

I exhaled hugely. "Well, *there's* your problem. Says right here on page twenty-three. The thing wasn't designed to go beyond five."

"Is it still under warranty?"

"What do you think?"

"Guess not." Sisyphus sat down on the edge of one piece of the broken rock. "I suppose I could get another one." He patted the surface of the boulder fondly. "Won't be the same, though. Me and Bessie ... "

"Wait a minute," Orson said. "You named your rock?"

Sisyphus hopped off Bessie and made a fist. "So I named my rock. What's it to you, fatso?"

"Nothing, nothing," Orson Welles, one of filmdom's greatest directors, said hurriedly. "Rock guitarists sometimes name their axes, so I guess there's nothing wrong with a Greek king naming his boulder."

Sisyphus relaxed. "Right, and don't you forget it. Anyway, me and Bessie have been together a long time. I've really just gotten her broken in, if you know what I mean."

I looked dubiously at the bisected boulder. Ironically, the millennia of stone hill rubbing against stone boulder had had the same effect as a gargantuan rock polisher. Bessie had become as smooth and polished as a bowling ball - without the finger holes, of course. The hill itself was probably several feet shorter than it used to be. Yep, Bessie looked pretty good ... except that she was split in half.

Sisyphus nodded to himself. He had made some sort of decision. "Look, Steve, I don't mean to be a nuisance, but I don't want another boulder. I want Bessie. Can you fix her?"

"Fix a boulder? And how am I gonna do that? SuperGlue?" I turned to Orson, who just shook his head.

"Well, why not?" Sisyphus countered. "You're Hell's Super. You're supposed to be able to fix anything. At least try, please?" The hulking Hellene looked like he was ready to cry.

I don't know where he got the impression I could fix anything. Sure, that was my job: Mr. Fixit for the Netherworld. That didn't mean I was any good at it, though. This was my eternal damnation, chosen specifically because I was lousy at this kind of work. Hated it, too, I mean really hated it, though that's about what you'd expect of an eternal damnation. Still, I had to try. "Fine, fine," I said at last. "But you've got to help."

"Sure," the king said, enthusiastically. "What can I do?"

"Well, first you can help Orson and me get the two pieces back together, okay?"

"Sure, I can do that."

That task was trickier than one might imagine. It wasn't just getting the two halves to touch; it also required a little bit of futzing around to get them to meet at the precise points where they had parted. Orson and I worked one half of the boulder and Sisyhpus the other. Our half alone seemed to weigh a ton. We ended up taking the limb of a nearby dead tree and, using a large rock as a fulcrum, applied all our weight and strength to lever the hemisphere into position. Then we chocked it up with some more rocks that were lying around. Sisyphus had no difficulty with his piece. After all, this was half the weight he was used to handling.

In about fifteen minutes, we had the two halves together. "Now, your highness," I said, reaching to my belt, "I'm going to need you to push the two pieces together as tightly as you can, closing the crack on this side."

"Okay," Sisyphus said, shoving the two bits of rock against each other until a wisp of smoke couldn't have gotten through.

I pulled two strips of duct tape, one from the roll hanging on a spool on the right side of my tool belt, the other from another roll on my left, and taped over the crack. "Orson, take over from Sisyphus."

My assistant's face puckered up as if he had been sucking on a lemon. "Come on, Steve. I can't handle that much weight."

"You and the duct tape can. Besides, you won't have to do it for long." Grumbling, Orson took our places. "Now, your majesty, let's deal with the other end." The king and I went to the far side of the boulder, he held the two pieces tightly together, and I secured things with two more strips of tape. "Now give me a minute to make a few passes around the rock."

I didn't need a minute. The tape flew from my fingers as I did a double-circumnavigation of the boulder, slowed only by my ability to run around the rock, dodging Orson and Sisyphus as I went. Then I had the two of them step back as I began to encase the entire rock in duct tape. In two minutes, everything but the top and bottom was covered. I had Sisyphus roll the rock over so I could finish the job. "There," I said, at last.

When all else fails, use duct tape. It was my fixit failsafe in life, and using it was the only thing I was good at in my afterlife.

Sisyphus scratched his head, dubiously. "I don't know Steve. Doesn't look as pretty as she used to."

"Hey," Orson said, still panting from his time holding his side of the rock together. "She's still gray and a little shiny. Besides, the tape will flatten over time."

"Sisyphus, I'm sorry but it's the best I can do. Why don't you give it a couple of test rolls and see what you think?"

The king shrugged then started shoving the boulder up the hill. He got to the top; the rock rolled down to the other side. He followed. He rolled it up, and the rock rolled down toward us - pretty fast too. We had to jump to one side to get out of the way.

Sisyphus came trotting down, a big smile on his face. "She may not look so good, but the old girl rolls like a dream. This'll do fine."

Whew. Close one.

"Okay," I said, handing Sisyphus a pen and the work order. "Sign here, please."

Sisyphus put a sigma on the form, in the "completed" box. "Thanks again."

"You betcha."

"And Orson, sorry I got a little hot there for a moment. Bessie and me, though, well, like I said, we go way back."

"It's okay," Orson said. "I should have been more sensitive. Thoughtless of me."

He and I made our goodbyes to the burly king and began wending our way back to the office. Steve Minion, Hell's Superintendent for Plant Maintenance, and Orson Welles, his trusty assistant, had triumphed again.

One work order down, an infinity to go, but that's life in Hell for you. Sisyphus had his rock; we had our work orders. He had his version of Hell; we had ours.

My friend and I headed for Hell's Escalator, a one-way affair that stretched from Gates Level, where St. Peter sorted recently deceased souls into lambs (Pearly Gates invitees) and goats (Gates of Hell inductees), all the way down to the Eighth Circle of Hell. As we walked, I noted that the day was an atypically nice one. The sky, or what passed for sky down here, seemed more clear than usual. Sure, it was still gray and smelled of gym socks, but I could see farther than was customary. The view from the Second Circle was spectacular that day, though not scenic, like a view from the Sears Tower or the Matterhorn or anything like that. Hell's spectacles tended to be a bit more grisly.

Off to the right, I could spy a large fiery pit with a gargantuan grill top. Hundreds of souls, bound in chains, were stretched atop it, like so many frankfurters. Beside the grill stood the giant Cyclops Polyphemus, who, like Sisyphus, was a colorful character from Greek mythology and another long-time inhabitant of the Underworld. He was dressed in a white apron and chef's hat, and his single eye monitored his charges as they sizzled on the grill. In his hand was a spatula the size of the digging bucket on a backhoe. Periodically, Polyphemus would flip over one of the souls in order to brown the other side. When one of these unfortunates was well-done - charred to me, but well-done to Polyphemus - the Cyclops would flip him or her off the fire and onto a massive platter. This would give the flesh of the damned soul time to heal, and then the giant would toss the raw meat back on the grill.

All of this, of course, was accompanied by plenty of wailing and gnashing of teeth. That's generally a requirement in Hell. All of us are really good at wailing and gnashing our teeth, seeing as how we've had lots of practice.

At least they aren't stuffed in a bun and eaten. That would be downright undignified. Extra onions. Hold the mayo. Ugh.

In the distance was the cone-shaped silhouette of Mount Erebus, which was sort of an anomaly among all mountains, earthly or otherwise. It hung upside down, suspended from the underside of Hell's First Circle, a gated golf community for virtuous pagans and unbaptized babies.

(Seems a bit unfair about the unbaptized babies, but the early leaders of the Catholic Church, who got to Christianity first and set up most of its basic constructs, are responsible for that. A lot of people don't like that babies are in Hell, but the First Circle is really very nice. Besides, I didn't make the rule, so don't shoot the messenger.)

The mountain is a frigid affair, a gigantic stalactite of ice that dominates the skyline, narrowing as it approaches the surface of Level Two, stopping just a few hundred feet shy of the ground. Erebus provides most of Hell's ice, which is used to punish the damned who in life lived in places like Florida, Hawaii, and Saint Vincent and the Grenadines (which to me always sounds like a Sixties Motown group). Others who get the cold shoulder include former Snowbirds, those northerners in the States who drive south in their RVs and spend the winters in more temperate climes. In other words, Erebus provides torment for people who hate to be cold.

Oh, devils and demons also use ice from the mountain for their martinis.

I remembered from a geography course I took in college that there was a Mount Erebus in Antarctica. At 12,000 feet it was taller than ours, but since it didn't hang upside down, Earth's version wasn't as impressive to me as our own mile-long stalactite.

Orson and I were going to take the Escalator from Two, where Sisyphus had his rock and roll gig, down to Five, where our office was located. We could have taken Hell's Elevator, but while it could traverse the Circles of Hell faster, it was less reliable. You could spend your entire day poking at the down button, trying to get the damn Elevator to stop and pick you up. And the Stairs, well, that was just way too much work. The Escalator was generally very dependable, and while we were on it, we weren't expected to fix anything, giving Orson and me a bit of a break.

"What do you want to do today, Steve?" Orson asked, as we passed some Gluttons on Level Two being force-fed cans of Spam.

I idly wondered why these souls weren't down on Three, in Glutton's Gap, where most of the gluttons tended to be gathered. Hell wasn't as tidy as Dante's *Inferno* suggested, though; I knew you could find sinners of every stripe in almost every Circle of Hell.

We came to the Escalator and hopped on. "I dunno. Fix some stuff, I guess."

"Well, that's pretty obvious," my assistant responded in that supercilious tone he would sometimes use. I had long ago gotten used to it, but I know it pissed off a lot of people down here. I don't even think Orson realized he did it. He was such a big shot in life that he had never quite gotten used to being a flunky down here. "I mean, what are we going to work on?"

We had just passed beneath the surface of Level Two, burrowing into the firmament that supported it. The air, already hot, since things tended more toward toasty than chilly down here, suddenly became superheated. I took a breath to answer my assistant and went into a coughing spell; it's hard to talk when you're sucking in super-heated air. Orson pounded me on the back, which didn't stop the coughing, but it gave him something to do, and he kept it up until the Escalator emerged into the air above Level Three.

"Like I said," I wheezed. "I don't know. Sisyphus caught me right after I clocked in, and I haven't had a chance to look at the work orders yet. Didn't even get to pour myself a cup of coffee."

"Ah." Orson stared off into the distance, daydreaming. "You know," he said, abruptly. "I wish Satan would let me make a film about Hell."

"Yeah, sure, that's gonna happen."

"No, I'm serious, Steve. Hell may be pretty horrible, but it's quite an eyeful. I'd think the devils, at least, would enjoy the movie, and Satan could use it as a recruiting piece to get more demons."

"Keen."

Orson harrumphed. "Stop being so sarcastic. You know he has a worker shortage in that area. He's certainly tried to talk you into being a demon more than once."

That was true. I like to think of myself as a nice guy, but if I don't like someone, well, I guess I have my nasty side. A couple of examples: Thomas Edison and Henry Ford were two of my least favorite people in Hell, and I'd certainly put those two through the wringer more than once. I chuckled nastily then caught myself.

I guess I'm not as nice as I think I am. The thought made me uncomfortable.

"Anyway, I could really do a bang-up promotional video."

"Would you do it in gray?" Orson preferred making black and white films.

"Uh-uh. There's way too much vivid coloring down here. You know, all the blood and bile and stuff. No, it would be Technicolor all the way. And my movie would make 'Satyricon' look like 'Bambi' by comparison."

I brushed some dust I'd picked up from that damn rock off my shirtsleeve. "Well," I opined, "there was that forest fire sequence in 'Bambi.' I thought it was pretty scary when I was a kid."

"Phtt! That was a *cartoon*, Steven." Orson gestured expansively. "Look around. This is the real thing!"

I didn't say anything for a while, and soon we were closing on the surface of Level Four. I noted the fire pits and the Sea of Thorns, where tens of thousands of the damned were impaled. In the air, two harpies sped by, sharp talons extended, as they chased a few understandably terrified souls. Off in the distance, Old Dependable, a perpetually-erupting volcano, spilled its fiery guts onto a town below. The screams could be heard even from the Escalator. "More like the surreal thing, I'd say."

"Absolutely!" Orson beamed. "It would make a great movie, and I wouldn't even need to get Harryhausen to create the effects. Who needs stop-motion dolls, when we have *real* giant apes, three-headed ogres, a volcano that just keeps on giving."

At that moment, Old Dependable's fire simply went out, as if someone had placed an invisible cone over the summit and choked off the oxygen. "Orson," I said, pointing toward the suddenly-inert volcano. "Look at that!"

Orson scratched his goatee. "Well, I'll be damned ... "

"That goes without saying."

"Yeah, but have you ever seen Old Dependable when it wasn't erupting?"

At that moment, the Escalator took us below the surface of Level Four. "Well, now I can't see anything."

Orson grabbed my arm, a little more tightly than he needed to. "But that's never happened before, has it?" he wheezed, the hot air no doubt scorching his lungs.

"No," I gasped. And it could mean only one thing.

Trouble.

Printed in Great Britain
by Amazon

40696315R00175